THE SHORE

THE SHORE

A NOVEL

SARA TAYLOR

HOGARTH

London New York

HOGARTH is a trademark of the Random House Group Limited,
and the H colophon is a trademark of Penguin Random House LLC.

Originally published in Great Britain by William Heinemann, a division
of Random House Group Limited, London, in 2015.

Library of Congress Cataloging-in-Publication data is available upon request.

ISBN 978-0-553-41773-9
eBook ISBN 978-0-553-41774-6

Printed in the United States of America

Book design by Lauren Dong
Jacket design by Elena Giavaldi
Jacket photograph: Joseph Kayne

10 9 8 7 6 5 4 3 2 1

First United States Edition

To B. A. Goodjohn,
for all of the Friday mornings

CONTENTS

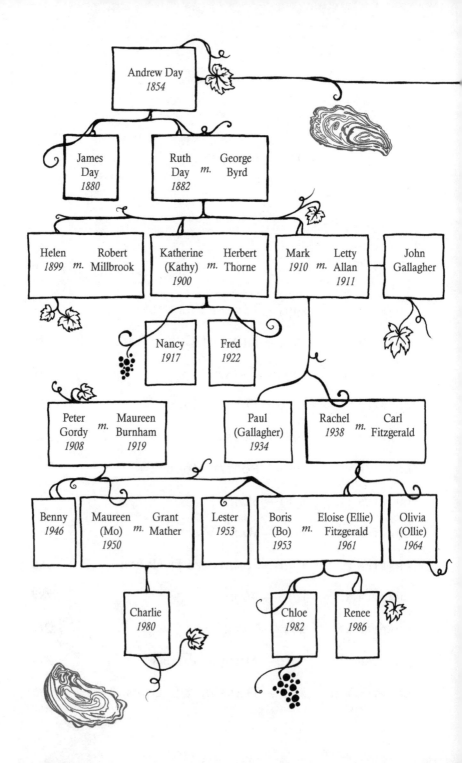

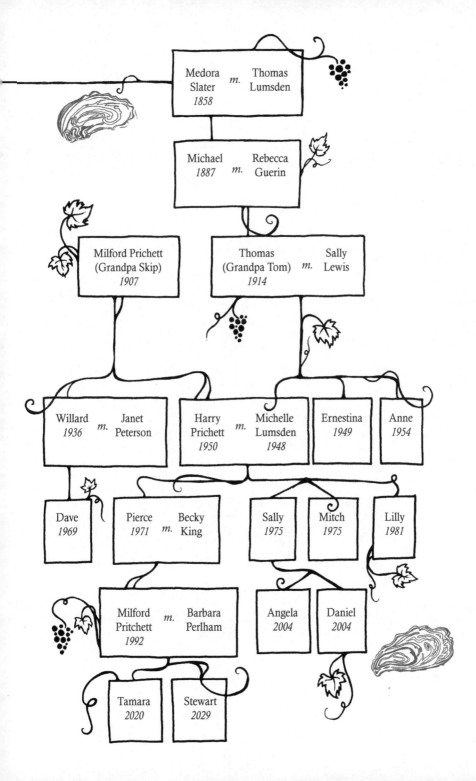

THE SHORE

1995

—

TARGET PRACTICE

When news of the murder breaks I'm in Matthew's, buying chicken necks so my little sister Renee and I can go crabbing. There isn't much in the way of food in the house, but we found a dollar and sixty-three cents in change, and decided free crabs would get us the most food for that money. Usually we use bacon rinds for bait, but we've eaten those already.

I'm squatting down looking at the boxes of cupcakes on a bottom shelf when a woman steps over me to get to the register. Matthew's is small and the shelves are crowded in; when Mama brought us with her to get food Renee and me would have contests to see who could get from the front door to the grimy meat counter at the back in the fewest hops—I could do it in seven. She's a big fat woman, with more of an equator than a waist; she steps heavy, all of her trembling as she does, and for a moment I'm worried she's going to fall and squish me. She dumps a dozen cans of pork and beans on the belt and gets out her food stamps, then digs down the front of her stretched-out red shirt and pulls a wrinkled ten-dollar bill out of her bra to pay for a pack of menthols. "Hear what happened to Cabel Bloxom?" she asks the cashier. The cashier hasn't. "They found him waist deep in the mud in Muttonhunk Creek, had his face shot to pieces and all swole up with being in the water. His girlfriend had to identify him by the tattoo on his back." The cashier's eyebrows jump up, and her eyes get big. I keep rummaging among the cupcakes. The cashier can see me, but they'll probably keep talking anyway; being thirteen doesn't get me noticed any more than being twelve did. My necks are starting to drip blood and chicken ooze through their newspaper onto my leg.

"They know who done it?" the cashier asks as she picks up the limp bill and unlocks the glass-front tobacco case.

"Not yet. Police say they used a slug-loaded shotgun. They couldn't find no cartridges, though."

"That's a lot of help—everyone around here has one of those," the cashier answers, and she's right. We've even got one, sitting next to the .22 by the porch door, in case deer show up in the yard.

"And that ain't even the half of it." The lady leans in close, but her whisper is almost as loud as her talking voice. "They done cut his thang clean off!"

"Guess he won't be needing it anymore." The cashier's face is lit up like Christmas as she bags the cans of pork and beans; not much happens worth talking about on the Shore. The woman waddles out with her cans, and I straighten up from the cupcakes and plop my soggy packet on the belt.

"You hear that, Chloe?" the cashier asks me as she runs them through and dumps them in a reused plastic grocery bag from the Food Lion up the highway. Matthew's is the closest food store to home; it sits next to a taco van where the gravel turnoff makes a T with Route 13, halfway between the village of Parksley and the causeway to Chincoteague Island. It's also the cheapest food store I can get to, so all the cashiers know my name, even though I'm kinda fuzzy on all theirs.

"Couldn't help but hear it," I answer.

"Sorry son of a bitch deserved it, though. Probably someone's daddy or husband decided that enough was enough." I nod in agreement and count out my pennies and dimes, then take the plastic bag from her.

I walk my bike down the graveled road a bit before pulling the packet of chocolate cupcakes out of the leg of my shorts. They taste sawdusty, and the frosting's like vanilla lard, but it's better than nothing. There are two in the packet, and I put the second one in my pocket for Renee and start biking the three miles home. It's not a bad ride, if you avoid the dogs. Close to Matthew's there are single-story houses and trailers up on cinderblocks with cracked windows and mossy roofs—the sheds behind them could be toolsheds or could be meth labs, you can't tell until one blows up—but after the houses peter out the road curves through cornfields and you don't have to worry so much about seeing people. The road goes out to a creek, if you keep following it, and a dock and a cement slip for boats, but I turn off when I get to the farmhouse, the big place with the columns on the front where our landlords, the Lumsdens, live. Kids at school say the Lumsdens do black magic, call down hurricanes or dry up the sky or make it rain chickens, which I don't believe, but I don't like to hang around near their house one way or another. Lilly Lumsden is two grades ahead of me in school, and

she's nice, but her older sister Sally already looks like a witch—
sometimes I run into her on the dock or out in the woods, staring at the sky like she's listening to something only she can hear.

I stop and think for a moment about eating the second cupcake; Renee can't miss what she didn't know was coming to her,
and I'm hungry. But I put my feet back on the pedals and keep
going, down the oyster-shell road that meets the gravel road
opposite the farmhouse, cuts through the potato field, and runs
along the edge of the woods down to the little dock on a calm
side creek too shallow for boating where the Lumsdens sink
their crab pots.

Our house rises out of the heat haze like a turtle on the sand,
just a little brown hump showing over a clump of evergreens
and a few acres of potatoes. Some years they plant corn, and
some years they plant soybeans, but mostly this field gets done
in potatoes. They stretch out dusty green off to the left of the
shell road, and the brambles and woods stretch thick and dark
off to the right, and the knobbly white oyster-shell stretches out
in front of me most of the way home, making my bike jump and
judder and kick up dust. Mosquitoes swarm around me in the
stillness, leaving quarter-sized welts. I'm gritty all over by the
time I reach the end of the shells and have to get off and wheel
my bike over the grass, around the evergreens and mulberry
trees, and over to the screened-in downstairs porch. Our cat
Mickle wanders out of the bushes and rubs against my legs as I
drag the bike onto the porch through one of the big holes in the
screening, and I scratch him a bit before going inside the house.

It's a little house, our house, one room downstairs and two
rooms upstairs and a porch for each, and according to the phone

company and the electric company and the taxman it doesn't exist.

Renee's in the bedroom we share on the ground floor, and I throw her the cupcake. She crumbles it into little bites and eats it a chunk at a time while following me up the stairs. The dust is thick on my skin, and makes smears of mud on the dishrag that I use to wipe it off. She stays two steps behind while I dig in the kitchen dresser for the box of rounds and reach the .22 down from over the window—it's easier to handle than the shotgun, and the ammo is cheaper—and wanders after me out onto the upstairs porch.

"Thought we was going crabbing when you got back," she says, her voice gummy and front teeth black with cupcake. The ripped screen door slams behind her.

"We are," I say, and put the box of rounds down on the porch rail. "Just let me do some target shooting a bit. I'm feeling nervous." I line up five rounds like Daddy does, flat base against my thumb and tip against my pointer finger, pinched in a row, and slot them into the magazine; they make a silvery sound as they slide down.

"What's going on?" she asks, and hauls herself up to sit on the porch railing. I've told her not to, it would be so easy to tip off backward and fall, but she won't listen. She doesn't like sitting on the one splintered bench we've got, and aside from that and the rain bucket the porch is empty. There ain't any mosquitoes up here, and we catch a good breeze. Behind her, the marsh stretches silver and gray and bright lime green, veined with creeks that reflect the blue of the sky, out to the gold smudge of barrier islands and white smudge of breakers at the horizon.

Off to her right is more marsh, the turtleback road down to the dock, with bits of roof or window from the trailers on the other side of the creek, the ones I'd passed on the ride home, flashing between the leaves if you really looked hard.

"Guess who got his self shot?" I answer her question with a question, and chamber a round.

"Who?"

"Cabel Bloxom." The lawn is a big, raw square of marsh grass, soggy and soft in places, hacked short and littered with junk. I sight on a pink Kleenex box down near the far left corner, then set my foot up on the lower railing, so I can brace an elbow on my raised knee.

"You're kidding," she says. I let a long breath out, and squeeze the trigger. Little clumps of dirt jump up. High and left. The hot cartridge pops out to my right, arcs inches above Renee's knees, then lands and rolls before falling through the splintery floorboards and hitting the downstairs porch with a little ping.

"Nope. Someone shot his whole face off. Get down from there, the cartridges are going to burn you." I decide not to tell her the part about his missing bits. Squeeze. High and left, but closer.

"But if he's dead, what have we got to worry about?" She hops off the railing to sit on the bench behind me and be out of the way, her heels on the edge of the seat and knees tented up to keep her bare legs away from the splinters.

"There's always someone to worry about. Anyone that knows that we're out here alone, for starters." This time the box flips. The next two aren't centered, but they hit.

The Shore is flat as a fried egg; on a clear day from our upstairs porch it feels like you can see into tomorrow, and usually you can just about see the dark smear that is Chincoteague Island off to the northeast. We are one of three islands, off the coast of Virginia and just south of Maryland, trailing out into the Atlantic Ocean like someone's dripped paint. We take the force out of the hurricanes, grow so much food that a lot of it rots on the vine because there's too much to pick or eat, but people say that the government doesn't ever remember we're here, that we get left off when they draw the maps. Accomack Island, the big one, is closest to the mainland, has edges laced with barrier islands that change shape and size with each passing storm, a highway up the middle with bridges to the mainland on the south and north ends, and little villages all the way up its length, and that's the island we live on. Then comes Chincoteague Island, off the northeast coast of Accomack. It's much smaller and squarish, not quite a town but bigger than a village, where most of the people with money, people that weren't born here but came across from the mainland, have summer homes; in the winter it's just as empty as anywhere else. Assateague Island is the farthest east, where there used to be a village but where no one lives anymore since it became a national park. It's long and thin and has the sandy beach that you can swim from, and the wild ponies. All three of the islands together is the Shore.

I take the gun with us down to the dock, unloaded, with some shells in a plastic case in my pocket. If I can't get it loaded in time I can probably beat someone's head in with it; the bitch is heavy.

The tide's running fast and clear, and we can see crabs underwater, walking sideways along the bank. Usually we drop a chunk of raw flesh, bacon rind or chicken neck on a string under the dock, but if we're fast we can net some of the walking ones too. The hardest part is getting them to let go of the bait. It's like they don't realize they've been caught; all they think about is getting the food to their mouths. They're pretty—chalky white with smudges of bright blue like someone's brushed them with ladies' eye shadow—but they pinch like a motherfucker. Sometimes we net up two at once, a male as broad as the length of my hand holding tight to the back of a tiny little female. I always pull them apart and throw the females back.

No one comes to bother us, and we fill an old detergent bucket with crabs. They're mostly just under keeping size, but we aren't having any of the deputies over for dinner or anything. On the way back we root around under the light brown crust of topsoil in the field next to the house and pull up handfuls of potatoes the size of eggs. You dig from the sides of the hills, so the plant stays standing up; it makes it look like there're still potatoes there. Daddy says it keeps the Lumsdens from getting downhearted about having nothing left to harvest at the end of the year.

Daddy's home when we get there, and I sneak the .22 back to its place over the window, and the rounds into the top drawer of the kitchen dresser. He thinks I'm too young to hold it, let alone shoot, but Mama showed me how when I was five. He's brought a package of discount chicken with him—he doesn't often remember to get food—but we put that away for later and cook the crabs instead. I don't eat chicken if I can help it. We've got three plants out here, and seeing the trucks stacked with cages full of birds to be slaughtered, all huddled up, half-plucked and sick-looking, some of them dead already with their heads dangling through the bars, just turns your stomach. Daddy works in one of the plants now, on the killing floor. Way before that he and Mama worked construction, fixing up old houses to be sold, but she got kicked off because she was pregnant, and then he got kicked off because no one was buying houses anymore, and he could only do the heavy labor, didn't know electrical work like Mama did. He hates the plant, the killing floors more than anything else, but it's the only work around.

We found a pullet that had gotten away, once, and kept it as a pet till it became a hen. Its chest grew so big that it tipped over on its front and couldn't walk, just flapped around in the dust in the front yard. Mama said it was 'cause of what they fed it at the farm, and wrung its neck to put it out of its misery. We buried it in the backyard with the other dead things, mostly birds and rabbits; the stone's still there.

Daddy's in a brooding mood, so we crack our crabs quietly and suck out the meat without hardly making a sound, then rinse off the dishes in the buckets on the upstairs porch and skibble down to our bedroom. He can find out about Cabel Bloxom on his own.

Renee spreads out on the floor on her tummy with a library book. The floor is cement, painted green so it's slick, and it bleeds cold like an ice cube all summer long. I settle on our bed instead, with a pencil and some sheets of paper with printing on one side I got from the library. There are spricklets in our room sometimes, and I don't like having the space under the bed looking at me, with the fluff from the box spring hanging down like Spanish moss. Even with the spricklets, downstairs is best—Daddy's room is upstairs next to the kitchen, and once we've gone to bed he won't come looking for us. We can hear him walking back and forth up there, and the cupboard opening and closing, and the radio humming.

The light coming through the paper blinds turns blue-purple, and I get bored of drawing. Renee is falling asleep on her book, so I make her go pee before I pull our black plastic tape player and the little yellow flashlight out of the bottom drawer and let her choose a cassette. Mama bought some of them for us, from library sales, but our favorite one is the *Twelve Dancing Princesses*, and that one we have to keep checking out. Renee likes to whisper along with the story, but I punch her in the arm until she stops. Daddy is still walking around upstairs, but slower now. When the tape is over I make Renee go pee again—she's nine but she still wets the bed and I hate waking up in soggy sheets—and then we go to sleep.

It's gotta be midnight when Renee starts shaking me.

"Chloe?"

"Whaaaaat?"

"Do you think Cabel Bloxom is watching us?"

"What the hell, Renee?" I'm awake now. The moon is slanting through the rips in the paper blinds, bright white and cold-looking in stripes across our bed. She's up on one elbow and looking down on me, her hair falling in kinky ropes across her face.

"Like Mama said Aunt Ollie was watching us, when she died."

"That's the most creepy-ass thing you've ever thought of," I say. "And anyway, he can't watch us because he's in hell."

"Are you sure of it?" she asks.

"I'm sure of it." I roll over, and she's quiet. The moon drifts behind a cloud, and our room goes black. I'm almost asleep when I hear her again.

"Chloe? Am I going to hell because I'm glad he's dead?" Her voice is quavery, and I turn back over and try to stroke her face in the dark, like Mom would have done. I miss and poke her in the eye.

"Why're you glad?" I ask.

"He showed me a cat he shot once," she whispers, and I feel a heat rise up in my belly. "It was a little stripy one. And after that I just wished and wished someone would shoot him like he shot that poor cat." She starts crying now, but it doesn't last long.

"Well, you wishing didn't get him shot," I say. "His own meanness got him shot." She snuggles up to me.

"Who do you think did it?" she asks.

"Someone's daddy or husband, I reckon."

"How come?"

I'm not really sure how to answer this one. The moon rolls out again, slowly, and reflects in fat bands off the big round thrift-store mirror hanging over our dresser.

"You know how the deer have harems, and if a buck comes after another buck's doe, they fight?" I ask her. "Like that."

"Are you glad he's dead?" she asks, and I know she's thinking of what happened in the woods last year. Now I'm thinking about it too.

"Yeah, I'm glad," I say. "Now shut up and go back to sleep."

She flips over and wiggles her back against my chest, but now I can't sleep. I can't stop thinking about Cabel Bloxom.

I heard him talking before I could see them. We'd been hiding in one of the little clearings there are so many of in the woods on the edge of the marsh, and Renee'd wandered off and made me come find her. He'd found her first.

His no-color hair was sticking out the holes in a John Deere hat, and his T-shirt was smeared with black car grease. He had his back to me, and was down on his knees so to be face level with her. One hand was on the back of her neck, the other was just a shape creeping up underneath the front of her dress, like a snake under a blanket. She looked like she was swallowing a scream.

I didn't feel my feet touch down when I ran at him, too fast for them to hear. I hit him with all my weight and bit as deep as I could at the side of his neck; it was fleshy and my teeth went in. He jerked back with a shout and sent Renee flying.

"Run!" I screamed, but she was already tearing off toward the house.

He flipped me over his shoulder and I hit the ground hard on my back, my air gone. His hand was on my throat, pressing in, and all I could see was sparks. He started shouting then, calling me a wild animal and other things and hitting with his free hand. In my head he'd been just an overgrown boy, with a beard like he'd forgot to wipe the egg off his face after breakfast. But then I'd realized that while I'd been growing, he'd been growing too, and had gotten full and solid like a man. That scared me. Just because I'd known him since I was a baby didn't mean he wasn't dangerous.

My knee went up on its own when he leaned over me, and

his body went rigid. I kneed again, harder, and this time a thin little scream came out. He bucked, and I rolled away and got up, dizzy with trying to breathe again. He gagged, then threw up on the pine needles.

"You bitch," he spat. "You psycho bitch. You'd better watch your back."

I wanted to tell him to fuck himself, that my daddy would snap him in half, that I'd tell his mama on him and then we'd see. But it wasn't that way anymore, we weren't kids fighting over popsicles and sand toys. So I left him, ran after Renee with my breath raw and sick in the stomach, and after that when we hid in the woods I was always looking over my shoulder, feeling eyes that weren't there.

That's why I'm glad he's dead.

The sunlight wakes me up, but it feels like I never fell asleep. Renee's all spread out like a starfish the way she does, and I'm balled up at the foot of the bed with one leg hanging off. The window faces north, so it's real early, and I lay there thinking of nothing until I hear Daddy walking around upstairs. His footsteps move back and forth slowly, but I can tell by the way the pan hits the camp stove that he's in a good mood today, and for a moment I think I might go up and sit with him for a bit. Instead I wait for the front door to shut and the crunch of his car tires on the oyster shells before I go upstairs. There's a chicken breast on a plate for us next to the camp stove, still steaming, but I wrap it in waxed paper and put it in the cupboard. Don't think me and Daddy have said more than ten words to each other since Mama.

Anyone that knows enough to wonder where she's gone

thinks she ran off to Atlantic City, to Norfolk, to anywhere that's not here. Not that there's many people who care; her mom broke ties with her family before she was born, and her sister, our Aunt Ollie, died of cancer when I was nine. Daddy doesn't talk to his family anymore, though sometimes when he's really drunk he talks about how much he misses his twin brother; I don't know if I believe that he has a twin brother, I don't want there to be two of him.

I wake Renee up and feed her potatoes from yesterday night, then make her wash herself. Our library books are due back today, but she's sleepy and quiet, and when finally I ask if she just wants to be left home alone she says yes. I don't like leaving her more than I have to, but it's miles to the library and I'm not about to drag her against her will.

There are deer in the potato field when I set out, walking because I don't have a bike lock and someone would steal it if I left it without one. They're not more than a stone's throw away, and for a moment I consider going back in and shooting one; they're damn tasty. But I can't field dress it myself even though I know how, and we don't have a freezer, so I have to let them be.

It's a breezy day. Skylarks are dipping over my head, and the sky is the kind of curved blue that seems to go on into forever. Raspberries hang dark and heavy in the underbrush, and I stop every now and then to shake down a handful and squish them between my tongue and the roof of my mouth so I can swallow them without chewing. There are no more raspberries once I turn off onto the gravel road, and I skip along fast until I come to Matthew's, where I have to turn again and follow the highway—two lanes each way, divided by grass. Locals drive carefully because there's no sidewalk so people and animals walk on the sandy edge. I can tell who's just passing through on the way to the beaches at Chincoteague and Assateague Islands by the way they roar down the road and swerve just enough to make me jump into the ditch.

There are more farmers' fields and stretches of woods along the highway, with here and there big houses with driveways of their own, set back from the road a bit, where the richer people live, and even though I don't belong here I feel safer than I do on the walk to Matthew's. Everyone's inside, enjoying their air conditioning. There are turnoffs now and again, graveled tracks back to the marshes or real roads with more houses down them, and I take the ones I know are shortcuts, to get away from the highway for a bit. Cicada hum rises around me, and I get lost in the picture playing behind my eyes. That's why I don't see the other kids till the rock hits me in the side of the head.

"Listen when I talk to you!" John-Michael threw it; Gabby and Russ are behind him, caramel-colored because it's summer, but just as ugly as they were on the last day of school.

"I'll listen when you talk something other than shit," I say, and Gabby and Russ get big-eyed. They'd gone after me the whole winter; I'd wanted to fight back, but Daddy had said that if he got called into school because of me he'd kill me dead and bury me in the backyard, so I'd taken it all lying down. Now, with no teachers around, I don't feel like being so accommodating.

"Whatcha bring your ugly face around here for?" He picks up another rock, but I dodge this one.

"It's a public street, dumbass. I can walk it if I want." I can fight him, but then I'll have to fight Russ too, probably, and then Gabby will bring someone's mama, and she'll talk to Daddy, or the police, or both, and it will all go to hell.

"People walk on the street," he shouts. "Get back in the ditch with the other stray dogs."

"If I'm a dog then you're a pig, shit-for-brains," I shout back. "Your mama must have fucked a prizewinning boar to squeeze you out." That stops him for a moment, and I start running toward the highway, but the backpack weighs me down. Another rock hits me square in the back of the head, and I stumble onto my hands and knees.

"Shut your mouth!" John-Michael is screaming now, and I know his freckled face is all red. "You're nothing but trash, you should have been run out years ago!" I hear the pop of his sneakers on the road as he runs for me, and I stagger up. He's fast; he gets a handful of my hair and yanks, spinning me around. His other fist is cocked back. My knee jerks up reflexively, and John-Michael folds up with a scream. I don't wait to watch him throw up, like I know he's going to, I just run like hell.

They don't follow me, but I don't slow down till I find the highway again. My stomach is all giddy butterflies now, and I stop with my hands on my knees to get my breath back. There's no way Daddy's not going to hear about this.

The library is clammy and cold; goose bumps rise up on my skin while I drop our books in the return slot. The librarian smiles at me, and I notice how dirty my feet are, how my knees are all grass-stained and my shirt has butter down the front from dinner a few nights ago, how my hair is all tangled up, and I'm embarrassed. It's never till I'm standing in front of a stranger that I notice how awful I look, like when I'm alone I go a little blind.

No one's in the children's section, so I sit there for a few hours, enjoying the cold and flipping through picture books. I still like them, more for the pictures now than the stories, but it's embarrassing if Renee isn't here. When my head starts feeling muzzy from too much up-close seeing I fill my arms with enough to last us a week and go out to the front desk.

"I bet you're glad school's out?" It's one of the newer librarians, and she moves slow, stacking the books square before scanning my library card and checking for fines. It isn't really my library card—it has Mama's signature and name on the back, Ellie Fitzgerald Gordy, almost rubbed off now—but the librarians who know she's my mom don't mind, and the rest think that it's my card.

"Kinda. Summer gets boring sometimes," I answer. My grades are awful, but I don't mind going to the Combined School out on Chincoteague. The bus driver likes me and we get free lunch.

"It's a good thing you're reading all these books instead of watching TV. Your brain would melt out your ears like molasses." She checks *Twelve Dancing Princesses* in, then scans my card and checks it back out to me.

"I like books better anyway." I don't mention we don't have a TV because we don't have electricity; the librarians still act like we're normal. She helps me stack my books in the backpack, then I hang around a bit by the magazines before leaving the air conditioning behind.

Now there's nothing really to look forward to; the walk home is always longer. There's a cornfield across the road from the library, with a stretch of wood beyond it and the main highway beyond that. The stalks are dead still, and the road is empty. I could keep going down that road and be in the center of Parksley in seven minutes, but all they've got there is the courthouse and the sheriff's office and the jail and even though there's real sidewalk that looks too clean to walk on, all shaded with bright pink crepe myrtles, I don't have any reason to be there. The breeze has died, and the air is full of greenhead flies and massive mosquitoes. I eat the potatoes I brought, sitting on the curb in front of the library, but my stomach still feels empty.

Mama took us to the library every Tuesday. There were sandwiches afterward, and a Thermos of iced tea. We built a nest of pillows and blankets in our room when we got home, then curled up in it and read our books all afternoon, until Renee fell asleep. Then Mama and I would sit on her bed and she would read me the books I liked that Renee wasn't old enough for and let me braid her hair. It was really long, past her pockets, and so kinky it held my braids on its own. Our hair is like that too, mine and Renee's, long and curly, though Renee is salt and I'm cinnamon: she has white-blond hair and white-blond skin, like Daddy's, and silver-blue eyes, like Mama's. I'm darker than Mama, hair and eyes and everything. She told me that she'd explain why that was, when I was older. We read about pea plants and Punnett squares in science last year, so I know that blue eyes and blue eyes can't make brown eyes, but I still want to know where my brown eyes came from. Now that I'm older she's not here to explain.

A new breeze picks up, and I'm drowning in stomach-turning stench. One of the plants, Perdue or Tyson or I don't know, is across the highway from town, behind the cornfield and the dark band of trees, and when the wind's right the whole town gets hit square in the face with that smell. It smells just a little bit like chicken soup, and a whole lot like dog food, with the inside of a molding coop mixed in.

In the time when Mama still took us to the library Daddy brought us a cockerel as a pet, just a day old and the yellow of a hi-lighter. It rode home in his pocket. Renee named him Suet, and after we fed him he slept like an old man on a park bench, his beak resting on his fat belly. He got to be a pretty good guard rooster, attacking the dogs that would come after Mickle, cutting at them with his spurs and generally making life unpleasant. Mickle was just a kitten and smart enough to not pick any fights, and they got along pretty good until a fox got Suet. There was blood and feathers all across the yard, and Renee just cried and cried for days. When she finally stopped crying, we asked Daddy to bring us home another cockerel. By then he'd stopped working at the hatchery and had gone on to work at a processing plant, and he'd started smoking his little glass pipe on his days off so his skin was all claylike and he smelled like cat pee. He was in a bad mood when we asked, so he told us how they get all the new-hatched chicks out on a table, and check them to see what sex they are, then all the cheeping cockerels get pushed into a grinder, alive, and get chopped all to pieces. Renee stood looking at him for a moment, then opened her mouth and just screamed and screamed until he smacked her. He and Mama got into a fight about that, later, and he smacked her too.

I keep to the shoulder of the highway instead of taking the short-cut that goes past John-Michael's house, and even though he and the others aren't anywhere I can see, my stomach still does flip-flops. I walk by quicker than usual, and don't slow down until I turn off the pavement onto the gravel by Matthew's. There's a skinny brown dog sniffing at the smear of roadkill down the center, and his head snaps up when my feet make that first crunch. He trots over and takes a sniff at me. I shy away. I don't like dogs. I've been bit too many times. I trot along by the ditch on one side, he trots along by the ditch on the other side, and I watch out of the corner of my eye. My gut goes like a big chunk of ice, like it does when I'm scared.

After we get past the little houses he cuts into the cornfield, and I can relax again. It's late afternoon and the air is heavy and damp, like a wet wool blanket put over your head on a hot day. It's like breathing pea soup. I look for raspberries again, but the mosquitoes are out now, and I can't stay in the bushes for long. Rabbits watch me from the path, their noses twitching as they nibble, waiting until I'm feet away before going lippety lippety out of range. Mama called the tiny ones "bunnylettes."

Mickle darts out of the brambles and across my path, gunning for a little rabbit. It sprints into the corn, and he drops and licks himself, pretending that that's all he really meant to do. I nudge him with my sandal, and he flops over to show me his belly, then trots along butting his head against my ankle every few steps. He's a grown cat now, a bit lazy and slack in the belly, and he does most of his real hunting at night. I sometimes find the smears of blood and tufts of feathers or fur that he leaves, and make sure Renee doesn't see them.

There's a frantic rustle in the cornstalks, and the dog that followed me bursts from between them. Mickle freezes, paws spread out on the ground, and the dog leaps at him. My cat screams, and I jump on the dog, pulling him away from Mickle. We wrestle, and his front legs flail and scratch at me and his back ones coil up and shove me away and I snap my neck back to keep my face away from his wild, waving mouth. Library books scatter everywhere, and I smell sour and green and fear and hear us both snarling, too angry to be scared anymore. We roll in the dirt and shells until I get him around the shoulders and get his ear in my teeth, and bite down hard. He slows his bucking then, and I roll us to the ditch and fling him at the corn. He scrambles to his feet and lopes back at me, but I've got my backpack off now, still half-full of books, and I catch him square in the chest with it. When he gets up this time I come at him, and he turns tail and springs into the corn.

Our library books are dusty on the ground and dented at the corners, but not torn at all, and I wipe them off as I pick them up. Mickle is waiting for me a few yards on, curled up and licking at a torn place near his tail. I bundle him up like a baby and carry him the rest of the way home. I can feel the places on my legs and butt that are bruised from rolling on the oyster shells. The scratches on my arms have started swelling.

Renee makes a fuss over both of us, but I don't tell her that there's a dog going for our cat. While she feeds Mickle the chicken breast Daddy left, I take the .22 out again and practice hitting the tissue box. It has a heavy, solid, comfortable feel to it.

I listen all the rest of the day, and until I fall asleep, for tires on the oyster shells, but other than Daddy's, none come. I want to think that John-Michael's mother isn't coming, won't tell Daddy what I did, but I know he's going to find out. If she didn't come today then it only means that she'll come tomorrow.

In the morning I don't hear Daddy moving around upstairs when I wake up, and it takes a bit before I remember that it's Thursday, and he's going to be home all day. I go up to get us food anyway.

Pink light crisscrosses the kitchen floor; there's a grapefruit sun rising out of the marsh. Up here is all big windows, so you can see out to the barrier islands. Daddy's sitting on the old wooden bench outside with his back against the window, swirling a glass and watching the sun. He might go out later today, but it's not something I can bank on.

There isn't much upstairs: a gray couch that feels like a potato sack faces the view out over the marsh, and behind it against the wall is the kitchen dresser, next to the door to Daddy's little room. The table is square and from Goodwill, and it stays pushed up against the half-sized wall that keeps you from falling into the stairwell. All our chairs are from Goodwill too, and they wiggle when you sit on them. The red camp stove is still sitting out on the pressboard counter from yesterday.

Daddy got our icebox from a junk shop; it's the kind that you have to put a big chunk of ice in every few days, and mostly he remembers to get it. There's a dented package of chicken breasts in the front, which he probably brought home last night, and I think about Suet a second. Back behind it there's a dozen eggs, less two, and one of the big discount packages of bacon ends. He forgets about food for days sometimes, and this is more than we've had around at once in a while. I boil six of the eggs on the camp stove, then fry up a handful of the bacon ends, one eye on the shadow Daddy casts across the floor. It shifts and rolls as I dump the bacon ends into a pile of paper towels, and the door creaks open as I wipe the pan into the trashcan. I keep my head down and keep rubbing at the bacon crust. He comes over, twitches the towels open; I can hear the piece of bacon crunch in his teeth.

"You and Renee going somewhere?" he asks.

"Out in the woods, maybe down to the creek," I say.

"If you go, catch some crabs for dinner," he says.

I don't say anything.

Renee is awake when I come downstairs, dressing Mickle in doll clothes. He bolts for the door as soon as I come in, trailing lace, and I undress him before turning him out into the yard. We pack up our food, a blanket, and a few books in my backpack, then I have to go back upstairs because I forgot to get us water.

While I'm filling our bottle from the big jug I hear tires. Daddy's sitting at the kitchen table, staring into a mug of black coffee, but this makes him get up and go downstairs. It's Stevo. He pinches my cheeks sometimes, and usually has strawberry candies in his pockets, but his tar-tooth grin makes me nervous in my stomach. Stevo's brother cooks and he deals, but Daddy gets it from them cheap because they've been friends for a long time. I can hear them talking, in that bouncy, happy way they have, and in a few minutes they'll come up and play a hand of cards and have a pipe. I wait as long as I can, then go back downstairs. They're standing in the little square space between the front door, our bedroom door, and the stairs, and when I stop on the bottom step Stevo grins at me and runs his hand over my hair.

He smells like cat pee even worse than Daddy, and his skin is red like raw meat or poison-ivy rash. He's skinny too, skinnier even than the models in the magazines at the library, almost as skinny as the starving kids in *National Geographic*. He's alone this time, but I know that after the sun gets higher more cars will probably show up, lots of women and some men and teenagers, all of them with the same scarred-up skin and greased-up hair and smelling worse than he does. We want to be gone before they get here.

"How's life treating you, Chloe?" Stevo asks, and shuffles in his pocket.

"It stinks, thanks." All he has is a peppermint, but I take it and smile at him.

"I could take care of that for a little while, sugar," he says, then looks up at Daddy. "Ain't she about old enough to join us, Bo? Sweet little face like that, she could tweak as much as she wanted free."

Daddy looks down at me. I stare at the front of Stevo's pants so I don't have to look at his face. "When she grows some tits, maybe," Daddy says. Stevo runs his hand over my hair again as I scoot between them and go back into our room. Renee is sitting crisscross applesauce on our bed, and we climb out the window so we don't have to go past them.

We go to the same clearing we usually do, in the woods between the oyster-shell road and the creek; I lay down with a book once we've spread out our blanket, and Renee starts collecting up snail shells to decorate mudcakes with. It's too hot to move.

As the sun heads down it starts to rain, the light pattery kind that gets you soaked even though there isn't much to it, and I bundle up our books. It's too early to go home still, but after we've huddled together under a bush for about half an hour the patter turns to a downpour, and we decide we have to.

Daddy's car is still there by the side of the house when we get back. Everyone else has left already, but we can see the fresh ruts in the grass from where their cars were. We crawl back through the window and sit on the bed for a second, dripping and watching the rain. There are fast, light footsteps upstairs, and I can hear the drone of the radio. We dry off and change, then curl up on the bed, not talking, not thinking, waiting for the dark to come.

I'm watching the raindrops chase each other down the window when I see the long black car in and out through the evergreen trees as it rolls slowly down our driveway, Gabby and John-Michael's mother peering over the big steering wheel. I huddle deeper, then consider hiding under the bed. There's a knock on the door, and a chair scrapes upstairs. Renee looks at me, but I didn't show her the lump on the side of my head, so she doesn't understand what's going on. We listen as the front door opens, and the woman starts talking, but I can't catch all of what she says. She sounds angry. I slip off the bed and creep over to the door, slip it open just a crack so I can see.

She's standing in the doorway, with the rain pouring down behind her. Daddy can barely get a word in, but when he does it's mostly about how I've never been a problem before, always got on with her kids before, he'll talk to me and straighten things out. Her voice is calming down some when I see her eyes lock onto Daddy's hand. It's his little glass pipe; he's turning it over and over in his fingers like he does sometimes without really noticing. Her eyes go back up to his face a moment, and her mouth sets in a thin line. He's still talking, too quick, but then he notices the look on her face and his voice dies away.

"It appears you have the situation under control," she says.

His hand has clenched around the little pipe, and he moves it back behind him, but it's too late for that. "Thank you for your time." She turns, and I close the bedroom door without a sound and back away slowly.

The front door bangs shut, and I hear her engine turning over.

"Chloe!"

Our door pops open and cracks against the wall, and I spring away from the bed. In the dark he goes for Renee. I dart around him and up the stairs, scared giggles rising up in me like bubbles in a bottle of soda. Renee shrieks, "Daddy, it's me!" and his footsteps follow me up the stairs. He catches me by the back of the shirt halfway up, and throws me into the kitchen.

"What the fuck, Chloe!" I tuck and roll. "What the fuck, starting a fight so some uptight bitch will show up and call the cops?" He swings at me. I curl up tighter. "You know what they'll do with you if I get put away?" Renee's followed us up: I can see her behind him, kneading the front of her shirt between her hands and all crumpled in on herself. I want to tell her to get back downstairs and hide under the bed like she's supposed to, but I can't. "You think it'll be better, in a foster home with sixty other kids beating your ass every day?" Smack. "I got news for you, princess!" I scrabble to get out of reach, but he swings at me again and I fall against the kitchen dresser. Renee screams, high and shrill, and I look up as she jumps on his back.

Mama said to take care of her.

He claws her off and holds her by one chicken-bone wrist, half off the ground. "And you stay out of this!" he roars in her face. That's more than she can handle, and she pees herself there on the kitchen floor. I'm all curled up useless against the dresser, wanting so bad to jump back up but my head and the scared in my stomach is weighing me down, and I don't know what to do. He's smacking at her now, and she's making noises like a dying rabbit.

I try to yank myself up, but the dresser-drawer shrieks out and splits open on the floor next to me. The hunting things roll everywhere; I scrabble for the scattered rounds but find the skinning knife, its black leather sheath smooth under my groping fingers.

I fling myself at his back, and bounce off. He's got his hands around Renee's throat, trying to make her stop screaming the way he used to try and make Mama stop screaming. She's gone loose and boneless, and I feel sick like a stomach full of vinegar as I wonder if he's killed her. I kick at his knees, stomp his bare toes under my heels, ram my elbow up into his belly with all my weight behind it, anything to make him let go. He stumbles when I get him in the gut, bellowing at me, but he drops Renee to grab at my hair. He punches me this time, and I reach up.

It's just like cutting a deer, only bristlier. Meat resists a blade in its own way, drags at it like an undertow drags at your feet. The look on his face says he doesn't feel what I've done, and I'm scared what he'll do when he realizes. I can feel his fingers bruising, smell his breath under the sour of his skin, but I can't hear past the sound of water in my ears. His words are bubbling out the slit in his throat, hissing red foam, but the artery matches the beat of his heart. My face is all wet, and my arms. He drops me. Renee isn't moving, but she's curled herself into a ball, so I know she's alive. I try to pull myself over to her, but

I can't move anymore. He slumps forward across my legs and hips, and now I can hear a sound like dry wind and water on stone. Then it stops. The rain comes down.

It's later, but I don't know how much later, that headlights flash through our window as they come down the road to our house, bright enough that I can see gasps of things I don't want to see. There's a pounding on our door. Everything smells like copper. A man's voice shouts, I can't tell what it says. More pounding. The door splinters down. A gun comes up the stairs, with a woman in uniform behind it. She sees me, she sees the blood, she shouts behind her for someone to get a light, and pulls me out from under him. Someone else leans over Renee, but I let them.

"Honey, honey, look at me. What happened?" she asks me. "Where's your mama?"

"In the backyard," I tell her. She stares at me for a second. "He doesn't know I saw him do it."

People are running through my house, barking words at each other, looking at things. Looking at me. Looking at Daddy. He's not moving, all blood, facedown. Just like Cabel Bloxom was, after I shot him.

CHAPTER II

1933

—

THINGS I COULD TELL YOU

L ate-afternoon sunlight falls in heavy bands through the chinks in the barn walls, like the folds of the red velvet curtain at the Onancock Playhouse. When Mark squints his eyes, the hay dust swimming in the light looks like the mosquito fry in the rain barrel, floating up and down in aimless circles. He can feel the dust more than smell it, prickling thickly in the back of his throat and all behind his eyes. It prickles more than the hay beneath them, covered by the blue cotton tablecloth Letty brought, a smudge of red wine at one corner. It's rucked up a little, and he can feel the hay itself pricking at the back of his head. She's lying next to him, resting with her head on his shoulder, one leg thrown across his hips, and the prickling isn't quite enough to make him move. He hears chickens squabbling and scraping distantly.

The loft smells like long-ago Sundays, full of books and pet mice and wild tumbling games across the springy bales, and sounds like horses eating, so deliciously like the sound of peppercorns in his mother's mortar. It smells earthy now too, a soft damp smell like rising bread and baby's skin, offset by a sharp muskiness that he can never get enough of, no matter how deeply he breathes.

She stirs and sits up, pulling herself slowly from him, and though the day is hot he immediately misses the warmth of her. In their earlier exuberance her hair had fallen all about her face, and she slowly gathers it up again. He watches her do this, watches the languid movement of her glowing white arms, the trembling rise of her small breasts, the in and out of her softly rounded belly. The bodice of her dress is a pale green puddle around her waist, and he thanks God for dresses. The long filmy skirts catching on even longer legs, the smooth curving buttons up the front, the decorous nature of the garments. His mother says that only fast girls wear trousers, but this he's never understood: skirts seem so much more convenient, for men at least.

He reaches up and cups her breasts, runs his rough fingers over the velvet smoothness of them. They're soft, like the last apples in the back of the root cellar in the early spring, when time and darkness have condensed them into perfect handfuls of yielding sweetness. She sighs, and bends into his hands, and he wraps his arm around her so he can take an entire breast in his mouth and flick his tongue over the rising firmness.

"I should be getting back," she murmurs. "It wouldn't do for him to find me gone." He pulls her down on top of him and kisses her slowly, and she lets him. For a moment they lie there together, in their own tiny nucleus of heat and breath.

There was a time when they somersaulted across the springy hay together and made nests in the corners, waiting out rainy days. Their mothers were friends, the two families' homes near to each other and far from anyone else, and they'd been left to amuse each other since before they'd learned to speak. His sisters never played with them—Mark was the unexpected baby, ten years after Kathy, eleven years after Helen, six after his mother had given up on any more children—so they had *always* had the loft to themselves. Sometimes Letty made him play house with her, stuffing her pullover up under her dress until she looked like her mother in miniature. He had awkwardly mimed whatever it was he had thought men did all day, making long furrows in the hay and dropping in seeds, then let her bully him around their dinner table. He in turn bullied her into being kissed, even though he knew she wanted him to. It was part of the playing.

It had been accepted as fact, or so he had thought, that the game was practice for a nebulous someday, when the lump under her dress would be more than a fleecy red pullover, and he would know what it was that a man did. He had even looked forward to that day, in a sort of half-expectant way, when he would be kissing her gleaming cheek instead of his mother Ruth's steam-reddened jowl when he returned home in the evenings. He had thought that she would wait until he was ready, until he wanted to step into the role of Man. His parents weren't as comfortable as they had been before the Crash of '29, but they were still gentleman farmers, they still had some money, and he was comfortable being their son.

Then Letty had run away.

He had thought to wait until he was twenty-seven, twenty-eight, not because he would have been in any better position then—his uncle, James Day, had promised him the house he'd built in Belle Haven with the heart-of-pine floors and sculpted fireplaces whenever he chose to start a family— but because he wasn't ready to be a man yet, wasn't ready to shoulder the responsibility. He should have known that she would not wait.

Slowly he pulls the bodice up and helps her guide her hands into the short sleeves. As he begins to do up the glossy buttons he notices, for the first time, the purple shadows up her ribs and across her left breast.

"Did I do that?" he asks.

"No, it was there before," she says, and hurries the buttons into their slits. There are fingerprints around her wrist, dark ovals like smears of soot. He is ashamed that he didn't notice, that he'd hurried her clothing off so quickly that he hadn't read her body.

"He shouldn't be doing that."

"No, he shouldn't."

"I thought he would at least stop when—"

"He doesn't know yet." She doesn't look at him as she says it.

"Are you going to tell him?" he asks.

"He hasn't touched me in months . . ."

She sits for a moment, staring at the straw near his knee. He wants to reach out and touch her, but her body has closed in on itself, like a hen setting a clutch of eggs. He knows he should do something, should comfort her, should take charge. She isn't his wife, he doesn't have a right to defend her against her husband, but he knows he should do something to protect their unborn child. He should lay claim to it, face up to the man she married. He cannot.

"I asked Pastor's wife what I should do. She said to aggravate him less, be more obedient, and pray that God will soften his heart."

"You could leave him."

"And go where?" she asks bitterly. "Stay here, in this hay-loft? Give birth in the stall with the plow horse?" She doesn't know about the house in Belle Haven. Even if she did, she isn't the kind to make demands. She thinks that she should be able to take care of herself. After a moment, she says, "I have nowhere to go. And you have nowhere to put me. And even if you did, I could never marry you—he would never give me a divorce. The court would never give me a divorce."

It felt like being punched in the stomach when he'd heard about it. It was at church, of course. He hadn't seen her that morning, but there had been many Sundays when he hadn't seen her, so he'd thought nothing of it. Afterward, a neighbor woman had walked briskly up, calling his mother's name until she turned around, then whispered to her, but not so quietly that he couldn't hear, if she hadn't heard that Letty Allan had run off with the slick insurance salesman that had been bumming around town for the past few weeks, her parents' only daughter and him nearly twice her age. Of course they hadn't. The news had elicited the expected reactions from all present, but he'd gone around behind the church and been sick in a ditch.

The couple had come back when her father died, three years later, to care for her mother and run her parents' farm on the far side of the creek. When he first caught sight of her, buying a paper of quilting needles on a leaden summer Saturday, there had been shadows on her neck, and thumbprints on her arms. His stomach had jumped, then plummeted, and he realized that all the filthy dreams he'd had since she left had been about her.

He had thought that it would be the last time he saw her, that day in town. She belonged to someone else. She was beyond his reach.

But some weeks later she had come, stepping neatly over the stile at the bottom of the north field, to ask his mother for her recipe for chicken pudding. She hadn't stopped, hadn't said a word to him, but when she passed him, buried to his shoulders in a litter of half-born pigs, there had been a weight to her glance, a significance, that immediately erased all of the years between them now and those rainy hayloft days.

She had returned the next day, in the late afternoon. His parents had gone to see his mother's mother, Medora, and to drop in on Helen and Katherine and visit with the grandchildren, so he had been alone, lazily mucking out stalls. She had appeared at his side, taken his hand without a word, led him up into the loft and pulled him down into the hay. When they had played before at being adult they had lain close together, kissed hesitantly at each other's cheeks and foreheads, but this was quite a different fruit. Her lips were soft against his, her tongue probing and searching, and when it touched his own it sent chills through his stomach.

A part of his mind had resisted. He wanted to sit back up, hold her and talk about where she'd gone, what she'd done, what they would do now that she was back, but the feather-light pressure of her fingertips drove thought and logic farther and farther from his mind, until he finally surrendered. There would be a better time for talking.

As he watches her now he realizes that, so many months and kisses later, that better time still hasn't come.

She gathers her legs underneath herself, pushes up into the dusty air. He catches hold of her wrist as she rises—it's meant to be a tender gesture, but she stumbles and grabs his shoulder to keep from falling.

"I'm sorry, I didn't mean—I want to ask something."

"Yes?" Her face is open, waiting.

There are so many things he can ask, but what comes to his lips is, "Why did you leave?"

"You know why. I couldn't—"

He knows about her father but that isn't what he means.

"Why didn't you come to me? I could have gotten you away. Not very far, but still away."

"The way you're going to get me away now, now that I'm carrying your child?" She says it quietly, but the words sting. "The way you did when you found out about . . . this?" She touches her bruises lightly.

"I loved you, Mark. And I still do. But I know you too. I left because you weren't going to do anything, not yet, and I couldn't wait any longer. And I know you're not going to do anything now, either."

"But—"

She hushes him with a finger, a look.

"You're not ready. Fair enough. That's your choice to make. But please, don't question my choices."

She stands slowly, swaying to balance, feet sinking slightly into the hay, then bends to scoop up the tablecloth and fling it over one arm. He doesn't want her to leave on this note, but he doesn't want to provoke her, or give her husband a reason to add to her bruises by keeping her any longer. He scrambles across the loft to retrieve his trousers, and hops back to her to put them on. They stand together, for a moment, breathing in the dust of the loft and listening to the chickens. He leans down and kisses her, cups her belly in one rough palm, the curve of it firmer now than it was the last time. Then they go down.

Light cuts through the trees: the day has nearly gone. She scatters the chickens with her green skirt and climbs the fence crisply. Her home is more than a mile distant, the same white house with the buttery window frames that she grew up in, and he worries that she won't get back before her husband does. He watches until the forest swallows her.

He could follow after her, bring her back and make her stay with him. He could take one of the horses by the road, find her husband on his way back to their home and confront him. He could claim the child only they know she is carrying, drag her marriage into the public eye, heap shame on all three of them but possibly end the mess with her at his side and their baby in his arms.

He will eventually stand up to her husband, hide her from him when she cannot bear any more, take her to speak to the judges and the sheriffs and the marshal, sit with her through the court sessions and comfort her when the gossip gets to be too much. They will survive the shame, marry and live in the red-floored house his uncle built, have a daughter who will leave the same way Letty did, and find one day that they are old and no one alive remembers a time before they were married. But this will not happen until after the baby is born and walking, until after Letty tries to hang herself in the barn where they played, the place she'd run to for safety in childhood and in adulthood, until after he stops her. It will be too late, by then, for some things, but not too late for everything.

But now he turns toward his own home, to wait for his red-jowled mother and silent father, and a watery cabbage-and-potato dinner. The evening smells of woodsmoke and hay, but he carries her smell with him.

CHAPTER III

1992

—

RAIN

As she drives to the rest home Sally remembers the first storm she made, some ten years ago. She had been picking raspberries with her grandfather, in the thickets down the gravel road to the marsh, so it must have been June. She was wearing her twin brother's purple rain boots and the new dress her mother had gotten her from the thrift store in Modest Town, and she stopped every dozen steps to twirl a bit and feel the cotton skirt slap satisfyingly against her legs as it wound up. Mitch, who was ensconced on the living-room couch with his cast-encased foot propped up on mounds of pillows, had seen her going out in the boots and screamed that he could walk just fine, that Grandpa Tom could carry him, that those boots didn't belong to her and she'd better put them back or he'd drown her Barbies while she slept.

Mitch was lucky to have only one broken foot. Pierce, their older brother, had gotten him to jump off the balcony with her Rainbow Brite bedsheet as a parachute the week before by telling him it would make him fly. Now he was immobile for six weeks and she had his boots. She'd just grinned in the face of his whining and followed Grandpa Tom out the kitchen door.

If she looked back the way they'd come she could see the house, with its thick columns and sagging porch, where the oyster-shell road joined the gravel road out to the highway. If she looked hard she could track the white smear through the potato field, like a snail snot trail, to where it turned off into the woods to go down to the dock. The seam where the shells met the gravel was stark, the line of demarcation beyond which she was not allowed to wander alone. There was a tiny house past the very end of that oyster-shell road; Grandpa Tom had just rented it out to Mr. Bo and Miss Ellie, distant cousins who were expecting a baby, and she hoped that the embargo would be lifted enough to let her wander down and visit, when it got born. She liked babies, and her little sister Lilly was walking and wiggly and didn't like being held anymore.

Her mother had said that the people that lived down there were no-accounts, but no matter how she grumbled about it, Grandpa Tom rented to them just the same. They were family, he said, far back but still family, and even if they hadn't been they needed help. Daddy might manage the planting and harvesting now, but Grandpa Tom still owned the land, decided who could and couldn't rent the outbuildings scattered on the edge of the property and park their trailers on the boggy land by the creek that was too wet to farm. Daddy said he was a soft touch for hard-luck cases.

Grandpa Tom was waist deep in the brambles, his bucket already half-full, whistling "South Wind," and she squatted down to get the berries he couldn't reach because of the arthritis in his knees. The shade felt good; the leaves of the potato plants in the field across the road looked like they were frying. The chickens had followed them, and were scraping for worms in the dust of the road and the weeds of the ditch. A breeze came along, the thin, wafery kind that lasts for minutes at a time, and Grandpa Tom had said, "Go along, try with this one." She'd reached out her hands, like he'd shown her, and felt the breeze between her fingers like long strands of dried grass, only this time she felt it in her mind too, as if her head was an empty room with all the windows open and the breeze was wandering through it. She'd grabbed hold and twisted, and the breeze twirled in on itself, picking up the cut grass on the road, spinning a confused chicken around a few times, then straightening back out.

"Very good! I am impressed," Grandpa Tom had said, and she hadn't been able to stop grinning. She reached out again, and the breeze felt firmer, more substantial this time. She gave it a wrench.

Wind whipped the raspberry bushes, plucked the chickens, tore their buckets from their hands, threw her against her grandfather's legs like a wave at the beach. There was a silent pop in her jaw as Grandpa Tom yanked the breeze straight again, and just as suddenly everything was calm. She looked up at him. Raspberry juice splattered his face, and his shirt, and dripped down his mustache into his beard. "Always gentle, little bit. Messes are hard to clean up," he'd told her, and scrubbed her face with his blue paisley pocket-handkerchief.

She was seven.

There has been no rain in weeks. The creeks are sandy paths, the cornstalks wither in the sun, the air itself sizzles. The long black road down to Parksley looks wet in the afternoon light, reflecting back ghost images of the woods and houses; the double yellow line up its middle is blinding. Sally drives slowly, avoiding the drooping chickens milling about the shoulder of the road. People don't like it if you kill their chickens, even if they're pecking at roadkill on the double yellow when you do it.

She passes the Perdue plant, slows down at the speed-limit sign and holds her breath as Parksley slides by—the Foster processing plant usually reeks—turns off Route 13 above Onancock, then pulls into the long driveway of the Tasley Assisted Living Facility and Rest Home. It winds artificially through a long stretch of bright green turf, a man-made lake peppered with mangy ducks twinkling from between the trunks of manicured oaks. The home itself spreads out in front of the lake like a bunker, a dark, squat three stories of cement and reflective windows, with a scatter of private cottages for the more mobile residents behind it. It's on the bay side, so that the residents can get a view of the glinting water of the port, and the boats sailing in and out. She and Grandpa Tom both like the sea side of the island better, with its peanut-butter smear of barrier islands at the horizon, but rich people like the bay, so the home is on the bay. The cousins have pitched in to get Grandpa Tom into the home; he's rich on paper, but all of his money is in the land, and he wouldn't sell a square foot of it, even if it meant being able to afford a room of his own.

Their family is large, if loosely connected now, the descendants of Grandpa Tom's grandmother Medora and her two husbands. Grandpa Tom's three cousins have already passed on; Helen and Kathy in their own homes, but Mark, the youngest of the three, and his wife Letty had both died in the rest home some years earlier, rather than in their red-floored house in

Belle Haven. It was supposedly a more modern, civilized way, but Sally wasn't so sure she agreed.

Mark and Letty had had one daughter together, and desperately wanted more. Rachel had been a sweet little girl but when she got older she'd fallen in with a bad crowd, then run off and gotten married, then come back to Accomack Island for a while before running off again and abandoning her husband and two daughters. The daughters had never been allowed to meet their grandparents. Cousin Letty had a son from her first marriage that the family had also never met; when she'd sued for divorce her husband had accused her of abandoning their child and been granted custody. He'd kept her from seeing her son when he was young, and so thoroughly poisoned the boy's mind against her that by the time he was old enough to choose for himself he had no wish to see her.

Kathy and her husband had also had one daughter, Nancy, who had been so anxious as a child that by the age of fourteen she refused to leave the house. Grandpa Tom had taken them to visit her a few times when they were young; Sally only remembered a quiet, mousy woman, the apartment over Kathy's dressmaker's shop cool and dim and smelling of face cream and zwieback. Kathy's son had fared much better, and between him and Helen's four children there were more cousins than they could count or keep track of, and since they were all much older or much younger than her and Mitch, Sally never bothered.

She sits for a moment in the parking lot, soaking in the damp chill of air conditioning before cutting off the motor. She can see Mitch in one of the shallow alcoves in the face of the building, crouched with his back against the cement. He works selling imported wine at Morgan's Specialty Foods in Onancock and walks over to the home when he finishes in the afternoons. It's not until she gets close that she sees the phone at his ear, the crooked smile even though he's slowly rubbing his eyes with two fingers in the way that he does when he's had enough. She catches him in her shadow, and he mumbles a hurried goodbye before clicking off the phone.

"How's Brian?" she asks as she takes his hand and pulls him up. They're of a height still, though Mitch is barrel-chested and she's what her dad describes as "wiry as a polecat."

"What makes you think I was talking to Brian?"

"You only get that smile when you're talking to Brian. What are you doing out here anyway?"

"Grandpa Tom kicked me out when my phone went off for the third time. Said he wasn't going to die in the five minutes it took for me to answer it." The tinted doors open with a pneumatic hiss, and the glassy-eyed receptionist nods at them as they turn toward the elevators. There are couches and coffee tables and, for some reason, potted poinsettias in the reception area; the ceiling goes three stories up to a skylight but still the room is dingy, the furniture trying and failing to look homey. There's a litter of outdated magazines across the tables, and everything smells like orange furniture polish and dust.

"I didn't think you were allowed them in here, because of the pacemakers and things. Do you think Grandpa's figured it out?"

"Maybe. It's not like he'd say anything." Mitch met Brian at service camp two summers before, building houses for poor people in Appalachia in between praying and singing hymns. They'd stayed in contact over the winter, phoning and meeting up every so often, then went again to the same service camp the next summer. He'd come home with the smile, a smile Sally had never seen before, and though he kept it put away most of the time it always popped out when he'd been talking to Brian, or talking about Brian, or sometimes for no reason at all when he was sitting still and thinking. Their mother still points out pretty girls at mass and asks him if he doesn't want to date more, and their father tells her to leave him be, Mitch is a good, responsible boy that others would do to take notes from, Pierce being one. Sally suspects that he plans on getting through his entire life without ever bringing up the fact that he's just not interested in girls that way.

The elevator smells like vomit, Lysol, and cold medicine, and Sally mashes the button to the third floor until the door rumbles closed. As they lurch upward, her stomach is left somewhere in the lobby. She leans back on her hands on the waist-high handrail that runs along the wall, then kicks her feet up onto the one catty-cornered across from her and suspends herself above the antiseptic floor. Elevators make her nervous. Rest homes make her nervous; they're too much like hospitals, which also make her nervous. She suspects that one of the uniformed nurses will pull her into a padded room, strap her into a straitjacket, and no one will ever see her again.

When she was six, Sally came down with bacterial pneumonia. She had started feeling bad one afternoon and fallen asleep on the living-room couch while Mitch and Grandpa Tom played Chinese checkers in the kitchen; Lilly hadn't been born yet and Pierce was grounded to his room for doing something stupid. She'd woken up after dark with a raging fever. She remembers enjoying the fuss, as her parents always seemed so terminally busy. Her dad had bundled her into an old blanket that he didn't know had been set aside for rags and hauled her to the car, her mother running frantically after. She'd been wedged between them the entire drive to Salisbury, her father hunched over the steering wheel, muttering, her mother whispering that maybe he should slow down, just a little.

She hadn't been to Salisbury, which was off the Island and across the state line in Maryland but still the nearest city to home, since she was born. She hadn't been to a hospital since she was born, either, and craned around to see everything as her father carried her in. They'd filled out forms, talked to nurses, then set her down on a paper-covered table until a doctor could look at her. He came in with his hair all tufted up on one side, eyes dark with lack of sleep, and immediately told her to open her mouth. She'd cooperated, swinging her feet so they bounced against the rubbery cushion of the table, holding absolutely still while the nurse stuck her and filled little glass vials with thick dark blood for testing, until they brought out the medicine in glass eyedroppers.

"What are you giving me?" she'd asked.

"Excuse me?"

"What are you giving me, what does it do?"

The doctor had looked at her for a few moments as if she were a chair that had suddenly started speaking.

"Little girls should be seen and not heard. It will make you better, that's all you need to know."

She'd opened her mouth for the dropper and swallowed, then made faces at his back as he'd left the room. He was a nasty adult; all she'd wanted to know was what he was giving her.

It was just a hazy memory now, though Sally still felt a strange annoyance whenever she thought about that doctor too hard. The impetus had been planted then. She had no interest in medicine particularly, or the workings of the human body, but she loved chemicals and was dying to know what you could do with them. How they worked. How they cured people.

Grandpa Tom said, whenever she brought it up, that the world could always use another pharmacist or three, or, failing that, someone that knew how to make bombs and mix napalm. But what she hadn't mentioned, because she figured that he knew, was that you didn't get to be a pharmacist without school, and there was no school for pharmacology on the Shore, or even in Salisbury.

Grandpa Skip, her father's father, who lived on the mainland and didn't have all his money tied up in property even though he had several farms all through Virginia, had promised before she was born that he'd pay the way for any of them to go to school, so long as they worked hard and made good. So far, few of her cousins had taken him up on the deal. Most of them were content to stay where they'd been put, could not uproot feet that had been planted since birth in the thick, rich soil of the Shore. She liked to think that she felt even more deeply the thrum of tide in her veins, the pulse of the land, that the islands were more hers, and she more part of them, than any of the other souls who called them home could ever be. But even that pride could not scratch her traveling itch, make her want to stay forever. She wanted there to be a greater destiny, a more important role in her future than just filling in her grandfather's empty footsteps.

⌐

The door rumbles open, and they nod to the nurse at the desk as they go by. The family has been in and out since Grandpa was admitted. Mama and Daddy come when work lets them, and bring Lilly, because the tubes and machines scare her and she won't come with anyone but Mama. The cousins come in shifts and batches, solemn and respectful, and Grandpa likes seeing them though they don't know quite how to talk to him, since they didn't grow up around him. Pierce tries not to come, but his girlfriend Becky does, because Grandpa likes holding her baby and he's one of the few people in the family that doesn't scare her silent. Sally and Mitch drop by almost every afternoon; they've been in and out so many times and the staff seems so apathetic that they doubt anyone would stop them if they walked in buck naked and had a picnic in the lobby.

Their grandfather is awake when they come in, sitting up in the hard railed bed, pale blue blanket tucked up to his armpits, sketching glacially on a thick pad of paper propped against his knees, the hose bringing oxygen to his nose buried under his thick white mustache. Sally avoids touching the IV tube as she wraps her arms around his shoulders and kisses his hard cheekbone: he's shriveled since they brought him here, the rubbery Jell-O, tough meat, watery salads failing to stick to the bones that seem ready to poke through his papery skin. The sound of daytime TV from the other side of the privacy curtain cannot completely drown out the whirs and beeps from the heart monitor. He pats her arm and puts his pencil down; the sketch is of a very confused-looking rooster, mobbed by a clutch of chicks.

"Think your mother will like it?" he asks.

"Grandpa, I've never looked at a wall and thought, 'That

wall needs more rooster.' It's a good drawing, though." It is, nearly photorealistic despite his feathery, rough style.

"Your mama has." His voice is slow. "She thinks everything needs more rooster. Sometimes I wonder if the fairies didn't leave her." Their mother is the oldest of his three daughters, and they suspect his favorite, for all that he doesn't quite understand her.

He hands the pad to Sally, and she puts it down on his bed-side table, next to a plastic pitcher of ice water, a dozen or so cheap "Get well" cards, and the tin of Werther's in powdered sugar that has always sat on the dashboard of his red truck. He's not happy about the cards, says it's silly to send pictures of teddy bears saying, "Get well soon!" when they should say, "Hope you have a pleasant death!" but the nurses refuse to throw them away.

"Hasn't rained since May," Mitch says. Someone broaches the topic every visit, but not usually this early. He's pulled the chrome-and-plastic visitor's chair out of the corner behind the door and turned it back to front so he can straddle it like a horse.

"And what do you expect me to do about that?" Grandpa whips back. Sally has settled on the edge of his bed, and is shuf-fling a pack of cards on her leg. Mitch doesn't answer right away.

"Mama's garden is still putting out zucchini too fast for us to eat," she offers.

"That is the nature of zucchini," Grandpa says, and accepts the cards that Sally hands him.

"Tomatoes and eggplant too," Mitch adds.

"Your mama doesn't know what she's capable of."

"Are you sure you can't teach Pierce?" Sally asks. "It's not like he has any other place to go."

"Your brother doesn't know his behind from his own head," Grandpa snaps.

Sally hands Mitch his cards, and gives him a pointed look. This is the general opinion of Pierce, though as far as they can gather Grandpa was the first to hold it. Their older brother teased them, broke their toys, egged them on for years to fight each other or do stupid things like lick frozen metal or touch the electric fence, but he is still their older brother. When he turned eighteen he wandered off with Dad's old white Chevy and the wad of just-in-case money Mom kept in the blue willow teapot in the china hutch and bummed around Virginia for a year or two, always meaning to strike out west but never getting farther than the Blue Ridge Mountains. When he ran out of money and luck he wandered back with his tail between his legs, nothing to show for his fortune-seeking but Kermit the Frog tattooed upside down on his thigh, at least two warrants for his arrest, and a sheepish and silent girlfriend who, a few weeks after their arrival, gave birth to what they have to assume is his baby. Even if he hadn't run off, stolen, dealt drugs and been what Grandpa called "an all-round little pissant," he wouldn't have been any good. As children, when Mitch and Sally had gone to bed with crying headaches from the weight of the rain in the sky or walked restless up and down the front porch waiting for a storm so far out at sea that no one could see it, he'd run around like nothing was happening. If anything, growing up had further deadened whatever connection he had to the natural world.

"What about Lilly?" Mitch asks.

"You're joking, aren't you?" Grandpa scoffs. "She's eleven years old, and she's yet to show any sign of talent or gift. Enough of this. Start the game before I die of impatience."

They roll the tray table over so that it hovers above Grandpa's midsection and lay out the deck and discard pile on it, Sally sitting carefully on the bed near his feet, Mitch kneeling on the chair nearer to his head, all guarding their cards. The first round of rummy is played silently, except for the beeps of the machines and the hum of the TV on the other side of the curtain. None of them like the room—it's small and Grandpa says it smells like old people—but they can't take him out in the heat the way they did in the first weeks of his residence at the home: he has too many wires and tubes to drag along. They ignore the heart monitor, the dialysis machine expectant in the corner, the painkiller drip and bundle of tubes and valves taped to his forearm. They ignore the scratch of the blankets, the thick, plastic feel of the mattress and the creak it makes when Grandpa shifts to lay down three aces, the wheezing breath of the man on the other side of the curtain, the click of nurses' heels in the hallway. They are back at home, at the kitchen table in the yellow house where they've grown up and their mother grew up, playing cards to pass the time while the rain pours down the windows, their parents at a church meeting or harvesting potatoes or across the water in Salisbury getting saw blades.

"You're saying it's up to us, aren't you?" Mitch asks as he lays down a run and three sevens, then gathers up the cards to shuffle again.

"No, I'm not saying it," Grandpa says. "You're smart enough between the two of you to have figured it out for yourselves by now." Sally blows a raspberry to indicate what she thinks of that.

"Your daddy and I were talking about setting up a little distillery—state of Virginia's selling licenses for that sort of thing now. They used to make it out here on the sly during Prohibition, used anything that would ferment. We thought a little romance like that could go a long way, make people want to try it. Those white sweet potatoes you two like, they'd probably make vodka that tastes like sugar cookies. A body could make a lot of pocket money out of something like that."

"Are you trying to bribe us to stay on the Shore?" Mitch asks as he deals.

"Not 'us,' just one of you," Grandpa says. "Y'all have always lived on the farm, and y'all always will be allowed to, but I have to deed the place to someone, and I want to deed it to someone that I know is going to be staying."

They stay until visiting hours end, then reluctantly go down to Sally's car. Mitch has failed the driving test twice, but Sally passed as soon as she was old enough; their father rebuilt an old white Toyota for her to use, but only because she'd gotten all A's in the first three years of high school, and only because he'd promised, and if she ever gets into trouble with it they'll both be right back to walking.

While waiting at the stoplight to cross Route 13, she leans back in the driver's seat and tentatively reaches her mind up into the sky. The air is thick with humidity; she can feel it aching to come down, but instead it continues to build and roll away, to drop over the ocean and the coastal cities, leaving their broad stretch of farmland dry. She can tell that Mitch is doing the same thing.

"Remember that story Grandpa told about the time he went to the mainland?" Mitch asks as the light turns green.

"Did it have a tattooed lady and a bottle of Jameson in it?"

"Nope, after his grandpa died, the one about how he met his wife."

"He probably told me one time or another. Remember it to me anyway."

"Well, when he was about as old as we are now——" in his stories Grandpa always seemed to be about as old as they were now—"he found that he'd got pretty sick of dirt farming and dirt farmers and dirt farmers' daughters, so he decided to make out for the mainland and see if things weren't better there," Mitch begins, in fair imitation of their grandfather's story voice. "His daddy and grandpa had died by then, but he left his ma and brothers and sister behind, figuring between the lot of them things would get tended to. He put the things he couldn't do without in an old mending bag, got in his beat-up pickup truck with the rust hole in the bed, and started heading south. When he got to the southern point he paid a fisherman to take him across the bay in a Carolina skiff."

"Less detail, more pith, we're almost home," Sally cuts in as she turns onto the gravel road by Matthew's Market. Miss Ellie is walking along the shoulder of the road swinging bags of groceries, her daughters following after, and Sally veers wide to avoid hitting them. Miss Ellie is thin but broad-shouldered, her kinky hair hanging past her waist, and she raises her hand in greeting as they go by; she and her husband still rent the little house on the edge of the marsh. The younger daughter, Renee, small for her age but maybe five or six, walks in step behind her, both hands clinging to her back pockets. The older daughter, Chloe, almost ten now, jogs along behind them, a grocery bag banging against her leg. Sally never did get to hold them when they were babies; now that she can cuddle Pierce's kid all she wants she finds that she doesn't crave the warm weight of a baby in the way she did when all she had were dolls.

"He spent two weeks in North Hampton and Virginia Beach, getting drunk with Navy men and getting to know a lot of lonely women, and when he sobered up he heard that a hurricane had nearly wiped the Shore off the face of the map. So he took the loneliest of the lonely women, got her to marry him, and came back in a hurry, and that was the last time he left the Shore."

Leaves go whipping by, and Sally sits up straighter so she can see the scrubbed white tombstones in the middle of the masses of thick green soybeans. "And the moral of the story is we're stuck here?"

"Either that, or if you get drunk in North Hampton you'll meet your one true love and lose your crop to hurricane," Mitch says.

"But there was only one of him," says Sally. "There's two of us. Together we can make things work—"

"Can you see me bringing Brian to live here? It would be a disaster."

They park by the house, behind a truck with its engine in pieces, and sit for a moment in silence. "Think he was serious about the farm?" she asks.

"And the vodka. Completely. I saw the paperwork on Dad's desk."

"Sounds like he's trying to bribe us."

"Sounds like whoever stays behind is going to be set for life." Mitch hops out and slams the door. "Just not exactly in the way they would choose."

After her first try and the resulting whirlwind in the raspberry patch, Grandpa had gotten Sally to practice whenever they had a chance, to reach out and tug at the wind, drag out the tide, pull rain down from the sky in little patches, just to see what she could do. Most times she had pulled too hard, drowned her mother's tomato patch or blown the chickens all across the yard, but he'd never seemed disappointed or frustrated with her.

After Mitch's broken foot had healed, Sally had triumphantly shown him how she could raise a wind; he'd tried to outdo her and sent one of the hens straight through the toolshed window. Crying, he had brought what remained of the chicken to Grandpa and, after the funeral, lessons had involved both of them. They had always spent a lot of time together, just the three of them, but after that Mitch spent more time at Grandpa's heels and less time sitting in the corner by the oven under maternal instruction to think about what he'd done wrong this time. Perhaps it was because, after the parachute incident, he was wary of taking Pierce's advice on any matter.

They'd raised baby whirlwinds, and made pillow-sized rain clouds, but nothing big, nothing serious. Grandpa had made it plain from the start that playing small was a good thing, and would give them practice, but anything bigger than their pocket storms would throw the entire Shore out of whack. If you were going to mess with the weather, you had to be able to control it, keep an eye on it at all times, calm it down or rile it up as people needed, not just pull and tug when you felt like it and forget about it the rest of the time.

⌐

They go to see him again the next day; the drawing pad is still on the bedside table. He's staring out the window, and doesn't move when they come in. The machines beep quietly, regularly, like breath. Sally goes up and touches his arm—his skin is cold—and he turns his head toward her. His eyes are unfocused, searching, but after a few moments they lock on her, and he smiles. It's a dialysis day: he's always worse on dialysis days.

"Hey, little bit," he says.

"How you feeling?" she asks.

"I been better."

Mitch pulls out the pack of cards, but Grandpa shakes his head.

"I was thinking," he begins, "about when your mother was a little girl." His breath is a wheeze, and comes in bursts. "I tried to teach her, I really did. But she didn't want anything to do with the wind and the rain and the snow. She was like your grandmother, always with her hands in the dirt."

They think there is a point to this story, but they aren't certain what it is. So they pull the stiff-backed chairs up to his bed, and tell his own stories back to him all afternoon.

He has always told them stories. Family stories, about his childhood and their mother's childhood and how they all came to be, and more private, half-mythic stories that they know instinctively are not to be shared; people knew vaguely what they could do, but it didn't help anyone to strew reminders about.

The story of his grandmother Medora was of both types,

and they did not know how much of it was strictly true. She was a come-here, he said, and a wise woman, the mixed-race daughter of a Shawnee Indian and a white landowner, who knew native herbs as well as she knew medicine. They got their gift not from her, but from her second husband Thomas, who passed it down to his son Michael, who Mitch was named after, and Michael's son who was their Grandpa Tom.

Her first husband built with her inheritance the house in which they still lived, with its broad, sagging porch and thick peeling pillars, but he despised her for the color of her skin and soon took up with another woman. She avenged herself—she hadn't killed her husband, but their grandfather always skipped over the details of that part, saying they were too grisly—and then ran out to the marshes to take her own life. Instead of dying, she was found by the first Thomas Lumsden, who had a European father but a native mother. This man, who could heal the ground and the sky the way she could heal the body, fell in love with her and hid her in the trackless marsh.

The poor knew where to find them when cures or rain were needed, and she stayed hidden from the rest, biding her time. Before Michael was born her first husband's history caught up with him: a wanted confidence man, he was traced to his grand house and arrested in the middle of the night. She had come out of hiding then, and since she could prove that all of their estate was in truth her inheritance, to which he had no claim, her husband's creditors could not touch it to cover his debts. Her revenge never came to light, Grandpa said most likely because the man was too ashamed of what she'd done to him to make it generally known.

They still live in her house, still keep the dark wood of her medicine chest oiled, but even though they have these tangible reminders of her she has a mythic quality in their eyes. They cannot trace their lineage any farther back; Thomas had been part of a vast but loose tribe, his wife had come to the island with no familial ties. Perhaps, once before, their cousins would have also inherited the gift, would have shared out the duty. Now they are the only ones left.

There's a dry wind blowing the next day, some cooler than it has been all summer. Sally scuffs her feet in the dirt on the edge of the turtleback road. A call has just come through from the rest home: her grandfather is in a coma. Mitch went straight to his room when he heard, Mom went to the home, no one else was around. The greenheads are swarming; she isn't sure why she went for a walk.

She remembers something that happened, when she was eight perhaps. Grandpa had a little cottage of his own, and she would sit on the countertop in the morning and watch the coffee to keep it from boiling over while he did other things. She remembers the sharp smell of the coffee, and the rising foam of bubbles around the edges of the pot, and her grandfather's voice in the background. He was on the phone, walking up and down across the kitchen, stretching out the spiraling cord like she and Mitch would stretch their slinky between them. His voice was strained, tight.

"I really am sorry, Vince, but I can't do anything about it. There is no water up there—the sky is bone dry clear out to the mainland. I know your irrigation pond is empty, mine is too, but I can't do anything about it right now." The voice on the other end bled through, and he stopped his pacing to bend against his hand, as though his back were hurting him, and listen. The voice was harsh, angry, almost panicked, and Sally thinks it may have been the first time she ever heard a grown man sound truly afraid.

As he listened to the voice on the other end of the phone, she reached up into the sky, felt around a bit, and found that what he'd said was mostly true—there wasn't enough water in the air for a storm. Curious, she reached out farther, and bumped the coffee saucepan. Her hands jerked to the handle to keep it upright before she realized that she'd only bumped it in her head: the part of her that felt the wind had found the water in the coffee. It had begun to steam gently, and she dipped her mind into it. Her grandfather had his back to her, so she poked at it some more, bullied the coffee until it began to climb reluctantly into the air, forming a soft cloud like a ball of molasses candy over the pot. Her grandfather mumbled apologies into the phone, hung it up, and turned around to see a tiny brown rain shower falling neatly into the saucepan from two feet up, Sally smiling guiltily.

"And what do you think you're doing, missy?" he'd asked.

"If you can put the water in the sky, why does it matter that there's none there now?" she'd asked. The cloud had sprayed a fine mist of brown on her nightshirt sleeve, and she began to suck the sweet stain out.

"I wish it was that simple, little bit, that I could just give them rain whenever they thought they needed it. Reach farther."

She did, stretching her mind until it ran thin as watercolor paint, until it bumped against a massing, angry wetness far out to sea.

"Feel that? That's coming in a day or two, and none of them know it yet. I'm not going to be able to stop it, but I can calm it down and spread it out enough so that it'll be more good than harm, if the ground isn't waterlogged when it gets here. We have to give people what they need, not what they think they need."

Sally remembers this now, and she thinks that she understands.

She thinks about the moment the day before, when he looked at her and his eyes focused. When he said her name. Then she turns her thoughts upward, into the heavily laden air. Moisture. Cloud, even: mare's-tails. She remembers a phrase from grade school, and stretches out across the bay, to the city where her grandfather once drank away the memory of rain. Condensation nuclei. And there it is: auto exhaust and smoke and coal dust, hanging lightly in the air. She finds a breeze, gives it a twist, and pulls the particles across the bay like teasing knots out of her sister Lilly's hair. It is a gradual process, and her pace slows as she waits. The ambient moisture begins to bead and grow heavy, a million pregnant bellies. Then, she brings it down.

The first drop she catches on her tongue, and then the million others plummet after. Suddenly the wind is whipping by like the gale she raised when she was seven years old, and the raindrops are falling like hailstones, stinging her face. She breathes deeply. It smells like her grandfather.

CHAPTER IV

1876

OUT OF EDEN

I t was June, and the air in her father's house in Franklin County, Kentucky, was thick with unfallen rain, had a physicality to it that made breathing difficult. It was the sort of day for which porch sitting had been made, but her father had dragged Medora up to her room by the hair just after breakfast—she'd managed to say something, or do something, or not do something, that riled him. At eighteen the dragging was quite undignified, but preferable to the other physical manners in which he sometimes expressed his temper.

Her room was more pleasant than his company, in any circumstance.

When it had become clear that he wouldn't be coming back to let her out for a good while she had stripped nearly naked, skinning off dress, shoes, stockings, and layers and layers of petticoat until all that was left was her thin muslin chemise, so that she felt peeled and, if not new, at least not so hot. She'd displaced her masses of curling green potted plants, morning glory and English ivy, columbine, aloe, clematis, and the trailing philodendron that threatened to pull the curtains down, so that she could roost on the broad windowsill. The anemic breeze served only to make her chemise stick to her gleaming skin, but one of her grandfather's books was open across her legs, with more stacked from the floor to her hip yet untouched. She spent an inordinate amount of time in this room, in this manner; she often thought that her father might as well brick her up like a nun, for all the time she was given the run of the place; at least then they'd keep from touching off one another's tempers.

The sound of an unfamiliar voice outside made her look up, twitch the edge of the curtain aside just enough to let her see without being seen.

He was a tall young man, younger than most of the men that came to see her father on business, and dressed more expensively as well, in city clothes with the stiff and shine of newness still in them. Her father walked beside him, leading his stallion Mercury with ease and comfort in his shoulders, even though he had to be stifling in the double-breasted waistcoat and jacket that he wore. Watching her father and Mercury together made Medora think of old couples walking hand in hand; Andrew Day simply looked like a man leading a horse he wasn't too sure about. They stopped a few feet off from the porch, where she could still see them, and her father rested a hand on Mercury's cheek while they talked. There was a tentativeness to Andrew's movements, a flutter in his too-big hands, made all the more pronounced by its contrast to her father's deliberate gestures. He was clearly there about the tobacco, rather than about the horses.

Afterward she thought that in that moment she should have felt something, or her heart should have jumped, or some organ should have given a flutter, the way the hearts and organs of young women in books always did. Or maybe not. It wasn't love, just opportunity, she felt that afternoon; the sight of him as he led his gelding up toward the house had simply set her mind to turning. When he stepped up onto the porch and passed out of sight she held still for a moment, staring into the middle distance, then turned back to the *Medicinal Herbal* and continued reading about the uses of *A. vulparia.*

That he was the means by which she would escape her father's house she concluded over the next few hours of reading, though she had not yet determined how. She wouldn't embarrass herself by trying to seduce him; the idea was inherently ridiculous. Matters of birth aside, she was not the type gifted in the tools of seduction. Her coarse black hair was shot heavily and prematurely with silver, and fought its way out of any arrangement. The years of contention with her father had set her face in a sullen grimace, which even concentration and a mirror couldn't fully remove. She stooped, she squinted, she stepped heavily. Her bones were large and solid, and when she bothered to winch herself into company-worthy clothes she looked even more ridiculous, more manly, for the juxtaposition between her coarse darkness and the lightness of fine silk. Her shoulders, hands, and face were broad, her skin a shade or seven too brown. She'd known from childhood that the usual feminine methods would not work for her, long before Calley, her father's housekeeper and the woman who had mothered her into adulthood, had begun to tell her that she'd have to make her way by her wits rather than by her caboose. He was a man, but a businessman: they would have to negotiate.

Her dinner was brought up to her that night. She could not tell, and didn't care especially, if it was because she was still in disgrace or her father didn't want his half-breed bastard at the table with a new business associate. Women, ministers, local families, none of them visited anymore, though Medora vaguely recollected small, golden-haired children rolling with her younger self on the parlor rug while a mushroomy man in a clerical collar and his reedy wife sat nervously on the horsehair sofa. Her father was no respecter of persons when it came to exercising his temper, and only men about the horses, or men about the tobacco, or men looking to buy or sell or sit on the long open porch in the evening air sipping bourbon until the heavy moon hung low over the horizon came round anymore. This did not bother Medora. She spent the majority of their visits locked in her room, its plain paper beginning to peel, the bedstead and two of the windowpanes cracked, plants in chipped pots and teacups and jugs slowly massing and reaching toward the window, her handful of childhood toys put up on shelves above the empty fireplace and their place on floor and bedside table taken by drifts of books gradually migrated from her grandfather's study. It lacked the dusty sumptuousness, bordering on excess, of the rest of the house, but it was her space.

Medora's parents had never married. Her mother had been one of the few remaining Shawnee, who wore dresses and pinned up her dark hair like a white woman, mended clothes and worked the fields, kept her eyes on the ground. That's what Calley had told her. Medora herself remembered little: still, dark eyes watching her through the kitchen window, a seamed hand reaching out for her own, feeling of "mother" like a pile of warm down quilts. The smell of the pipe that she smoked while sitting opposite the kitchen door, back braced against the chopping block where Calley beheaded chickens, waiting for Medora to come out to her.

Her father frequently entertained himself with female hands, but they had all been careful or had men of their own, so until Medora came along there had never been issue. Her mother had no husband, no family, did not cover up her condition, named him openly as the father, and from Medora's birth he held a grudge against them both. Her mother worked her father's fields with Medora tied to her back at first, but when the girl had grown enough to totter barefoot up and down the rows of tobacco he had sent one of his overseers to bring her into the house. He had expected her mother to give her up with little argument; she'd bitten the overseer's arm bloody, and two of the hands had carried her away and locked her in a curing barn to keep the man from shooting her like a mad dog.

It was not usual for a gentleman to claim his bastards, but her father had ceased to abide by the dictates of "usual" years before, and he could think of nothing that would hurt the woman more than laying claim to their child. Medora had been handed over to Calley, who had not yet graduated to housekeeper but was undisputed mistress of the kitchen, with instructions to keep her quiet, out of his sight, and away from her mother. Calley had taken charge of the toddler without comment, made sure she was kept clean and fed and happy—and assiduously turned her back when the Shawnee woman appeared at the kitchen door.

Medora was five the first time that her father found them, herself and her mother, sitting together on the kitchen stoop. Calley had gone down to the root cellar just moments before, which saved her from dismissal. The sound of his raised voice brought her back at speed; she tucked Medora's face under her apron and held her still there as he shouted, threatening to have the Shawnee woman arrested if she came near the house again. Medora didn't see her father throw her mother into the kitchen yard, but she heard it, heard the impact of her mother's body against the ground and the air leaving her lungs in a rush. She had tried to fight her way free, but Calley held her tighter; a moment later she was glad of this as her father then directed his venom at them, cursed Calley's incompetence and threatened to have her arrested as well if it proved that she'd been abetting covert meetings. Only when he had gone back in the house was she allowed out from under the apron; it was the first time she had ever seen tears in Calley's eyes.

The visits did not cease, but they became shorter, more clandestine, only occurred when Calley was out of the kitchen completely. They were not caught again until one late winter night when Medora was perhaps seven. They had been sitting by the fire, wound in each other's arms, and her father came unexpected into the room; when she was older Medora looked back and guessed that someone must have told him that he would find them together. This time Calley was too far to hear, and so no one kept the child from watching, from hearing, as crockery shattered and furniture cracked. Even so, Medora's memory of that night was blurred, except for the moment, sharp as glass, of looking through the kitchen window into the night and seeing the vague lump of her mother's body, crumpled on the frosted ground. That was the last time Medora saw her.

Calley had not been dismissed as he had previously threatened, but he had taken Medora out of the kitchen and brought her into the house, to be tortured into the form of a Southern lady much in the way a French gardener would shape a box hedge. She should have been married off as soon as she was old enough, to one of her father's overseers or some man of similar station. She should have been sent to foster with a family, perhaps one of his cousins, where she would have had the benefit of a mother. He should never have brought her into his kitchen, certainly not into his parlor. She often wished, after he had decided to take notice of her and make her into his idea of a lady, that he had left her in the kitchen, pretended that she was Calley's daughter. She did not understand why he bothered with her, whether it was out of stubbornness, out of the same perversity of nature that had made him take her from her mother in the first place, or if he did indeed feel some affection, some responsibility for her, if he were perhaps doing by her as best as he knew how.

Her upbringing came in stops and starts, and frequently she was sent back to the kitchen and out of her father's sight, where she had cheerfully helped in whatever way she could and hoped that he would forget about her. Those banishments were the happiest parts of her childhood; she had helped Calley can and jar and absorbed the woman's knowledge of herbs and natural medicine seemingly by osmosis.

But eventually her father's temper abated, no matter how severe the cause had been, and she was always called back into the house to sit stiffly, behave properly, and sneak off to occupy the tedious hours surreptitiously in her grandfather's medical library.

Medora was let out of her room before breakfast the next morning, and contrived to have a chance encounter with the stranger on the back porch while her father was mixing his pre-breakfast julep in the dining room. Maybe she should have simpered, preened, looked coyly over her shoulder and said something poetic about the dew on the narcissus. Instead she walked up to him and candidly stuck out her hand and introduced herself. He was taller and broader than she'd realized from the upper window, but still too thin in the beard and around the middle to be many years past twenty.

His handshake was weak, and though he managed to tell her his name without hesitation—Andrew Robinson Day, Andrew after his father and Robinson after his mother's most beloved fictional character, an introduction she found a little excessive—his brief fumbling for polite small talk gave her physical pain.

"It is . . . I should say . . . very pleasant . . . a very pleasant morning for—I suppose you would ride, you do ride, that is . . . yes?"

"I do enjoy a turn about from time to time. It is a wonderful way to get some air, I find. Are you yourself quite fond of horses?"

His answer was lengthy but amounted to "no"; she let him fumble through a comment on the weather, the hospitality of her father, and the becomingness of her dress before losing her patience and making her proposition.

"If I may be forthright, Mr. Day, I do believe that you and I may be of some use to each other. If you would be so good as to ask me riding this afternoon, we will be assured of privacy and have the chance to discuss further—my father tends to nap just after dinner." She went back inside before he could respond, and remained demurely quiet through breakfast, carefully keeping her eyes down. He walked out with her father after the meal on his habitual review of the property and, sensing opportunity, she slipped up to the guest bedroom that the young man was occupying to undertake her own review.

There was nothing of interest in the pockets of the clothing that he had recently worn, and nothing but the usual necessities in his valise, but his document case—cordovan leather, gently scuffed at the corners, well made but with a flimsy lock—proved interesting. She didn't dare lay out the entire contents, for fear of getting caught by Maisie, the upstairs maid, when she came to neaten up the room, but she did flick through the papers and booklets, pulling a piece out now and again to read it fully before sliding it back and moving on. She left the room with plenty of time to spare, and as close to the way she had found it as possible, overly anxious about being caught; she didn't care what the repercussions might be if she was found snooping, but if her father became party to what she had found in the case then she would lose what leverage she had.

When she told Andrew Day that her father tended to nap after the noon meal what she had meant was that he tended to be insensate from drink. The decanter came out with the salad at one o'clock, as usual, and was depleted and refilled before the chicken and the collards, also as usual, so that by the time the table was cleared, and ripe, velvet-skinned peaches had been brought out in a creamware basket, her father was nodding. She excused herself to her room and changed into a riding habit, an aging black costume originally belonging to an aunt, then waited for the young man on the side porch. There was no question in her mind as to whether he would come, and when he finally appeared the delay was instantly explained by the temerity with which he held the reins of the two horses that were leading him across the lawn, the stableboy following some feet behind, visibly suppressing merriment. She studiously turned her face away as he mounted, but she could hear the clumsiness of it, and she set a slow pace as they started down the long drive, their backs to the house. He sat like a pile of rocks, twitching as his balance changed, but this did not keep him from telling her about his business.

He was a partner, apparently, in a company in Indiana with too many syllables in the name, that had a new, better way to grow and cure tobacco that would make her father even richer if he decided to throw in with them; all they needed was a little starting capital, but the returns would be worth the expense. She supposed he was trying to impress her, or was nattering away out of nervousness, or perhaps both. She nodded periodically, but didn't pay much attention until the house was a fading speck behind them and they were deep under the locust trees near the edge of the plantation, and she pulled her mount around and addressed him.

"You certainly have a lot of bank accounts for an up-and-coming company, don't you? A whole book of checks from the First Bank of Altona, and from the Rockville Holding Corporation, and the Golden Merchant Bank, and about a dozen others." He froze as she said this, and she could barely keep the smile off her face. "Now I know that since the war half the money going round has 'Confederate States of America' on it and isn't worth a tinker's dam, but I've never seen bills quite like yours. If one of your banks is printing them up special for you, they certainly aren't printing up too many."

"You've gone through my papers, haven't you?" he finally asked.

She didn't respond, but nudged her horse into a slow walk, and his followed.

"You've gone through my papers. Admit it, you have!"

"This is what I'm thinking," she began slowly, as if he hadn't said anything. "There is no First Bank of Altona, and you've never once set foot in Indiana."

"Now see here—" he tried to break in.

"If I had to bet, I'd say you're from Boston," she continued, speaking over him, "or Albany, or one of those sorts of cities, and you haven't left it more than once or twice in your whole life. You wouldn't know what to do with a harvest of tobacco if it stood up and called you Papa, but that doesn't matter, because you're planning on finding a way of walking off with your pockets stuffed with real money before the next crop even sprouts. You, sir, are as crooked as they come."

He was taken aback, spluttering, growing red in the face. His horse danced under him and he rocked unsteadily in the saddle, but she held perfectly still.

"We can be useful to each other," she said. "You want money, I want to be anywhere but here."

When they returned to the house nearly three hours later, her father had not been pleased. Apparently, riding off in private with a strange young man and no one to watch over them was something that she was white enough to be forbidden. That evening she went to the kitchen while Andrew Day and her father played cards, and let Calley brush her hair while she rested her head in the familiarity of the older woman's cool gingham lap. Her bedroom was her prison, as comfortable as she had made it, but the kitchen was her home.

"You're headed for trouble, m'dear. Sure as winking," the old woman said to her, but Medora closed her eyes and leaned her head down, enjoying the feel of the brush. She knew what she was doing.

"They's worse places to be, child. Hate the old man all you like, least you don't have to sleep next to him. Least you can close the door against him."

"I'm being careful."

"Girl can't be careful enough. No way to win against them, men will always come out on top. Don't you believe a thing he or any one of them say."

There had been a very limited amount of improper behavior on their ride, and none of it had tempted her, though she kept this information to herself. After her confrontation with Andrew, they'd dismounted to walk their horses slowly and discuss business. Or she had tried to discuss business. He had at first defended himself, explaining that he was the last of a long and noble line, impoverished by war, whose honor remained untarnished but whose name was somewhat sullied by the limited funds of its final scion. Pedigree meant nothing to her without money—if she hadn't been born mercenary, she had been brought up to it—and when she showed no interest in his he began to make court to her, first talking about her dusky beauty, at which she nearly laughed, then how well she sat a horse, and finally in desperation attempting to kiss her. Her slap had all of her muscle behind it, and he settled, somewhat sullenly, to discuss the means by which they would remove themselves, and a decent amount of money, from the premises.

"You don't have to tell me twice. I saw what he did to my mother," Medora answered Calley.

"Just being sure, m'dear."

After their private ride, Andrew stayed for a further two weeks. She had made clear in that initial interview that theirs was solely a business arrangement, but as the days wore on he seemed to be less interested in their plan and more interested in getting his hands on her. At first she let him hold her hand, just so he'd stop bothering her about it. Then she let him stroke up her arm, until by the end of the first week all he had to do was set his palm on her skirt-draped knee to make her stomach jump. It wasn't love, she knew, but a sort of feline want, a purring and a pulling that she hadn't felt before. She was relieved when the day came for him to move on, though it would only be for a short time—in order for him to speak with a few other plantation owners, he had told her father, and to make a full report to his business associates. She enjoyed his attention, but she had been giving in far too much.

When Andrew left, immediately after breakfast on the sixteenth day since he'd arrived, his goodbye to her was polite but perfunctory, and she wondered for a moment if he would keep up his end of their plan. In the days after he left she frequently found herself staring into space, reading the same line of a book over and over, not exactly pining but wanting something that she couldn't name. She told herself that it didn't matter. His absence was part of her plan. A month rattled by, two months: she still ached, still told herself that the aching was inconsequential. Whenever she closed her eyes in that time, she saw her mother.

Her plan required her to obtain a specific sleeping draft from one of the local doctors, and she found it poetic that, after a lifetime of sleep so deep and absolute that Calley had several times drenched her to be sure she wasn't dead, she was suddenly and for the first time wakeful in the private hours of the night. She had planned on simply lying to obtain the medicine, but when she went to see Dr. Parsons, everything she told him was true. He listened to her description, her tone as light and girlish and stupid as she could make it, of her restless nights and the exhausted days that followed them, and gave her a bottle of chloral hydrate with instructions to be careful with the dose. She had other purposes for it, but that first evening she'd taken the amount he recommended; it made her feel so leaden, so heavy, that she tucked it away in her drawer and thereafter mixed herself one of Calley's herbal drafts, strengthened with brandy from her father's decanter.

Nine weeks after his departure Andrew Day returned, with good news from his associates and additional backers to boast—or so he told her father. On the day that he returned she stole to the kitchen, chose one of the largest knives, and sharpened it on the whetstone while Calley was out of the room; then she saddled Mayfly and went for a long ride down the carriage drive, beyond the pecan trees and millpond, to where her father's working horses were kept.

She behaved coolly toward Andrew over dinner; his conversation was entirely business. After supper she followed them to the parlor where a decanter was opened and the cards were brought out. If she didn't know better, Medora would have thought that Andrew had never left, that the long period of waiting had been one especially wracked and sleepless night. She settled in her usual place, the corner chair just behind and to the left of her father's shoulder, a heavy book in hand, to quietly play the part of a lady. Bets were made, cards were drawn, Andrew glanced across at her and she deliberately turned her page. He raised, and won the hand.

The evening wore on, the men bent companionably over the table and the decanter between them slowly emptying, Medora with one eye on her book, the other on her father's cards. She'd never played herself, but her regular presence on such evenings, with no company of her own, had left her with a solid understanding of the game. When the cards were right she turned her page and Andrew won the hand.

When her father's pile of chips had vanished, he tossed down his cards with a laugh.

"You show much improvement since your last visit, Mr. Day."

"You have been most kind to me, sir. If the stakes were higher I'm certain you'd have long since cleared me out."

"I doubt it," her father answered flatly as he emptied the decanter into their glasses.

"How about higher stakes then? You're a betting man, you've probably grown tired of such small potatoes."

"And what would you propose? My finest stud? Half of next year's crop?" He let out a barking laugh. "I know better than that, young man."

"I was actually hoping, sir, for something much more valuable." He glanced up at Medora, who continued to study her book.

"And what would you be wanting a cross-grained, plain-faced, vile-tempered wretch like her for? If I'd had any sense I would have sold her to the Gypsies when they'd have taken her, or boiled her into a pudding while her bones were still soft." He shuffled the cards.

"A wife now, a plantation later," Andrew said. "It sounds as though you're none too keen on keeping her."

"You certainly are making assumptions about the dispensation of my property—and my inclination to ever die," her father chuckled.

"She is your only child, is she not?"

"Though that appellation would usually indicate certain behavior on the part of the appellee—" his voice rose and he leaned back in his chair—"such as 'duty' and 'respect . . .'"

"Father, really—" Medora began, but he raised his hand and she was silent.

"I own the wretch to be my child. And though I'm loath to think of her inheriting the lot, the idea of my estranged relatives getting their fingers on it disgusts me more. At least the harridan knows a good mount when she sees one." Her father began dealing the next hand. "It should rightfully be the losing man that gets her. They're like elephants, women are. Everyone likes to look at them, but no sane man is about to volunteer to keep one." He was silent for a moment. "But I'll take your bet. Best of three. Medora against, what, fifteen thousand? What's your offer?"

Medora kept her eyes on the page—as they drank, as they haggled playfully, and as the cards were taken up, fanned out, and rearranged in the men's hands. She turned her page and sealed her own fate.

⌒

That night, she slipped out onto the front lawn, down the path lined with crepe myrtle, to her father's personal stables, her nightgown pooling and drifting around her like a mist. She touched her fingers to the nameplate on each rough door as she passed: Aise, Coco, Mayfly, Lapis, until she came to Mercury's stall.

He towered above her as she led him out, past the tobacco fields, down under the pecan trees, toward where her father's working horses were kept. The long stable, the corral and the exercise track, the small millpond, all glowed silver in the darkness. His skin was hot, and she led him gently into one of the sets of stocks and looped his halter around its thick wooden frame so that she could strip off her nightgown. The knife was where she had left it, high in the fork of the nearest tree. For a moment she considered him: huge and perfect, the smooth nap of his skin like darkly glowing velvet, his eyes gleaming wetly at her in the dim light.

Her father loved this horse. Every morning, before his breakfast julep, he strolled down to the stables, stroked Mercury's cheeks and kissed his velvet nose, walked him through the early mist, oversaw his feeding. He had made a bed in the stallion's stall and nursed him through a fever the previous year, and when he had stumbled back to his feet after days of dull half-consciousness her father had broken into silent tears. They had pranced together at her side when her father forced her onto Lapis in the hope of making her a horsewoman, and though she had learned to ride almost as well as he did she did not find with any of the horses the bond her father had with Mercury. She doubted that many men found with their wives the bond he had with Mercury.

She reached up to stroke his flank, felt for a moment the pulse and tremble beneath his skin, the sheer aliveness of him, and she couldn't do it. Then she pictured her father flinging her mother down the kitchen steps, and the way he had come at her so many times through her childhood and adolescence. She raised the knife.

Hot blood sprayed her arms, sticky and viscous. She didn't know if the sounds she heard were from the horse, or in her own ears. He bucked, pranced, tried to kick in the tight space of the stocks, then stilled.

They were soft in her hands, and much larger than she'd expected, even though many times before she'd watched the field hands gelding horses, bulls, sometimes smaller animals for the sake of practice or boredom. For a moment she considered taking his cock too, but dismissed the idea: it would require teasing the organ out of its deep sheath, and though she knew she could, she doubted Mercury would cooperate now. And he might bleed to death from that.

He had already stopped bleeding, and she watched as the last few drops splashed into the dust beneath him. She was drenched in sweat, though the night was cool, and shaking, and she left him in the stocks to throw herself into the millpond on the far side of the stables. She laved the water over her hands and arms, rubbing at the congealed blood until it melted away, and emerged dripping.

The shift clung to her skin as she carefully led Mercury out of the stocks, up the path, and back to his own stall. She stabbed the knife deep into a bale of hay, then pried one of the nails from the wall of the small storage room at the end of the stable. With a rock, she pounded it through the velvet skin of the horse's scrotum, into the wooden nameplate on the door of the stall, pinning his testicles where her father would be certain to see them. She retrieved the knife and walked slowly back to the house, and suddenly she felt as though she could sleep where she stood.

They were at breakfast when the explosion came. She was bent low over a boiled egg, hunkered down, expecting it. Andrew was more upright, unaware: she hadn't bothered to tell him, it was her private revenge. It began with a rustle in the hall, and voices, and became a slamming and a shout as her father exploded into the room and caught her up. Her chair went over behind her, the back cracked in two as it hit the floor.

"You whore! You she-devil! What have you done?" He shook her by the arm, but she hung inert, eyes unfocused over his right shoulder. Andrew sat silent at first, but when her father struck her across the face he started up, more in shock than outrage.

"You shall not treat my fiancée in this manner!" he thundered, and her father threw her back against the wall.

"The more luck for her she is your fiancée, or else I'd tear her limb from limb and stake her out in the field for the crows. Get the wretch out of my house, let me never hear her name again!"

Medora gathered herself up, straightened her clothing, then

went to retrieve the case she had packed the night before. When she came back down her father had sunk into a wing-backed chair, silent, his face set and stony, the muscles in his jaw jumping; he did not speak or look up at her as she passed, and to Andrew he addressed the curtest of farewells.

Once out of her father's hearing range she instructed the stableboy who had followed him into the house to hitch up the gig, and he hesitated only for a moment before obliging. The drive out to the railroad station was unmarred by speech, but once the boy had left them Andrew breached the silence.

"Forgive me, but I do not remember our plans for egress involving any forays into gelding, amateur or otherwise."

She did not reply, only looked at him, openly and directly, until he finally looked away in discomfort. He did not bring the matter up again.

They rode the train to Frankfort, disembarked in a light shower and went directly to the tiny room, let out by a deaf older woman but near the railroad station, that Andrew had arranged for them. And then there was nothing to do but wait.

For Medora it was an alien, almost surreal, experience. At home her wallpaper had been peeling, but here the walls themselves were cracked, and insects scuttled in the dark corners and climbed behind the walls; even the air tasted unhealthy, and there were strange stains on the mattress. She had not realized before quite how rich her father was, how tidy Calley kept everything, and for the first week she could barely bring herself to touch anything in that room, even the floor. The filth, from the streets and the air and the people themselves, seemed to cling to her skin, so that she felt constantly dingy and dreamed of her crisp white bedsheets and coppers full of boiling water and the freshness and quiet of first-thing-in-the-morning air. She couldn't imagine how such a press of people could tolerate living in a city, knowing that they would most likely never escape.

They had bought cheap silver bands at a pawnshop the day after they arrived in town, but every time Andrew broached the subject of marriage she put him off; the only thing that she could think of that might be worse than living with the man was relinquishing the right to leave him. The first night they slept on opposite sides of the bed, fully clothed, with their valises and the document case in a neat row between them. Medora assumed that they would continue as they had begun, but as the days of quiet waiting progressed, and the pennies in Andrew's ragged purse began to run out, he grew bolder.

She was not entirely lacking curiosity. She wondered what it was that drew women to men, what the fizzing in her belly would become if he ever did more than lay his hand on her clothed knee. But she had been raised well, at least in this. Calley had made sure of that. It was his role to press, and hers to protest, and for once she fulfilled her prescribed role. But every moment of it felt like acting, as though she were upon a stage for the benefit of a single audience member. They posed as husband and wife, and having her father's consent made them so close to being married that she didn't think it mattered that they weren't. He pressed, and she resisted, and his temper wore thin, until one afternoon he declared that if she didn't dispense with her sensibilities and stop acting like the well-bred woman he knew she wasn't he would use the rest of their money on whores while she slept on the street. It was with mostly feigned reluctance that she gave in.

Immediately afterward she regretted it, and nearly told him to take himself and his whores to hell, but pride kept her from saying a word. Calley had been right in calling it "the wifely duty," and for the first few days she couldn't see how it could be construed as anything else. Once she yielded it seemed that his hands were always on her, that she had given her unequivocal and nonretractable permission for him to enjoy her how and when he pleased. But after a few days, as she began to adjust both to the concept and the actuality, she found the ridiculous side to it, the humor of Andrew's urgency and concentration, and eventually she found herself enjoying it, even having fanciful daydreams of quiet cottages with deep, downy beds and soft, cuddly babies. There wasn't much else for them to do, and the waiting weighed heavy.

The telegram came some nine weeks after they fled the house; Andrew had been sure to send a letter to her father with their address as soon as they'd arrived in Frankfort, and the lawyer had found it in his office and notified them as next of kin. The old man had been found slumped over at his desk, the empty decanter fallen and smashed, apparently drunk into his grave as his physician had predicted. He had barely amended the will that he had made when he first inherited the property, not thinking that he would live forever by any stretch of the imagination, but giving little thought to his mortality or his dependents. There was the standard provision made for a hypothetical spouse, which he had not bothered to correct, with further directive given that the remains of the estate pass to his natural daughter—the wording made it extremely clear that this was categorically to prevent any of his estranged family from making a claim, rather than through fondness or concern for Medora. She was slightly surprised, when it was read out to her, that this stung, just a little. She hadn't expected outpourings of affection, but she had thought she'd meant a touch more to him.

When the telegram arrived she sat for a long time on the edge of the bed in the rented room, staring out the window. He would have drunk himself to death sooner or later: a julep for breakfast, a bottle of wine at dinner, bourbon and water in the afternoon, and usually a full decanter between supper and sleep. The bourbon was kept in bottles in the cellar, rack upon rack of them, which were brought up a bottle at a time and decanted by Mose, the houseboy, as it was needed. The night before their expulsion, before her castration of Mercury, she had crept down to the cellar, blue glass vial of chloral hydrate in hand. She counted off the bottles, calculating from years of experience how long it would take her father to finish each one, and chose one that she guessed would be opened in two months. That it had not been sooner, she supposed, was fair indication that his rage over Mercury had been temporary. She had briefly considered dismembering the horse entirely and leaving the pieces for her father to find scattered across the front lawn. But this would have led to immediate disinheritance, if he hadn't killed her first. Though the gelding had enraged her father, had come against that which he most loved, it had not caused him to suffer any tangible loss. If Mercury had been one of her father's racehorses, a prize stud, rather than his personal mount, there would doubtless have been repercussions. That had been the one risky part of the plan, her father's reaction. But it seemed that she had played all of her cards right.

When they arrived at her father's house Medora closeted herself with the lawyer, emerging hours later with a carefully worded document and a smug smile. She would not marry Andrew, though she would continue to pose as his wife; if he wanted access to her money he could, if he wished, sign the agreement that she and the lawyer had drawn up, which would make him the official manager of her property and funds, otherwise he could test his luck and see how long he could remain in her good graces. He had not been happy, at first threatened to expose her for a murderess, but changed his mind when she reminded him that he would be charged as an accessory, and after a satisfying display of temper, he relented.

For the first time in her life Medora avoided Calley as best she could, and for the first time in her life the older woman offered up little more than a distant expression. In the week immediately following their return Medora had descended to the kitchen once, squeezed into her old spot near the hearth with her black mourning dress crumpled like an overly dramatic flower around her, tried for a moment of normality. Calley was taking an inventory of the entire kitchen, from the spice vials to the laundry cauldron, and did not acknowledge Medora's presence for twenty minutes. When Calley finally did look at her, Medora wished that she hadn't: the gaze was piercing, painful, conscious of all of her faults.

"Have you been using what I taught you?"

"Ma'am? Haven't needed to, ma'am, no one's been ill of late."

"I don't mean that medicine. Do you remember what I taught you, about women's herbs? Have you been using it?"

Medora's bewilderment must have shown, because the woman sighed deeply and pressed her palm to her forehead, in the attitude of a despairing saint. This type of displeasure was familiar, easier to bear, and Medora hunched forward on her chair and listened eagerly as Calley explained the alchemy of tansy, parsley, raspberry leaf tea, the black magic of a woman's body. The original lesson had come, most likely, when Medora was young enough to think that she would never need to know such things, could not understand why someone might want to prevent children from happening. Now there was an urgency to the recitation, a quiet desperation in Calley's gestures as she handed Medora packets of herbs to smell and touch. There was no margin between theory and practice now; Calley did not ask if they had been married in their absence, if the marriage or lack thereof had been consummated. In the end there was too much for Medora to remember, too many details that were vitally important, so Calley took some of the blank leaves of paper meant for the inventory, had her sit and copy out the instructions like a child in school, fold them small and slip them between her chemise and the skin of her belly; she did not need to say that they must be kept secret.

Medora did not return to the kitchen after that. The task of going through her father's library, his papers, his records, was immense, and she was no more inclined to leave Andrew alone to it than he was inclined to be left alone; when they were in bed at night he whispered that the servants seemed to know, that they stared right through him, and Medora whispered back that they knew nothing, that they just didn't like him. Even so, she found it uncomfortable, the gazes of the people that she had known all her life, felt a judgment in them that she did not want to confront.

They settled the affairs of the plantation as quickly as possible, selling the horses, dividing up the land to be rented to tenant farmers, disposing of what they could not or did not want to take with them of her father's estate. A pair of steamer trunks sat, fully packed save for daily necessities, in their bedroom for a full month before they were able to leave. Andrew's first suggestion had been that they go west, start anew like everyone else with a past to forget; Medora vetoed this immediately, due to the likelihood of her being recognized immediately as half-Indian and the possible consequences of such. She objected also to foraying farther south—too hot—and north—too many Yankees—leaving Andrew with one cardinal direction in which to search for their future.

"Not a city, please, not a city. Or a town, if you can manage. Find us a place in the countryside. I don't care if we grow tobacco and raise horses, I don't care what we do, but please, find us a place that I can think of as home."

On the day they left Medora sought out every member of the household, said a private goodbye, but Calley was nowhere to be found. Medora knew that this was because she did not want to be found, and she could not determine if the cause was distaste for partings or due to lingering disapproval of her own decisions. It was with mixed feelings that she eventually resigned herself to leaving without seeing Calley one last time.

They took the train east until they ran out of country; the line terminated in Norfolk, and Medora did not hesitate in expressing her opinion of the grim city.

"Keep your peace, woman, we haven't arrived yet," Andrew responded jovially, but for the first time she realized that she was at the mercy of his whims. He bought her a pot of coffee and some muffins before taking her to the ferry landing, checked to be sure that their trunks had been properly stowed and then settled her solicitously in a place near the rail with a good view.

The mainland receded slowly in the spring mist, so that when the vague, marshy outline of Accomack Island appeared she felt as though she had entered the fairy realm she had read about as a small child. Andrew had bought land for a plantation north of the county seat at Parksley, the acreage already tilled and planted, the foundations laid for a house and the outer walls curing—a couple had intended to set themselves up there, much as they were about to, but the husband had fallen ill and was confined to a sanatorium in northern Maryland. Andrew engaged rooms for them at the health spa at Wachapreague, as the season was just beginning and it would be six months before their house was finished, and there Medora was left to her own devices for most of the day, while her faux-husband went off to tend to their business.

The role of lady of leisure did not sit well with her, and after the first week, which was occupied entirely with casual conversations with the three other women in situ and with thumbing through the frankly asinine books that were kept on hand as light reading for gentle ladies—Andrew had arranged to have her own library shipped only when the space for it was finished—she felt as though she would go mad.

She unearthed her old riding habit from the bowels of her trunk, asked that a horse be saddled—one with an interesting temperament, please, she would prefer something with a little more character than an armchair—and declined the offer of an escort. On that first day she rode out to the beach on the ocean side of the island, dismounted to walk along the sand

and watch the breakers lave the shore, and felt, for a moment, wholly content.

The first two years on the island passed quickly for both of them, Andrew occupied with playing plantation owner, Medora luxuriating in her new-found freedom. There was more room for eccentricity on the Shore, more of a blind eye turned to peculiarity. Even after their home was finished and furnished Medora continued to foray out to the wilder places of the island, to the beaches and into the marshes, collecting unfamiliar plants, speaking freely with the poor farmer's wives whom she met, unfettered by social convention. Her cook and the housegirls quickly grew used to her tendency to sit with them during the quieter times of day, to her presence in the corner of the kitchen, and it was because of this that they discovered her secret knowledge, and she discovered that Andrew had been unfaithful.

The former event came first, about a year after their arrival. It was women's conversation, in the evening after supper, with cups of coffee and the cook's pipe lit. One of the kitchen girls was a year married that month, and she laughed that all the older women had told her to enjoy the tupping because it wouldn't last, but damn her if she couldn't get her husband to keep his hands to himself; it was a miracle that she hadn't yet fallen pregnant. Medora had thought about this while the conversation wandered elsewhere, then stood to take her leave and drew the girl out of the room after her.

"I'm sorry if I've offended, ma'am, I didn't mean to be uncouth," the girl began, anxiety in her voice.

"There's nothing to apologize for, sweetling, I just had a thought." Now out of hearing of the kitchen, Medora turned to her. "Do you truly wish to keep from falling pregnant?"

The girl nodded.

"And do you truly know no way of keeping this from happening?"

"Only that he should leave the church before the final hymn has been sung," she answered timidly.

Medora laughed at the euphemism, then led her up to the library, where her medicine chest was kept.

She told the girl to be careful with the herbs, to tell no one where she had gotten them, and so it was mere weeks before women began appearing at the kitchen door, poor women and ill women and women that couldn't trust or afford a doctor, asking if the mistress was in, asking if the mistress could help them.

In their third year on the island, James was born, a calculated mistake on Medora's part. He was a perfect baby, round and quiet, dark-eyed and dark-haired, but his birth marked the end of peace in their house.

If Andrew had taken up with another woman in the beginning, when they were waiting for the telegram and arranging her father's affairs, when she still despised him, she doubted that she would have cared. He was just her means then, the method by which she had escaped her home. But as she played the part of the happy wife she felt the role grow on her, until Andrew became as much hers as her own skin, not necessarily something she loved or thought about, but something she could not do without. Pregnancy and childbirth only bound her more closely to him. In the months that she was round with James, Andrew was attentive, fawning almost, and ridiculously mindful of her health and comfort. This care had abated somewhat after James's birth, when he had seen the shade of the baby's skin, the satin darkness of his feathery newborn hair. She had been too busy with James to care how Andrew was occupied, counting his tiny fingers and toes over and over, stroking his fat cheeks and holding him even while he slept, even when she could have easily laid him down and taken some moments for herself.

Andrew began talking about his family name then, its long, proud history. She had stopped listening whenever she heard the word "honor," much as she had when her father mentioned "duty," until the day that the cook drew her into the cold room, shut the door so that no one could overhear, and told her that rumor had it her husband had been tumbling one of the female hands. She considered, and decided to keep her peace for the time being.

Ruth was a true accident, born two years after James. When Medora had discovered that she was pregnant again she had hoped that the baby would be a boy, would be fair, would satisfy Andrew and cause him to cease the dalliances that he still thought she was ignorant of, that the house staff kept her privately apprised of. Ruth was as dark as James, but Andrew seemed taken with her regardless, and for some months he kept to their bed, treated her again with tenderness.

It was when Ruth was nearly two years old that the woman who did their washing told Medora that her husband had been seen about with Gracie Cole, not taking advantage of her, as he had done with the others, but courting her in earnest, if in private. Tumbling the servants she could blink at, so long as he kept them out of their bed; her father had kept the field hands' daughters in terror for as long as she could remember, it was behavior that she could accept as a given for a man of means. Women more common than herself, with no name and no fortune, were no threat to her, but Gracie was the daughter of a mainland gentleman, brought over every summer to enjoy the sea breezes. The young woman was white as notepaper, blond-haired and gray-eyed, slender and graceful: the perfect mother for the dynasty of which Andrew dreamed, a woman he would not be ashamed to take with him back to the mainland. All he needed to do was get rid of Medora.

On the night she chose to confront him she went to the study immediately following supper, locked the door and stared at a page of the *Medicinal Herbal* as the house closed up around her. When all was silent she shut the book, walked slowly to their bedroom. He was still awake, sitting at the secretary desk with his back to the fire, scribbling out business correspondence by the light of an oil lamp.

"Come to bed, my little wife?" he asked her merrily.

"How long have you been courting Grace Cole?" she asked.

"Pardon?"

"How long? How many gifts have you given her—books, kid gloves, fancy hats? How many sweet nothings have you whispered in her ear?" He did not respond, kept his eyes trained on the page that he had been writing.

She continued, her voice lower but thick with feeling, "How many times have you promised to make her your wife once you've gotten rid of me?"

"I don't know what you mean. What would make you think this?" His tone was even, but his skin had gone waxy, his expression static; she knew he was lying.

"Did you tell her that you'd get an annulment? Sue for divorce? Were you going to have me committed as a madwoman? Maybe you told her that we never married, is that what you did?"

"Surely you can understand—"

"Surely I can?"

"I have a right to see my family name continued."

"You have two children, two children as perfect as children can be. We can have more if you want more. What else are you lacking?"

"Legitimate children, for one thing. Pure-blooded children, for another."

Her rage was incandescent, so that afterward she could not remember the particulars of what she said, what she did. She knew that their talking continued for over an hour, increased in volume with no thought for their children sleeping, that they stalked about the room, that a bottle of cologne had been thrown, a mirror broken. That she had scratched at him, and that he had hit back at her with a closed fist, that she had tried to get at him with the fireplace poker and he had wrenched her shoulder out of its socket in getting the implement away from her. She remembered the sting of her palm when she slapped him, that the words "half-breed daughter of an Indian whore" had been why she had slapped him, that when she had tried to slap him a second time he had caught her wrist in one hand and her throat in the other, pressed on her windpipe until her vision went dark.

He had shaken her then, forced her downward. She felt heat on her back and side, and realized that they were against the fireplace, that the hem of her skirt was already smoking, that he was pushing her downward, choking, into the flames.

It felt as though the fire were under, rather than against, her skin, as if he had set her bones themselves aflame. Her left arm was pinned beneath her, she could smell her hair frizzling, she could not breathe. Then the cloth of her dress blazed, a wall of quick flame in front of her, and he released his hold on her throat.

She erupted from the hearth, trailing live coals as she rolled on the rug, smothering the flames, screaming in fear because she could not feel the pain yet. He was still for a moment, as if stunned, watching her and clutching at the hand that he had scorched in holding her there against the fire. He reached for her again and she surged to her feet, flung herself out the door and down the hall. She could smell the fire, she could feel the fire, even though she couldn't see flames anymore. She stumbled, fell bumping down the entire flight of stairs, staggered to her feet and fled onward: he would kill her, she knew it, if he got his hands on her again. Faces appeared as she ran through the house, familiar faces, shocked faces. The cook reached out to stop her but she sprang away, ran like a frightened colt, through the wide front door, down the sandstone steps, out into the marsh, still screaming.

CHAPTER V

1984

—

Boys

O n your way to Stella's you see the boys again. They're climbing the apple tree on the green next to Onancock Methodist church, the shorter one pulling himself up into the branches while the taller pushes him from behind. As you pass by, the taller one waves to you, and you lift your hand to wave back but then smile instead, and hurry on. People already think you're a bit slow, even though you got through eighth grade just fine. No sense in confirming it by waving at someone no one else can see.

It's been a while since you've seen them, though they're never gone for too long. They've been around since your childhood, like the talking birds that perched on your bedroom door and the mermaids that held their arms out to you, calling you to join them in your grandpa's pond. But while the birds and the mermaids have faded away the boys are still with you. The taller one looks like he's seven, the same age as Cabel Bloxom, the kid you babysit, and the little one is just big enough to run around on his own. Maybe they're the residue of all the acid your mom dropped, all the grass your dad smoked, before they found religion. A remnant of magic in your DNA like the fairy dust you believed in when you wore a pink tutu to school and wrote your name in yellow crayon.

The windows of Stella's are still frosted with morning condensation, and you have to resist rubbing your sleeve over them as you go in the back door and find your apron. You've been working the sandwich counter here since 1979, when you were fifteen: five long years in the same apron, grinning at the same customers, smacking down bologna and ham and cheese like you're dealing cards, every day of the week but Wednesdays. Most people would feel stifled, stuck in the town where they grew up with no hope of ever getting out, but you like the familiarity. Stella doesn't let anyone give you a hard time, even when you give them Cheddar instead of American cheese or forget that they were drinking Coke and not iced tea. She lets you stay in the back mostly. Some people still give you that look, the one that says they remember what you did. It isn't that hard to remember; your parents still won't talk to you.

As you tie your apron around your waist you wait for the feeling of your shoulders unkinking, the way they do every morning just as soon as you get in front of the sandwich board. Today the tension of the outside world stays with you, resting like a block of cement across the back of your neck. As you check the bread and get ready for the lunch crowd you think it was stupid to expect this to go away like your everyday worries always do.

Stella bustles into the kitchen, a ticket clutched in her lean brown hand, and smiles good morning to you.

"Could you do a couple salad eggs pretty for old Mr. Wallace? He was wanting deviled but I told him we wouldn't have any till lunch." Jack Wallace had begun planting clams when he was a barefoot teenager too poor to afford schooling; now well into his seventies and selling his harvest for nearly a quarter of a million dollars each year, he still came by Stella's most days.

"Yes, ma'am. I could devil a couple quick but they wouldn't be chilled right."

"Anything you do is fine, he loves his eggs."

She spikes the ticket above your workstation, then takes a tray of rolled silverware and turns to go.

"Miss Stella—" You roll a hard-cooked egg between your palms and skin off the shell, shy to talk. "Can I ask you a favor?"

"Something wrong, Izzy?"

"Can I borrow ten dollars against my next pay? I've got a bit of a problem and I don't want Donnie to know just yet."

She gives you a look when you say it, but when she comes back to get the plate of sliced eggs, arranged carefully over lettuce and tomato wedges, she slips you two crumpled fives along with the next order ticket.

Ellie doesn't say anything at first when you ask for a ride to the pharmacy in Salisbury later that day. You can see all the words on her face, though. Why don't you ask Donnie? Why didn't you go to the pharmacy across from Stella's? What are you going to get, anyway?

"Eh, why not?" is all she says, and swings her daughter Chloe up under her arm. "I'll go get my car."

Ellie went to the same school as you. She was one of the tough kids, who spent more time in the principal's office for bloodying someone's face than in her classroom seat. Her dad was a deadbeat and her mom was a psycho, so no one much cared what she did as long as the cops didn't show up. Then her mom ran off for the mainland and she left school to take care of her sister Ollie. It wasn't until she got pregnant and you got thrown out that you became friends. She had a forbidding look to her back then, a terminal case of bitch face you'd heard it called, so when she and her husband Bo moved into the little house on the far side of the creek you were surprised at how friendly she was. It was a shotgun wedding, or so people said, but you pretend you don't hear her and Bo fighting on still nights, just like she pretends not to hear Donnie pretty much every night. Sometimes you wonder what would happen if everyone stopped pretending.

As you wait for her to come back—it's a good walk by road, even though you can see her roof peeking through the trees across the water—you watch Cabel, the boy you babysit, throwing stones into the bowl of an old handicapped toilet Donnie found pretty soon after you moved in. The yard is littered with junk, cracked or rusting or covered up with tarps, that Donnie's found or stolen but hasn't gotten around to selling yet. He fixes cars, off and on, but salvage is where he gets most of his money—or where he says he gets most of his money. You suspect he deals in things more illicit than stolen bathroom fixtures, but you don't want to know. You feel bad about the handicapped toilet—Ellie mentioned once that they were expensive, not the kind of thing that someone would junk if it still worked—but there isn't anything you can do about it.

Cabel is a caramel-colored boy, skin tanned darker than his pale hair, so thin that you can see the muscles in his back and shoulder twitch and roll as he lifts his arms to toss the rocks. His dad is a sleazy skirt-hound, Ellie told you, knocks up his girlfriend and then moves on to the next one; she knows be-

cause she worked construction with him, before she got pregnant. You can tell when Cabel has been visiting him because he
comes back with a meanness that hangs around for a few days.
He's sweet, though, generally speaking: sometimes he brings
you handfuls of raspberries and honeysuckles he's picked, or
the shells of bird's eggs and glittering mica fragments because
he knows you like pretty things, asks if he can play with your
hair and falls asleep in your lap while you read to him. You've
always had a soft spot for little boys. Donnie was like him once,
you suppose, and Bo too. But something happens in the gap between boy and man to turn all that sweetness bitter. You wonder if it's a necessary hardening, like a tree's shedding of leaves
as winter approaches.

Your eyes unfocus in half-thought, catch a slice of movement beyond the trees, focus with a snap as the boys appear.
Maybe they were there all along. They look at you, and you
look at them, and you want them to come over and sit with you
as you wait for Ellie to come back. The twisting in your stomach has kept you from eating anything all day. But they watch
you from the tree line, as if to say everything will be all right,
or maybe that they do not know if everything will be all right.
A rock clunks against porcelain. You decide to get up, to go to
them, but hear the crunch of gravel under car tires.

Ellie drives a liver-colored boat that rocks as it hits the div-
ots in the road. The cloth of the ceiling is caving in, and you
tell Cabel not to pull at it as you strap him in next to Ellie's little
girl. She's not quite two years old, with curling hair the color of
cinnamon and wide, staring eyes that she turns on him warily
as you buckle the strap. You pray that they don't start fighting.

The drive to Salisbury is long and slow, the air inside the car moist and heavy. The heat puts the kids to sleep in the first few miles, and for that you are thankful. Ellie chats with you about this and that, but there's awkwardness to the conversation, and eventually you both just sit quietly, watching the mile markers zip by.

A few miles outside of Salisbury Ellie turns down a side street lined with crepe myrtles and stops in front of a pharmacy. You sit for a moment, breathing the sticky air and willing yourself to get up, to go in.

"I'll go with you," she says as she pulls the key out of the ignition. It's a statement, rather than an offer. Her thighs have stuck to the vinyl, make a peeling sound as she climbs out of the car. "The kids'll be fine for five minutes."

Even though it's small, the inside of the pharmacy overwhelms you, and you wander for a few minutes before realizing that what you're looking for is going to be behind the counter, and your stomach plummets toward your knees. You can feel Ellie beside you as you walk toward the back, look for a moment at the tall, gray-mustached pharmacist, and then to the cabinet behind him.

"Can I help you, miss?" he asks.

"I need a pregnancy test," you mumble, staring at the chips in the edge of the Formica counter, and he turns to the shelves behind him. Ellie steps up next to you, takes your hand and squeezes, and you're glad she came in with you. You can feel the heat rising in your face, and you wonder how Donnie can stand to buy condoms. Knowing Donnie, he probably jokes with the pharmacist about what he'll be using them for. Men are allowed to joke about things like that, you've discovered. They're expected to, even, to strut and gloat a little bit when they have the opportunity, with the right audience. You could have gone to the local pharmacist, not bothered Ellie with driving, but someone would have seen you if you had. Even if the pharmacist himself hadn't mentioned it, Donnie would have known before dinnertime, come slamming into the trailer demanding to know why and when because it's not his fault. You're hoping that you're all worked up for nothing, that you're not pregnant, that he'll never have to know that you came here, bought this shameful thing.

The test comes in a tan box, but the pharmacist puts it in a plain paper bag before handing it to you and taking the ten dollars you borrowed from Stella. That kills you more than anything else; you could make those ten dollars stretch so far.

You wait until Donnie leaves for work in the morning, then open the test on the kitchen table. It's in a clear plastic box: a plastic ampule, an eyedropper, and a test tube in a stand over a little mirror. You read the instructions twice—it requires the first urine of the day, which you knew already, and takes two hours to register, which you didn't—then go pee into a clean juice glass. All night it felt like you'd burst if you had to hold it in another moment, but now that you're finally allowed to you're so nervous that it's five minutes before you can scare up a drop. Only three drops are needed, measured out with the eyedropper and shaken up in the test tube with the liquid from the ampule. It looks so innocuous when you're done, the test tube just sitting there over the mirror. You leave it next to the sink, behind the sugar tin, slide on your shoes and walk the mile and a half to get Cabel so his mother can get a nap before she goes to work at the Perdue plant on the killing floor.

He's in a quiet mood today, and you get him to help you clean a bit before you sit down together on the kitchen floor with a set of tiddlywinks. You keep your eye on the plastic clock over the sink as he chatters to you and flips the winks, only half-hearing anything he says, and when the two hours have gone by you pull yourself abruptly up from the floor, walk over to the sink, and slide the sugar tin aside.

A dark ring has shown up in the bottom of the test tube, and even though you open up the directions and read again to be sure, you know it's positive. The rushing in your ears drowns out the sound of Cabel talking, and you grab the edge of the counter to keep from tipping over.

The first thing he asks is how the hell you're so certain. When you show him the test tube with its incriminating ring he wants to know where you got it, where you got the money to get it, who took you to get it, because he would have found out if you'd gotten it in town. His voice gets louder and louder, until you're cringing away from him, all but hiding under the opposite side of the table. This makes him angrier, he's not some monster that you have to hide from, and as you mumble an apology and straighten up he goes into the bedroom.

When he comes back he smacks a wad of bills down on the table, crumpled ones and fives with a few twenties and fifties shuffled in, creased and layered together like a handful of last year's leaves.

"Was saving for a motorcycle," he says, "but that can wait. Get rid of it."

"Why?" you ask.

"Why?" he says.

"Why not keep it?" Start a family. Get married. Be what your mother expected you to be. Watch your own children during the day instead of other people's. Have a reason to end the arguments.

"I ain't gonna father a bastard. You can always have another one."

"I want this one!"

His fist comes down on your upper arm, but you don't flinch away. You've pushed him too far, like you always do. He curses, grabs your wrist, and wrenches you across the room so that you bounce against the opposite wall, but you've become stone. You hear none of it.

Maybe one day you'll learn to read his moods better, learn to sense when he's running out of patience, learn to stop pushing him until the storm comes. There will be bruises, on your arms and other not so visible places, in the morning, and neither Stella nor Ellie nor any of the people you see throughout the day will say a word about them, the way you never say a word when Ellie's skin blooms purple-green. Even so, you know they'll see and wonder what you said, what you did, how you failed to keep it together this time.

As he calms, you find yourself nodding along with what he says. He leans in to kiss you, to embrace you, ashamed of his outburst. Then he draws you into the bedroom: you always make love after a fight, to make up for the screaming. You let him touch you, slowly peel your blouse off, without saying anything. You want to think, to go someplace quiet. The last thing you want is the soft-shelled crab feeling of him on top of you, but it's so easy to touch him off again, and you're freshly scared, recently reminded of what those fists can do. It hurts in a sharp, shredding way when he enters you, but you roll your selfness up from your toes and tuck it into the very back of your head, leaving your body empty, and the pain goes dull. Your eyes flick across the ceiling and around the upper edge of the wall, settling nowhere in an attempt to escape from the sound that is more a sensation of his hot, wet breath on your neck, the grunts and chuckling moans as he pushes into you. His hands on your shoulders burn.

A movement catches your attention, and over Donnie's sweat-flecked shoulder you see the older of the boys, freckled face framed by the tiny trailer window. His eyes meet yours, their stillness making him seem infinitely sad, and you focus on them. The pain gets worse, and you want to say something to Donnie about it, except the last time you did, things didn't end so well. The boy steps through the wall, and even though you don't want anyone to see you like this you're glad that he does, that he knows, that someone knows without you having to put it into words. He puts his hand on the pillow next to your head. His eyes look like the quicksilver from the thermometer you dropped when you had mumps, still and moving at once, silver and glinting, and you focus on them, time your breaths to his, watch him so closely that for a moment you think you've become him.

It hasn't always been this way. Once you were a good girl, and went to church with your mama five days a week, ate the wafer and prayed to God that you'd escape eternal hellfire. She said that was what happened to girls who lied about washing their hands and cleaning their rooms and whether they'd eaten the last cookie weeks before and put the packet back empty in the cupboard. She'd not done right by your older sister, she'd been foolish then, but by God she was going to do everything she could to make sure you turned out holy.

You never meant to lie, but you could never remember what you'd done, or hadn't done, or had been meant to do but hadn't really been listening when you'd been told to do it. You knelt on the time-stained pine floorboards of the Catholic church in Parksley and prayed like nothing that you wouldn't burn up in hell, but your mama shook her head over you, said that you'd never be saved if you didn't get over your lying ways.

When you got older you started noticing boys, and boys started noticing you, and Mama started noticing you noticing each other. She scared them off for a few years, but when you started working at Stella's Donnie Hammond took the opportunity to follow you around, get you alone so he could stroke your hair and arm and tell you how damn pretty your cloud-gray eyes were. He told you that just one kiss, just one touch, wouldn't get you in trouble, and even though you didn't believe him you let him touch you, and kiss you, because you wanted to know what his hands and lips felt like. You had never guessed anything could feel that good.

Mama'd told you that boys would try and make you do dirty things, but she'd never told you exactly what they were, or that you'd want to do them, so when Donnie started pulling you closer and moving his hands under your clothes you didn't know what to do. So you did nothing. And after you'd done nothing once you had to keep on doing nothing.

You'd sat near each other in mass for years, your mother and his mother were both in the Altar Guild, you'd been in the same class at school until he'd dropped out to learn how to fix cars; Mama thought he was a good Catholic boy. He told you it was just plain mean, letting him touch you special one day and then saying no the next. And it weren't no use, Mama would have said if she'd known, stopping after you'd started. You'd already proved you weren't a good girl; you weren't worth anything anymore. You decided that you might as well enjoy it.

Except once he'd gotten you to go all the way, he didn't take the time anymore to run his hands over your quivering skin, to kiss you long and slow, the way he had at the beginning. He got straight to the main attraction. You felt cheated that you didn't enjoy this as much as you had the touching, even though it was supposed to be the big thing, the biggest thing. But you didn't know how to tell him that, how to ask for something different, or what to ask for.

You were seventeen when you finally got caught. It was in your dad's toolshed, on a rainy day when there hadn't been anything to do. Donnie had come to find you, and by then you'd found the nerve to tell him that even if he was your secret boyfriend you didn't want to do it anymore. He'd told you not to be that way, that he'd try harder, make it nicer for you, almost cried, and you'd relented. When your dad came in you still had your shirt on, but there was no good excuse for the rest of it.

Mama scattered your clothes on the front lawn, smashed your porcelain ballerinas on the sidewalk, the rain mixing with her tears and sticking her long gray hair to her face. You could feel the eyes behind the curtains on the prim little street in Parksley where you lived, hated them for enjoying the spectacle. You gathered up the muddy skirts and blouses without saying a word.

For a while you stayed with Donnie at his parents' house in Tasley, a few miles south of Parksley and still close enough for you to walk to work, but the priest and the women got after his mother until she decided that she couldn't help the two of you live in sin anymore, and had Donnie's daddy kick you both out. Donnie found the trailer quick after that, a dented sardine tin with a rotting kitchen floor and barely enough room to change your mind, and found a farmer that would let them park it cheap on his land. With what you made at Stella's and what he made fixing cars, you could just afford the rent. There wasn't anywhere around that cost less to live. There weren't any other options.

The first time you walked into the grocery store after your mother threw you out, the eyes felt like cigarettes being put out on your skin. You'd thought it would be the men who would stare, but instead it was the women. Even though you guessed half of them had done the same, been touched and kissed or more and liked it, none of them had been caught. You felt the weight of their judgment on your shoulders as you picked through the basket of dented, marked-down cans. You'd known them all your whole life, but not a soul spoke to you, until Ellie asked if you were planning on making a casserole with those beans. Her belly was round and firm with Chloe, the copper wire twisted around her wedding finger in place of a ring still shining, her guarded, acne-scarred face the most beautiful thing you'd ever seen.

⤚

Donnie falls asleep afterward, and you squirm out from under him and sit naked at the kitchen table, looking at the mound of bills. You have no idea how much is there. You have no idea how much an abortion costs. You'll have to get Ellie to give you a ride down to Norfolk, or up to Salisbury; you're not sure if either place has a doctor that does that sort of thing.

A shadow moves across the screen door, and you jump to cover yourself. You thought that it was Cabel, come like he does sometimes to ask for a drink or a snack or just some company because his mother's passed out and her boyfriend is elsewhere, but it's the boys again, one on either side of the doorway, watching you impassively as you contemplate the money on the table. For a moment you resent the thickness of the stack, the careless way the bills are crumpled and folded together, in light of your pilled-up thrift-store clothes, the dented, marked-down cans of beans and vegetables in the cupboard, the hole in the corner of the kitchen floor that you've covered with a piece of plywood to keep Cabel from climbing through it when he visits you. The way Donnie takes your pay, every cent of it, for the rent, and demands to know what you've spent money on if there's less than usual.

A baby seems a nice thing to have, one day, but even though you're not sure you want one right now, you're also not sure if you want to get rid of the one you're carrying. Even if Donnie married you now it wouldn't make people forget what they know about you, how your parents threw you out and how you've been living in sin. They need you, need someone to be better than, to point out when their own lives don't go quite as planned, to carry the communal disdain. Getting married right now would only give them something new to talk about, as most of them can count to nine, even if they have to take their shoes off to do it. And if Donnie was going to marry you, was planning on marrying you, he would have done it by now.

The sky is softening outside, dimming at the eastern edge; the summer evenings are long. The boys have slipped through the wall, come to stand on either side of you, look at the money as you shuffle it. You want them to hold your hands, make you feel better, like how your daddy used to stroke your forehead when you had a fever, but they never do. Their eyes are all the comfort you get, but usually it's comfort enough.

As quietly as you can you slip back into the bedroom, move quickly in the tiny gap around the bed as you dress. As you close the door behind you, you don't look back at Donnie stretched out and asleep on the bed.

You head south down the edge of the highway, the walk you take to work every morning, toward Parksley and your parents' house, cross the highway just before you reach it and follow the main road into Onancock; you haven't been to Parksley since they threw you out. It's a good walk but you take it slow, breathe the soft marsh air deep into your lungs and watch the patterns the wind makes in the tops of the corn. At one time you thought that this would be your forever home, but now you're not so sure. Behind you as you walk you hear the light crunch of feet on the sandy shoulder of the road, and you know if you look back you will see the boys dogging you, the small one on the older one's shoulders, his bare feet swinging.

Stella's looks full but you know it's not busy: the post-dinner crowd is lounging back in their chairs, sipping the dregs of coffee and toying with half-eaten slices of pie and cheesecake, not wanting to order anything else but not wanting to leave. Stella herself is behind the counter, and you grin and dig into your pocket as you cross the dining room. You think of Ellie as your only friend, but from Stella you've never gotten the judging look the other women give you.

You set a crumpled ten on the counter. "I wanted to give this back to you," you say.

"Thank you, Izzy," Stella answers as she puts the bill into the drawer, "but you could have waited until you came in tomorrow."

"I'm not so sure I'll be in tomorrow, Miss Stella. My problem has gotten bigger than I thought it would."

She gives you a long look, and you know that she's taking in the raw spots on your face from where jaw and cheekbone scraped the rough wood of the table and she's coming to her own conclusions. You don't correct her.

"Well then. I'm sorry about that, Izzy. And I want you to know that, when everything clears up, you'll still have a job here."

She makes you wait as she packs you some sandwiches and counts out the pay she owes you, and you stand embarrassed by the counter while she does. You don't want to take charity, but you know that you need it, even with the roll of Donnie's money pressing against your thigh through the pocket of your dungarees. It's going to run out sooner or later, even though it's more money than you've ever seen in one place at a time.

The sky darkens to indigo as you walk back along the highway, skip the turning to your own home, and continue down the gravel road toward Ellie's. You half-expect to hear her and Bo fighting, first as you step onto the crushed-shell road, then again when you cut through the grass and under the evergreens, but the only sounds are the crickets and the frogs and the rising rattle of cicadas. When you come around the corner you see the dark shape of her sitting on the stoop in front of the screened-in porch, not smoking or drinking, just leaning back and looking at the sky. You sit down on the cinderblocks next to her.

"Whatcha doing out at night like this?" you ask.

"Just getting some air," she says, and you don't know if she's lying to you or to herself or if it's the truth.

"Took the test," you say, short and sharp. "It was positive. Donnie wants me to get rid of it. I don't know if I'm going to."

"So whatcha going to do?" she asks. Her eyes bulge a bit when you show her the money, and you find the look satisfies something deep inside you.

"Come with me?" you ask as you tuck it back deep in your pocket.

It's only a moment before she shakes her head.

"You'll get farther on that if you're alone. We'll just drag you down."

"You sure?" you ask.

"You can melt away on your own. Get set up before the kid comes if you keep it, have some place to recover if you don't. Donnie will huff and puff a bit, but he'll never get off his ass to find you. Me on the other hand—" she flashes the wire ring, now dulled and dented—"if I run off, he'll hunt me to the end of the earth and bring my head back on a plate."

"Really sure?" you ask again. You don't want to go alone.

"He hates me and he wants me and he hates that he wants me. If I stay right here I'll be fine. Besides, I don't have a big fat bankroll—we'll eat through that twice as fast, and you're the one that really needs to get out of here."

"I want you to go with me." As you say it you know it's urgent, it's important, and you know that she isn't going to.

"I can give you a ride to the bus station in Salisbury," she says, and pulls herself up. "Let me get my keys."

She holds your hand the whole ride north. Her eyes are straight ahead, she doesn't say a word, but her hand in yours is warm and firm and comforting. You lean back and grip it tighter.

At the bus station she waits as you buy a ticket—she doesn't want to know where to, so Donnie can't make her say if he comes asking—then squeezes you goodbye. Then she's gone, and you're left waiting alone on the hard metal bench in the outdoor terminal.

As you stare at the ground two forms walk into your peripheral vision, but it isn't until they sit down on either side of you, isn't until you look up, that you recognize the boys. Part of you thought that they would have stayed behind, thought that they were tied to the land, to the marsh. They look at you, and you feel a momentary pang of guilt, knowing that Cabel will be expecting you in the morning and you won't be coming. Then the little one reaches out and takes your hand, and so does the older one. Their skin is smooth and cool against yours, and for a moment you forget that no one else can see them.

Your bus comes, and you show the driver your ticket before climbing on and taking a seat near the back, and the boys follow you and settle on either side. The bus won't be leaving for a while, but you feel too exposed outside. It's tomorrow already. Your eyes close on their own, your head rocks back against the threadbare purple headrest, but just on the edge of sleep you feel it: the hot, wet breath on your neck, fear knotting your stomach.

CHAPTER VI

1991

—

PORTER MOUNTAIN

They'd been on Porter Mountain for a day, a day and a half, before his cousin Dave showed up. Laying low, Pierce called it. Just for a while. He'd neglected to mention that his cousin would be coming to work on the fences, patch leaks in the roof, and generally get the place back in shape. The farm belonged to Pierce's disgustingly rich grandfather, and all the cousins reportedly had his permission to use it as they needed. Pierce and Becky had gone there for a few quiet weekends and clandestine afternoons, when they could afford the gas or when her parents were hovering more than usual. Becky loved the Blue Ridge Mountains, loved being out of touch and out of reach of anyone who could want to find her, but staying in a stranger's empty house had made her uncomfortable, no matter how short the visit. Pierce said that they were allowed, and she didn't think that he was lying to her, but he so often lied to himself about the things he wanted that she wasn't sure if that were the case with the farm.

Then Donnie Hammond, Pierce's dealer back home, had been arrested and Pierce suggested going to the farm as an option preferable to going to jail. She hadn't liked the idea of using someone else's house as a place to hide from the law while living in sin, but arguing with Pierce was useless; he always brought the conversation back around to her performance in bed, and she automatically lost. So she hadn't said anything, either when he first mentioned it or while they bought groceries for the trip or on the way up the mountain. She sat over near the passenger door as they wound slowly over the rutted logging paths, her forehead pressed to the window, looking out at the trees whipping by.

It was a charming place, she had to give it that: an old-fashioned kitchen, tiny parlor, and master bedroom on the ground floor, with two little rooms like an afterthought above. The front porch looked out on a small meadow, with the mountains rising beyond it, and no neighbors within sight or holler.

On the night they arrived, they cooked bacon, eggs, and rice together over the old wood stove, almost smoking themselves out of the kitchen in their efforts to light the fire: it had become a point of honor that they not use the little electric range that sat in the corner of the kitchen. Afterward, with dirty dishes still spread across the table and grease congealing in the frying pan, Pierce pulled her to the top of the bald hill behind the house to look at the stars and the smudge of the Milky Way, and she almost forgave him. It was easy to forgive him when he had his arm around her, and it was quiet enough that she could hear his breath rasping in his lungs. They messed around a bit, up under the naked sky, but he hadn't felt like doing more. For once she didn't want to push it. The fields around the house were rented out to valley farmers for cattle grazing, and on their first visit, when Pierce had pulled her down to have sex on the dead grass in the front field, one of the bulls had smelled them and chased her all the way up to the porch, his erection flopping almost to the ground. Pierce had joked about making her fuck it so he could make some money off the film, and she'd become acutely aware of the presence of all the bulls since.

The front bedroom and its enameled brass bed frame had been used by generations of Pritchetts, and the part of her that did not quail at the thin, stained mattress quailed at the idea that Pierce's grandparents had once spent private nights together in that bed. Pierce fell asleep almost immediately, naked except for his boxers, curled up like a dog with his smooth back radiating heat. She had tried curling around him, but there was no give in his shoulders, so she'd turned her back to him to avoid sliding into the dip in the center of the bed. There were no sheets, and it was too hot for the quilt, so Becky lay uncovered, looking at the turning stars through the slotted blinds as pinfeathers slowly worked their way through the mattress and etched into her skin.

The popgun sound of a truck door closing woke her, though Pierce only stirred and settled again, and she lay bewildered, sick in the stomach and head aching from the sunlight streaming through the cracks in the blinds, as a set of heavy footsteps clunked up the front porch. A long, bulky shadow fell across the blind, and a watery blue eye peered at her through a gap between two bent slats. She shrieked and rolled into the space between the bed and the wall, clutching her arms over her breasts. Pierce jumped up, cussing, then called out, "Thought you were getting here tomorrow," and stumbled to unlock the front door.

They exchanged what Becky assumed to be the usual cousinly banter while she scrabbled around the room for her clothes, which were clammy and limp from the humidity of a Virginia morning. Embarrassed and shy, she'd managed to draw out getting dressed until after they'd brought Dave's things in from his truck and ensconced them in one of the upper rooms, and began rummaging through the fridge for breakfast things. He kept looking across the table at her with curiosity while they ate, but she hadn't responded. It seemed that Pierce had told Dave as much about her as he had told her about Dave.

As she filled the cast-iron sink with hot water to wash the dishes, they discussed what had to be done around the place. The family had apparently come together some weeks before and decided Grandpa Skip, a landowning octogenarian who lived with his much younger girlfriend on a Georgia plantation and castrated his own livestock as a hobby, was simply too old to be expected to keep up with all of his far-flung properties alone, and Dave had been delegated to repair and winterize the house on Porter Mountain; Pierce had apparently volunteered to lend a hand. Becky offered to clean out the upper rooms and the attic, even though it was hotter in the house, and the cousins agreed that it was a good idea before going back to their discussion of barbed-wire fences. She stayed at the sink, soapy to the elbows, chipping burned scraps out of the bacon pan until the front door banged behind them.

The stairs were silent, which surprised her: in such an old house she expected an atmospheric creak. They'd never bothered with the upstairs, the times they'd come here before: the downstairs had always been more appealing, the narrow staircase dark and eerie. The first of the upper rooms contained nothing but a double bed draped in plastic sheeting and littered with dead ladybug husks, and Dave's suitcase, backpack, and pillow in a stack by the door. She gathered up the sheet and discarded the ladybugs out through the crooked window. This bedstead was enameled brass too, and made her think of Victorian women mooning about in dressing gowns, holding babies and teapots and pieces of embroidery. She wondered, briefly, if anyone had ever given birth in this room, walked the floor before this window between contractions while nervous men waited below, if anyone had run up and down the stairs with boiling water and clean flannel.

The second room had two beds, side by side, with shelves above them; their middles sagged gently like the top of her grandmother's red velvet cake. The gnawed plastic sheeting that covered the beds was scattered with pellets of green rat poison. She imagined brothers and sisters holding hands across the gap at night, and 1950s TV shows with married couples gazing chastely at each other from separate beds. This room had a tiny closet, a scant two feet square, with clothes still in it: thin polyester dresses and dried-out saddle Oxfords wrapped in yellowed tissue paper. She took up and shook out the plastic on the beds and the blue quilts underneath, but the clothes she left alone; it felt like too much of a violation to move them.

Leaning out the window with one of the quilts, Becky caught sight of Pierce and Dave stapling barbed wire to fence posts. They were shirtless, Dave's movements lazy and slumped in the heat, Pierce's more angular and jerking. For a moment she had a flash to the books she had read as a little girl, about pioneer families living out in the wilderness. Her mind's eye painted a black felt hat over Pierce's rust-stained Mohawk, and she fell back into the room, giggling.

As she watched them from behind the edge of the curtain, she remembered stories Pierce had told her in those unguarded moments right after sex, while they lay together exhausted and unable to tell where the other's limbs ended and their own began. He told her that he'd grown up in a dirt-poor, stone-dull farming community out on the water, a long, narrow island where all they did was watch corn grow and try to bang their sisters. He'd seen porn for the first time with a cousin: they'd found it in their uncle's workbench in the garage when he was six and the cousin not much older. He had so many cousins and she wasn't sure if he'd told her the name of this one. At first they'd been horrified, then curious, then had taken the magazine to the cousin's older sister, who had turned out to be a lesbian later in life but explained everything to them with solemn authority, turned the pages of the smut rag and pointed out illustrations as if she were a teacher in a biology class. This had only aroused the two boys' curiosity further, and they had tried what they saw on each other after putting the magazine back, first with their hands, and then with their mouths, taking turns back and forth until they'd achieved the promised results. The taste was odd, but the feeling was addictive. Their exploration had continued into their early teens, but they lived far apart, or as far apart as you could get on the Shore, so Pierce had taught what he knew to one or two of his best friends, the ones who could be trusted, the ones who he knew would never tell. This was all before he'd started doing things with girls, of course, and even if he'd kept at it for the first few years that he had girlfriends, well, he wasn't a faggot. A faggot fucked men, and he'd never done that, even though his cousin had once suggested that they try, just to see what real sex would feel like when girls finally stopped being icky, as the lesbian sister said they one day would.

There was a soft familiarity, a comfort, to their movements, almost like they were dancing, and Becky wondered if she was imagining it. Probably she would be suspicious no matter which cousin she saw with Pierce. It was too easy to read into a situation what you thought you would find, see light touches, tender glances, where there were none. Probably Pierce was getting in the way and screwing things up, and Dave was getting more and more annoyed; for a farm boy, Pierce couldn't do a thing with his hands, had all the manual dexterity of a rock. She went back to cleaning.

More insects came down when she shook out the folding ladder to the attic, and she swept them up before climbing into the dark under the shingles. Here the air held a weight of its own, fixing the breath in her lungs like a cork in a bottle. Humidity made it impossible to find the point where her skin ended and air began, and she slumped down for a moment as her eyes adjusted to the dirty light filtering in through the streaked window in the peak of the roof.

Piles shoved into the corners clarified into heavy steamer trunks, mounds of cloth, black plastic trash bags, jumbles of children's toys, squirrel-gnawed blankets, and cardboard boxes. Wicked roofing nails poked through the paper backing of the insulation packed between the joists, like blackened witches' fingers, and she instinctively bent into a half-crouch, even though she was beneath the peak of the roof. There was no order to the attic—it seemed that things had been thrown in piecemeal and forgotten about—so she began by clearing a space in the center in which to work. Some of the trunks were empty, and she lined them up close under the slope of the roof and began stacking the stray tools and toys into them. It made

Becky think of her mother kneeling in her and her sisters' room, sorting and re-sorting their dolls and toy food and plastic jewelry into labeled bins, every week inventing a new system, one that would finally keep them all organized.

Most of the chests were packed with clothing, even older than the pieces she had found in the closet. There were silk dressing gowns and lace bodices, high button shoes and kid gloves, white wool scarves riddled with moth holes and heavy skirts with mysterious stains. Up against the roof she uncovered a cracked full-length mirror, and for a few moments considered propping it up and trying on one or two of the old dresses, the way she and her sister had done when they were younger. None of the clothes would fit her though, made as they were for a different time and a different body type. Becky was solid, thickly muscled, breasty no matter which diet she tried, and she wasn't up for the feeling that always accompanied her attempts to try on something she liked only to find that she was just as fat as she thought. Pierce didn't say much about it, except when they were fighting, but she knew he preferred skinny girls, short girls, girls with small, perky, single-serving-sized breasts.

She couldn't see Pierce and Dave through the diamond-shaped window under the peak of the roof, but if she closed her eyes she could hear them, the rise and fall of their voices as they cursed at the barbed wire or laughed over some shared story. The window framed the mountains, purple with cloud shadows, the image marred only by the telephone line cutting through the trees at the bottom of the front meadow. The lines went right over the mountain, the trees and brush trimmed back beneath them, and for a moment she wondered what would happen if she picked up her backpack and just walked out, followed the path of the power lines straight down the face of the mountain, stuck out her thumb by the side of the highway, went back to her parents' house in Lynchburg and refused to explain where she'd been for the past few days. Her parents would scream, and beg, and cry. The police would get involved, because Donnie would have sold Pierce out within hours of landing in custody. Donnie drove a sweet motorcycle and had a big mouth, and she was a bit surprised that he'd gone so long without being busted. He rented space for the trailer he lived in from Pierce's other grandfather on the Shore, one of those hard-luck cases Pierce said the old man was so soft for, young girlfriend and no place to go, though the girlfriend had wised up and left years ago. If Pierce went down he'd take her with him. It wasn't spiteful, it was just how he was, but after jail and community service— probably not prison for a first offense—it would all blow over. But even if she succeeded in walking away from Donnie and Pierce and their mistakes there would be other problems to deal with, problems that couldn't be plea-bargained into a few hours of picking up highway trash. And Pierce had become necessary to her, in their year or so of not exactly dating, but association. She didn't think she could actually leave like that; there were far too many things left unsaid, too many loose ends to tie up. But it was certainly a tempting idea.

Beneath a drift of books melting slowly out of their bindings she found a birdcage, of the old dome-shaped pattern, coated in layers of gloppy white enamel so that it looked as though it had been rolled out of fondant. She set it in front of the window to get it out of the way, in the beam of light, then rested for a moment in front of it. In her mind's eye she filled it with gold-finches, flitting and twittering, then tiny monkeys, then little

men like Gulliver in the TV movie she'd snuck out of her bed
to see when she was nine. God, she wanted weed. Or opium,
though the one time she'd tried it she hadn't felt much. Whip-
pets. Acid. Hell, she'd settle for a pack of menthols and a can of
Coke, anything. She watched the cage out of the corner of her
eye as she shunted all of the chests into even rows and swept the
sanded pine floor bare, and it was the last thing that disappeared
as she backed her way down the ladder.

They had all worked through lunch. Her watch was still sitting on her bedside table back home, and Becky was surprised
to find that it was three in the afternoon when she came down.
The boys were sitting on the front porch drinking iced water
out of Mason jars.

"Want to go up the ridge and see the view before dinner?"
Dave asked her when she came out to join them.

"Of course she does," Pierce answered for her. She settled
down next to him and leaned into his side. "We go up there
every time we come." This wasn't entirely true; they usually
went halfway up, took in the view, smoked a bowl, and decided
that they'd finish the climb on the next visit. "Let's christen it
with a bottle of something this time though."

"And a joint," Dave added. He looked at Becky as he said
it, fishing for a response, she thought, but she didn't give him
one. She wondered if Pierce had told him about the bust, how
they'd been making their money—or rather, how she'd been
making her money. She'd started dealing out of the girls' locker
room her first year of high school, and was such a boring, honest kid in every other way that she had never been caught. She
was still dealing in her first year at community college when
she met Pierce, who was bouncing from restaurant to restau-

rant, washing dishes, and he liked to claim to be the backbone
of her business even if he'd never gone with her to pick up or
drop off. She didn't do synthetics, so even though he bummed
weed from her he kept meeting Donnie every few weeks on the
mainland side of the bridge to Accomack Island to pick up Oxy,
Ket, Ice, and whatever else he felt like, then sold his extra to the
other restaurant workers. She could have told him that this was
a risky and expensive way to do business, but he wouldn't have
listened to her.

They threw a bottle of wine, a corkscrew, and a pair of binoc-
ulars into a backpack, then crossed the side pasture and hiked
up into the woods. The game trail they followed led them along
the brow of the hill and down through a patch of swampy bot-
tomland before turning up the mountain. Pierce observed that
it was a good place to drop a handful of seeds and see what happened, which sparked off a discussion of all the places they had
lit up, best and worst. Becky was content listening, and eventually Dave stopped glancing at her as if he expected her to join in.

As the path got steeper the cousins began to discuss the farm
itself, how Grandpa Skip owned the entire mountain and had
probably never seen more than ten square acres of it, how far it
was from nosy neighbors or anyone that would care—the cattle
farmers never went beyond the edges of the cleared land—how
rich the earth was, how large the well was, and how empty their
bank accounts were. The trees around them grew stunted and
thin, until they crossed the timberline and waded out into the
tall grass near the top of the ridge. Becky fell a few steps behind, only half-listening since it was the sort of conversation

she'd had a million times before. Pierce hadn't done much with weed other than smoke it, but she'd saved seeds and played with sprouting them, nothing serious, more a botany experiment than a real attempt at growing.

The tooth winked up at Becky from between strands of dead brown grass like old men's hair, and she broke step to stoop and pick it up. The boys didn't notice, and she had to skip for a moment to catch up with them. It was a molar, complete with roots, thick and square, the crackled off-white of old teacups. Probably from a deer that the coyotes had gotten, not big enough for a cow. Or it had just died of old age, up here under the sky with the wind tearing its soul away and the foothills of the Blue Ridge laid out all around it. Not a bad place to die, considering.

"Whatcha got there, Beck?" Dave turned her hand over and she held it up for him. "That's cool."

"I can't believe I didn't see it," said Pierce and held out a hand for it. She pretended she didn't see.

"Dude, you miss half the shit that's going on around you," said Dave. "Neither of us were really looking."

They watched her slip it into her pocket.

"Think we'll need an irrigation system?" Pierce asked.

"Nah, we can just haul buckets till it sprouts—it's pretty wet down by the spring. And weed's a hardy plant. When I was like fifteen I used to dump all my seeds behind the toolshed back at Dad's, you know the place. Looked up one day and there was this six-foot-tall pot plant staring me in the face."

"Damn. How much did you get off something that big?"

Becky tuned them out again and listened to the wind across her ears. The grass was long and bent and silvery, waving like the surface of the ocean. It flowed away to either side of them, creating its own horizon. If she were to go off to the left, she knew that she would see down onto the clearing, the crooked farmhouse with its crinkled tin roof and pale purple globes on the lightning rods, the massive cows, Dave's red sedan and Pierce's dented white pickup that burned oil and had the ceiling falling in. If she looked at the right time she might see the farmer from the valley checking over his stock; she knew that someone came in the afternoons, drove up from the foot of the mountain nearly every day to refill the water troughs or chase the herd from one pasture to the other, but they steered wide of the house and she'd never seen them. Down to the right were more mountains, wave upon wave of them, and somewhere beyond, she knew, home. If she wandered closer to the edge she could see the telephone lines cutting starkly down either side of the mountain, then rising up the next one and disappearing over.

Once at the top they sprawled out in the silvery grass, the sun beginning to set behind them, out of breath, gazing down at the valley below. The mountains rolled on past the Peaks of Otter until they misted into purple haze at the horizon. Dave pulled a joint and a lighter out of his shirt pocket, and hacked meditatively at the striker. Becky flopped backward between them and stared at the sky. Every atom of her body tingled when she caught the first whiff of the smoke, and she hesitated for a breath before waving the joint away. She didn't smoke if she wasn't sure about the product or the people she was with. They passed it back and forth over her until it had burned down to a stub, then opened the bottle of grocery-store wine. That was easier to refuse; she'd never been able to stand cheap wine.

"If we can get a crop of half-decent shit, I know a guy back home that'll get us good money for it," Pierce said.

"Thought you said your buddy just got busted last week."

"Yeah, 'cause he's a dickhead. Not that one, I mean another guy back on the Shore. People call him Stevo. His brother cooks and he deals. They've got the sheriff and half the county in their pocket, he can move anything. Does cocaine and meth mostly, smokes a lot of it himself but he's a pretty chill businessman. If I get it back there, he can take it off our hands at a fair price."

Becky closed her ears to the conversation. She found it funny the way that Pierce talked like he'd done it all before: back home only Donnie had ever been his dealer. She figured that he'd been too scared of Stevo to ever buy direct from him, and now he was talking about setting up as a supplier to the guy like they were old buddies, going back to the place he'd run away from to make the kind of life he wanted. As much as he trash-talked where he was from, she didn't think she'd mind living there. Isolation made her feel safe.

There was a breeze up on the ridge, like thin, cold fingers, lifting her sweat-stiff shirt from her skin.

Pierce had taken her up to the farm for the first time a week after they met, a week before he decided that they were together. They'd laid sleeping bags out on the front porch and watched the sunrise, and had wild crazy monkey sex that she'd not really enjoyed, but she figured it was because she was new to it all and it would feel better as she got used to it. It was autumn then, and the mountain had been a blaze of red and yellow, and they'd sat on a fallen tree at one of the overlooks for hours, watching birds diving, and making out in an exploratory fashion. She fingered the tooth in her pocket.

The walk back down to the farmhouse was faster than the ascent, as they went straight down the face of Porter Mountain, rather than up the zigzag path over the ridge. The conversation had slowed, as had their movements, and Becky found herself casting around in the grass beside the path. Her friend Jamey called her a finder, said she was a living dowsing rod for picking up interesting shit. She found snail shells in the dust, empty shotgun cartridges, deer prints embedded in dried mud. They nearly stepped on a painted box turtle, but she left him behind. As they neared the farm the shadows deepened until they were moving through a vague purple twilight.

Something struck against her shoe as she followed Pierce, and Becky bent to unearth it from the tangle of long grass. It took a moment for her to register the curved shape as the jawbone of a cow, most of its teeth still set in their sockets. Insects and decay had bleached it white and scraped it clean, and she turned it over for a moment before tucking it under her arm and wandering after the guys. They were nearly back, and she could see the cows in huddles around the troughs as they climbed the fences and strolled toward the house.

Down in the meadow in front of the house was an old fire ring, and at some point in the course of the day the boys had filled in the missing stones and gathered up a heap of downed tree limbs. When she caught them up they had begun building a bonfire.

"Hey, Becky, go up and put some hamburgers together, will you?" Pierce called to her when she came in sight. "We're cooking out here tonight."

She considered telling him to do it himself, but thought better of it and went back up to the house, leaving the jawbone on the porch.

There was a smattering of stars high in the sky when she

came back with a plate of raw hamburgers, and the edge above the western mountains was fading to pale turquoise. The boys had dug up an old grill grate and balanced it across the rocks in a corner of the uneven ring, and she carefully dropped the discs of meat onto it, where they steamed and seared to the metal. She sat down next to Pierce and snuggled into him. His shorts had ridden up, and she traced over the upside-down tattoo on his thigh. A friend had done it for him, one time when they'd gotten really fucked up together.

"You've been pretty quiet all day," he said to her. "What's with this cuddly shit all of a sudden?"

"I need to talk to you about something," she whispered back to him.

"Like what?" he asked.

"It's kinda private."

"Anything you want to talk to me about, you can say in front of Dave," he said. "Go on. Am I not screwing you enough or something? Because we talked about that before."

She wanted to just lay it on him, to get back at him for getting her into this. She wanted to see him lose his shit right there, right then. She almost told him.

"Nah, it can wait," she said instead, and ran a hand over her firm belly. The smell of burning meat made her nauseous. "It's not like it's going anywhere."

CHAPTER VII

1981

SKIRT

She shouldn't have been wearing a skirt, Bo said to us after. It was her own damn fault. But what did he want Ellie to do, go to her aunt's funeral in dungarees and work boots? My guess is he didn't want her working with us at all, wanted her to keep her smart ass in the house where it belonged. Didn't matter to him that the fifties were over and done with; he probably figured she'd stolen the job from some well-deserving man with a family to raise.

It was a Thursday. We were fixing up a Victorian on the edge of Belle Haven. The original builders had crammed all the plumbing into the one wall between the kitchen and the bathroom, to save on cost and make things easier. We'd ripped out the wall between the two first thing, so the studs and pipes stuck up out of the floor like tulip stems after the flowers had died. Tiny had been set to take out the old handicapped toilet with me helping, and Chick and Bo were stood in the kitchen checking the joints in the copper piping.

Ellie didn't plumb. She was in the far corner of the kitchen levering up the heart-of-pine floor a board at a time, knocking out the nails, and stacking them on the porch next to the shoe molding she'd already ripped up. She pulled up the age-dark boards slow and gentle, easing apart the tongue-and-groove like she was bathing a baby. Bo would've ragged on her about that, but when she got done you couldn't tell the floorboards were secondhand except for the nail holes, and that made them worth more. Once the expensive flooring was out we wouldn't have to bother as much with carefulness, nothing underneath but joists and subfloor.

When we fixed up a house we pulled out the pretty bits first: the enameled cast-iron bathtubs with the claw-and-ball feet, the watery window glass, the hand-milled egg-and-dart molding. Our boss, Paul Lovett, sold all the little pieces off right away to retired city types that thought restoring a vintage house on their own would be a fun way to hurry up an early death, and couldn't bring themselves to finish it off with modern, mass-produced trim and fixtures. Then we'd fix the leaks in the roof and the shorts in the wiring, fit out the place with new Sheetrock, Kohler sinks, and double-glazed windows. When it was done, or sometimes just before, Lovett would sell it, usually to some young couple that wanted a historic home without all the drafts and falling plaster. More recently, the "just before" buyers had become scarce, and the finished houses usually sat for a few weeks, like dollhouses in the toy store in January.

We had a paint-splattered black plastic radio blaring old Country, so we didn't hear tires on the gravel driveway. Me and Tiny wrenched up the toilet and went to carry it through the kitchen and out onto the back porch when I saw the girl hanging against the doorway, hesitating to come in. She was tall and narrow, with too much pink brushed on her face trying to hide all the freckles. I'd seen her and Ellie together before. Since I was the only one that had noticed her I kicked the side of Ellie's boot as I passed to make her turn around. She popped up with her flatbar in hand to take a shot at me, then saw the girl in the door and changed her mind. They went out onto the rotting porch and Tiny and me followed them slowly, to get the toilet out of the way. They'd gone off under the oak tree by the drive-way, next to the girl's dented brown Chevelle, and some of their conversation drifted over. The tone didn't sound so good. We left the toilet by the back steps. I fiddled the knob on the radio down when I went past, hoping there was going to be some ex-plaining when they got through.

Ellie came back in, and we heard the girl's car pull out. Tiny had started in on the sink, and I was waiting to be useful, so we were all in a bunch around the old copper piping when she tapped Chick on the shoulder. No one else looked up, but I reckon Tiny and Bo were about as curious as me.

"My dad's sister died. Funeral's in Salisbury tomorrow."

Chick made an "I'm sorry" noise. The rest of us pretended not to hear. "How'd it happen?" he asked.

"Drunk driver. Ain't much left to bury."

"Wanna go home and we'll see you Monday?"

"Nah, I'll be good for the rest of today. Do need to go to the funeral, though, if you can spare me."

Chick nodded an affirmative. She went to the next room, the dining room before we'd emptied it down to plaster, and picked out the ten-pound sledge from the tools leaning against the wall.

"Hey, El, who was the hot skirt?" Bo shouted after her. "I'd sure like a piece of that!"

The sledge hit the wall; bits of plaster pattered to the ground. "My baby sister, you asshole." She pulled the fractured plaster free from the slender lathes, and whacked it again.

"No way in hell she's your sister, with that rack."

Whack, patter.

"Give lipstick a shot one day, maybe then someone other than your dog'll want to put his mouth near you."

"Go to hell, Bo." She stripped the wall to lathes and studs, shoveled up the fragments, then went back to pulling up boards.

Bo gave her hell pretty much all the time, but she stuck it out. Sometimes Tiny joined in, but Chick never said anything. Chick was foreman: he made sure the job got done, but he wasn't there to babysit. He probably would have shut them up if it had slowed down the work or if they'd started taking swings at each other. I was mostly glad they weren't going after me: I was barely nineteen and not more than a carpenter's helper. Bo really got into it sometimes, but Tiny usually just listened, a funny smile on his face. He was tall and skinny, worked fast and didn't talk much, but the way he watched people sometimes made me go cold all over. I'd run into Ellie once, having a beer at Charlie's one night, and asked her if Bo's bullyragging didn't get to her.

"I'd rather have Bo talking shit than Tiny looking at me the way he does," she said, and I decided I would've felt the same way if I were a girl. It wasn't like she had much choice; there weren't any jobs on the entire Shore unless she could stand line work at the Perdue plant making half the money even on swing shift. A lot of people were glad when all the chicken factories showed up on Accomack Island, but you can smell the stink from miles away, and take-home pay's so small it makes you want to cry. Bo or Tiny might've liked it, killing chickens eight hours a day, but I couldn't think of many other people who would.

Nothing went right that Friday. We got there in the morning to find that some jackoff had lifted the handicapped toilet from the back porch. That's three hundred bucks just walked off, probably coming out of Chick's pay, so he stood there cussing for a fair minute.

A skunk had come in after the half a peanut butter sandwich Tiny had left sitting by the radio, and sprayed Bo when we tried to kick it out. He changed clothes and doused himself with pickling vinegar from the little general store a ways down the road, but that didn't do much for the kitchen. We decided to ignore it and get on with the work.

Tiny and me had begun ripping out the baseboards in the bathroom, carefully; we'd found mice at other jobs, rotting lumps of fur and bone. The baseboards here were just flat pine, a broad one and a skinny one knocked together to make an "L" shape, so the wires could be tacked to the wall underneath it. They hadn't bothered to go under the walls when they wired the house for electricity, just run it along under the baseboards or poked it into the gap beneath the plaster. Since new plaster takes months to cure it makes sense to do it that way, but when you go to fix the wires you see that it's a snarled mess just waiting to start a fire, and if you're honest you rip it all out and start from the beginning. There were a few plastic-covered lengths here and there, but all the old wire was insulated with raw cotton and cloth strips. Some of it, around the light fixture, was burned and crisped from when lightning had struck the house.

Wiring was Ellie's job; she told Chick when she first started working with us that she learned it all from following her daddy around. She'd gone to the funeral though, so Bo took a crack at it so we could Durock the bathroom over and call it done. He shocked himself right off, and anyone could see that he didn't have the first idea what he was doing, so Chick told him to leave it and to take up where Ellie had left off prying up the kitchen floor, which he didn't like. A few hours later Tiny went out on the back porch for a smoke, stepped through a rotted patch, and fell through up to his waist into the spidery cavity beneath. When we pulled him out we found something else to worry about: an entire tribe of feral cats had set up camp under the porch. We turfed them out ourselves instead of wasting breath on animal control, and the beasts were docile enough until Bo started up the compressor while I had one draped over each arm. A compressor sounds like a jackhammer's little brother, and makes me start even when I'm expecting it; those cats climbed straight up me and tore for the woods out back.

Chick wandered off at that point, told us to take early lunch and a smoke break and headed down the road toward the village. He came back half an hour later with a handle of bottom-shelf whiskey from the ABC in Belle Haven, twice as much as he usually got, swabbed it on mine and Tiny's scratches, then passed it around so we could each take a swig before hiding it away for card night. The skunk had gnawed through the power cord of our radio, and when we realized that we almost packed it in right there. Working without music, even crap music, makes time drag on forever. The day was capped off with Tiny dropping one of the kitchen windows and shattering five of the six watery panes.

We all had headaches from the skunk spray, and should have taken that as a sign and given up for the day, but we stuck it out another hour until Paul Lovett showed up with the payroll. He and Chick walked off a way like they always did to talk over how we were getting on, and we could tell Chick wasn't happy by the way he ran his hand over and over through his crinkled black hair. Lovett didn't look too thrilled either by the time the wad of green was handed over. He hopped in his truck and crunched off back toward Parksley, and we all gathered up on the porch to collect.

"It's a low week," Chick told us as he counted out bills. "Some effer bounced a check on a load of windowpanes, so we're all taking a cut in exchange for a bonus when this place is finished."

"You could've run that by us before you said yes," Tiny cut in.

"It's a hundred now for a couple hundred later. Our other option was a permanent cut. The market's as stable as a drunk's aim—I'm getting us as good a deal as possible out of this." He handed over my pay.

"That ain't legal, is it?" I suggested.

"When you start paying income tax you can start talking 'legal,' kid. Don't tell me you do, 'cause I know none of us do." He looked at me in that sharp way he did, out of one eye, that reminded me of my grandpa when he was only partly joking. "Anyway. I buy the booze for card night, cut or no. Go home after instead of hitting the bars, you're even again."

"If you get through a Friday night on a hundred, you drink like a pussy," Tiny guffawed, then took a tenner from each of us and walked off toward town to make change for betting.

The rest of us went up to one of the bedrooms. First thing we'd done when we started on this house was strip off the decades of wallpaper laid thick one on top of the next, took every room down to the scratchcoat and swept the floor clean so we could suss the job and plan it out. Otherwise, we'd left the upstairs alone. It was a pretty room; the ceiling high and the windows large and trimmed in hand-milled molding, the heart-of-pine floorboards twelve inches wide and blood red from age, a fireplace with a mantelpiece all plaster curls and wreaths. The wiring on that circuit was bad, so we had a big battery-operated camping lantern that we kept with the tools; the early-summer sun had already dipped below the trees. Bo brushed bird shit and crumbled ceiling off the packing crate in the middle of the room before setting the lantern down. I'd brought up the milk crates we'd "borrowed" from Food Lion, and Chick wiped out the Mason jars that lived in a crooked line on the mantelpiece when we weren't drinking from them. We settled down on the milk crates and played a few rounds of Smack, waiting for Tiny to get back.

While we sat there we heard an engine down on the driveway, and a car door slamming. There was a cuss from the back porch, presumably at the lingering eau de skunk, then the sound of flip-flops thwacking up the stairs. Ellie showed up in the doorway, dressed in borrowed black and white: the top tight and stretched across her chest, the skirt safety-pinned on one side. She looked like a waitress.

"Damn, what the hell happened to the porch?" she asked.

"Good funeral?" Chick asked back, and cleared the table.

"Sucked ass, but I didn't expect any different." She threw herself down and stared accusingly into the bottom of an empty Mason jar.

"What the fuck are you dressed as?" This from Bo.

"A lady."

"Do you have peaches or baseballs stuffed in there?" he asked.

"Nah, they're mine. Where's the bourbon?" She rolled her jar around on the crate.

"We're waiting on Tiny to get back."

"Just a shot to start me off?"

"The bottle doesn't get opened until we're all here." Chick put his cards down and reached around to his pocket. "Figured you'd want in, so I gave him a ten for you." He handed over her pay, and explained why it was less than usual. She stared at him without responding; you got the idea that she didn't really care. Probably wore out from the funeral.

"We cleared a heap of cats out from under the porch today," I told her. "Clawed the shit out of us."

She didn't look up, just sat there with her arms on her thighs fiddling with the bent corner of one of the jokers.

"Should've nailed 'em all to the fence when we had the chance, like you do with weasels," Bo chipped in. Her head snapped up at that, but she still didn't say anything. "Fuckers're prolly tunneling back in already." He drawled it out one side of his mouth. "Guess we can save that for Monday. Think the nail gun's big enough? Pow! Right through the skull."

"You nail weasels to your fence, Bo?" Chick asked.

"My daddy used to, when we caught them in the henhouse,"

he said. "Kept the rest of the vermin off. Did it sometimes to the neighbors' cats, when they come around too often."

Ellie was tensing up; there was going to be a fight in a minute, and we hadn't even started drinking.

"Also cleaned a skunk out," I cut in before he could go on. "Chewed the radio cord all to pieces, sprayed Bo down good."

She smiled at that.

"Did it improve the stink?" she asked, and Chick chuckled. Bo scowled at her. "Thought that's what I smelled. Been sayin' we needed a radio what took batteries, so we could run it when the power's off."

Tiny came in with a sack of quarters from the laundromat change machine and a bottle of knockoff Coca-Cola under each arm from the gas station. Bo shuffled and dealt while Chick poured whiskey and Coke into the Mason jars and Tiny split up the quarters. Bo and Tiny had played three-card draw on payday off and on for years. Generally Chick played a few hands before going home to his wife and kid, and Ellie hung around for it when the mood took her. I'd felt odd joining in at first, and still did sometimes when it was just the three of us, like walking into church when mass was half said, and my hands and feet and laugh too big to fit comfortable anywhere. We kept playing till someone ran out of quarters, then Bo and Tiny would usually hit the bars, see if they couldn't get some action, spend as much cash as possible; mostly I went along with them.

The first few hands went fast; no one was in a good mood. Bo and I folded several times, but Ellie kept throwing out coins like a slot machine, and Tiny kept scooping them up. As soon as Chick handed her a drink she'd swirled it around and drained it. He poured a second round once we caught up to her, and we all mellowed out a bit. Bo and Tiny started ribbing each other, the friendly way they do when they've had a few, then Chick called them both fatheads, so they started in on him together. The three of them was pretty much raised together, so they've got a lot to rib him about.

When he was five dollars ahead Chick collected up his quarters and made for the door. "I'll see you all Monday morning. Fuck anything up tonight and no one will ever find the bodies." Bo and Tiny got up and walked out with him, not to leave but to go piss in the bushes out back. I had to piss too, but I liked sitting where I was more. The whiskey had made me feel loose in the joints and shiny all over, and Ellie was sitting across from me, her elbows together and her cards up to her face but the tops of her breasts just peeking over the neckline of her shirt, saying hello.

She smacked the cards down, ran her eyes around the molding at the juncture of wall and ceiling and took a deep drink.

"Pretty house, ain't it?" I said, trying to start a conversation. We could hear Bo and Tiny hooting at each other out near the back edge of the property.

"S'pose so," she answered.

I wanted to roll one of those breasts in my palm so much.

"Wonder what made them sell up."

"They died." Her voice was flat, and for a bit I thought that she was going to leave it at that, but when I'd given up on hearing more she continued. "My grandparents lived here. Ma said they were crazy, that they used to beat her and make her play in the snow naked. That they had a bunch of other kids, but they killed them all and buried them in the garden to make the vegetables grow." She paused for a drink. "Sounds like utter horseshit now, but when you're five years old you believe everything your ma tells you."

"Do you think she was telling the truth?"

"Are you kidding?" Her laugh is a sharp bark. "Ma was the crazy one. She lied about pretty much everything and everyone." She finished off her drink and, even though it was against the rules, I sloshed some whiskey into the bottom of her jar. "Didn't matter what was true or not, she never let us meet them. Didn't want them turning us against her. Like she hadn't done that herself.

"First time I stepped into their house was to rip it up."

She sat up straight of a sudden, scooped up her cards again, then drained the whiskey out of her jar so no one would know she'd gotten an extra drink. Then I heard what she'd heard, Bo and Tiny on the stairs, chuckling to each other and stepping heavy already, and by the time they walked in she was back to her normal self.

This was the time when we'd usually hit the bars and get trashed on our own dime. But between the short pay and the fact that we still had most of that handle of whiskey there was little reason to leave. We tossed Chick's seat against the wall, squared ourselves off around the crate, added an extra dollop of the hard stuff to each of our jars, and kept on playing. Ellie came out with a few ripe comments about the girls Bo and Tiny would normally be picking up at Shucker's Roadhouse at that hour, loud and bold now that the day's work was over. She teetered on her crate, and it seemed the whole world was a laugh. Bo cussed her, but Tiny looked at me like we both knew she'd hit a nerve and didn't have to push her point. After that she kept her mouth shut. We'd almost forgotten she was there until she handed over her last quarter, folded, then drained her Mason jar.

"Where you think you're running off to, sugartits?" Tiny asked.

"Got nothing left to bet with, have I?" she answered, and stood up real carefully. She'd been keeping up with us drinking, since no one got a refill till everyone was empty. I didn't think she'd make it to the door: she was broad-shouldered for a girl but more than a foot shorter than Bo, and all that whiskey didn't have nowhere to go but her head.

Bo looked at her close, like he'd forgotten her name and was trying to remember. "Sit your ass back down," he said. "You're set for another few rounds."

She slumped over, leaning against the packing crate, feet pigeon-toed and legs tangled. She wasn't going anywhere. "OK, wiseass, what am I betting?"

"Shirt's a good start," he said.

She shot up like she had rockets on her ass, but Bo reached out with one of his coal-shovel hands and pushed her down onto her seat. Tiny was staring at her, and I guess I was too. My face had started feeling fuzzy the way I liked a few hands back, and I didn't want the evening to end just yet.

"No fucking way," she said, and crossed her arms over her chest like a little kid. Her breasts did look like peaches, soft and juicy and just begging to be let free.

"'S'just a shirt," I said. "Win a round and you'll have it back right off."

She stared back at us.

"Got a third nipple or something under there?" Tiny asked.

"It's nothing we haven't seen before. Like he said, it's only a minute, just to keep the game going." Ellie kept her arms crossed firmly, and Bo reached for the hem of her shirt. She smacked his hand away, and Tiny fixed Bo with a look until he settled back in his place. "Make you feel better, I'll join you." Tiny peeled off his own shirt. His chest was caved in up the center, the skin yellowish and sticky-looking, with wiry single hairs springing up here and there like a boy's first beard. "You don't really want to pack in the fun now, do you?"

You could see the gears turning in her head, deciding whether to play along. I was staring hard now, and I knew it, right at the front of that shirt. She saw me, and she smiled, moved her hands down and cocked her head at me like she was going to take it off. My heart sped up a little. She gave a shimmy. Then she reached down and threw a black flip-flop on the table. The cards came back out, Tiny won the hand, and the second flip-flop came off. That hand she won, scraping the quarters into her lap, her knees spread wide so they could rattle down into the bowl of her loose black skirt. She bet with the flip-flop first this time, and Bo won it with a pair. Then we all went back to laying out quarters, slower now, but topping off our jars between each hand, not waiting for everyone to be empty. Then she was out again, and stood up to leave. Bo pushed her back down.

"We're not finished yet."

Ellie looked at us, blinking slowly, but no one moved or said anything this time. She hadn't slowed up with the drinking though she'd slowed up with the betting, and was rocking even more now. I was holding my breath. Bo and Tiny weren't pushing it, and she wasn't fighting it, and at that moment I would've shoved my whole pile of quarters into her lap, and thrown my share of payroll in after it, to see that top come off.

For a few long minutes she hesitated, looking at me, before slowly peeling her white shirt off in one long, smooth motion, and letting it puddle in the center of the crate. Tiny whistled, and she smirked and wiggled a little before picking up her cards again. She was as white as skimmed milk, but she had muscle. The stomach underneath the white band of her bra was hard like a man's, harder probably than any of ours, with all the beer we drank. I don't know what I had expected since she kept up with us day in and day out, but with work clothes on she'd looked like a shapeless lump, smaller but not really different from Bo or Tiny. Heat was growing low in my belly, and it wasn't the whiskey.

Bo smirked at her, laid down a straight, and scraped up the pot. She didn't look too happy then, and didn't move to take anything else off.

"How about the skirt?" Tiny suggested. Bo reached over and began pulling on her bra—it wasn't more than a strip of cloth—but she smacked his hand away again and scraped her milk crate back.

"Hang on, cool your jets," she said, got up unsteadily and turned her back to us. The skirt was long and full, and I couldn't really tell what her wiggling was doing until she turned around with a piece of white cotton crumpled up in her hand.

"That's as far as I'm going," she said before she put her underpants down in the center of the crate, and dropped back onto her seat. Bo and Tiny both catcalled her a bit, but she bent her head over her cards. I had a flush that time, but I folded without a word, hoping to give her a better chance. Tiny won anyway. He looked her in the eyes as he gathered up the quarters, but when his hand hovered over her underpants she snatched them away and jumped up.

"I've had enough. Gimme back my shirt, I'm going home." She reached for where Bo had it draped across his knee. He held it out of her reach, but instead of diving for it like he wanted her to she moved toward the door. He grabbed her wrist and jerked her down onto his lap. She fell onto him hard, and he snaked his free hand up under her bra.

"The fuck is wrong with you?" she shouted. Bo was rubbing his face against her shoulder, running his hands up and down. She kicked herself back up, but he held on to her wrist, laughing a little, like she was a fish on the end of a line. "Is this 'cause I wouldn't screw you again?"

Tiny and I looked at each other—that sure was news. I'd jumped up when Bo pulled her down; the room was unsteady, or else I would have pulled her away from him. Punched him, maybe. Done something.

"You sucked the first time, needledick, there's no way I'm giving it a second go-round."

That made him mad. He yanked her back down and bit her shoulder, then took the top edge of her bra in his fist and pulled; it tore in half with a ragged sound.

"Get the fuck off me!" she screamed.

Her tits were perfect handfuls; the nipples stood up like gumdrops. I tried to say something, reached out a hand. She snapped her arms down over them as she squirmed to get away from him. Bo threw her at Tiny, who caught her around her middle, the other hand on her tits. Bo tossed her shirt into the corner farthest from the door. She lunged for it, but Tiny had hold of her still. She kicked at him and tore away, stumbled, and fell down on her knees into the corner. Bo followed. His hand went almost the whole way around her neck. She clawed at him, making noises like the cats we'd cleared out earlier. He elbowed her in the small of the back and she went down, all her breath gone. He raked her skirt up to her waist, and ran his hand over the skin of her legs. The sight had me sick and giddy all at once, and it felt like my heart was going to beat its way out of my chest.

"You're going to go to jail for this, you bastard." Her breath was like sobbing as she said it. His free hand slid up higher, probing. Her back arched; she made a sound that would have been a scream if he hadn't been crushing her throat. "Please don't do this, Bo." It wasn't more than a whimper now.

"Going to jail? You think anyone's going to believe you over the three of us?" Tiny said. He knelt down over her, Bo's hand still around her neck, and fiddled with the front of his jeans. The sound of the zipper did it; she writhed like a snake for a second, hard as she could, but I saw the muscles in Bo's arm bunch as he squeezed her neck. She let out little clicking sounds, and Tiny pinned her ankles to the floor and knelt between them so she couldn't pull her legs together. He lowered himself down on top of her, slowly, and she sobbed just once.

He moved against her like all his bones had melted away, like a wave hitting the sand, soft and smooth and crushing all at once. His breathing was thick and wet, gasping, and it filled the room and filled my ears. She was perfectly still. Just her left hand, stretched out, the knuckles almost as white as the shirt they were clamped onto, clenching rhythmically like a heart beating there on the blood-red floor. That's the only part of her that moved. My stomach was churning, nervous and excited all at once, and suddenly I realized that I hadn't moved since I stood up, my jar of whiskey and not-Coke still clutched in my hand, watching like it was TV.

Tiny shuddered with his whole body and peeled himself up, and when she felt his body lift up off her Ellie scrambled to get her feet under her. Bo socked her in the middle of the back, and you could hear all her breath go out as she hit the floor, face-down. Then he was on top of her. This time she made a noise, a popping gasp as she tried to breathe with all of Bo's weight crushing down on her. He grunted and pounded into her with his whole body, like he was trying to go through the floor, or break her hips. Maybe he was. She scraped at the floor with her fingernails, and he pinned her wrists down, crushing them into the boards. He finished with a growl, suddenly, abruptly, and ground her body beneath him before pulling away. Blood smeared his shrinking cock, and he wiped it away with the tail of his shirt as he stood up.

"Your turn," Bo said, and I realized he meant me. She'd curled into a half-moon when he got off her, like a pill bug when you move its rock. I put my Mason jar down on the crate and moved toward her, slowly, like moving through a mass of throbbing cotton. It was a long way down onto the floor, but I wished it were longer. I stayed kneeling over her for a second so my head could stop spinning, but she didn't seem to notice I was there. Bo had knocked the wind out of her, probably.

Pressed together like that her breasts were even more like peaches, the white ones that are so sweet they make your teeth hurt, and I realized that I'd been looking at them out of the tail of my eye since I'd first met her. My hand came up on its own, and through the booze her breast felt like a peach too, soft and firm at once and slightly downy. When my hand touched her it was like she suddenly woke up. Her head snapped back, and she looked straight up into my eyes.

"Jake. Please don't do this." So quiet I probably imagined it. She wasn't moving now at all, just her chest rattling up and down. Those eyes looked right through me, asking me to do something I didn't know how to do in a language I didn't understand. I turned her over so I wouldn't have to see them.

I hadn't been that close to a woman, I realized, in months. I could feel the heat rising off of her; smell the warm bittersweet saltiness of her skin, tempered by the coppery cut of blood. Her long, curly hair had spread out on the floor in a puddle, and I pressed my hand into it to feel the springiness. All that hair. Like having an entire chocolate cake to myself. I lowered my face into it, and smelled her shampoo, something fruity. It warmed a spot in my belly, and all my muscles softened up until I was lying on top of her, cupped around her, breathing her in. For a moment I pressed myself against her to feel how warm and firm her body was under me, how curvy, and all I could think was Iwant Iwant Iwant.

Then I pulled myself slowly back up. Tiny made a derisive sound.

"Be a man," he brayed.

"Whiskey dick," I said. "I couldn't 'be a man' with a gun to my head." I stumbled back to the table and drained my drink.

Bo hitched up his jeans, then walked over to her and kicked her lightly in the side, to make sure he had her attention. "Say a thing to Chick or anyone about this and I'll tear you apart." I'd expected him to start in on her the way he usually did, but his voice was really quiet. Calm. Dangerous. "He wouldn't believe a word of it, anyway. Stupid bitch. Should've known better than to come here dressed like that, hey? Like dangling a bone in front of a dog. You only did it to show me what I couldn't have." He leaned over her, took a handful of her hair and turned her head so she had to look at him. "What just happened is your own damn fault. You were begging for it." He let her head drop. "Keep your mouth shut, or else."

He stood and turned for the door, Tiny after him. I hesitated a moment, looked back. Ellie was just lying there, not moving, not crying, and for a moment I wondered if she was dead. Then Bo called for me to hurry up, and I followed them down.

Monday morning when I got there, Chick, Tiny, and Bo were all pulling out the downstairs windows to swap them out for double-glazed, weatherproof ones. I got nervous as hell, then I saw her on her knees in a corner of the kitchen, rewiring one of the bathroom wall sockets, the one that shocked Bo on Friday.

"Was thinking you weren't showing up," Chick called. "That wild a weekend?" I went over toward Ellie. She wouldn't look up at me, even though my feet were inches from her knees. I nudged her, just a little. She wouldn't look up at all.

"Just cards, that's all," I answered Chick. "Same thing we always do."

CHAPTER VIII

1885

—

MANY WATERS

The sun was in Medora's eye. If she hadn't just gotten her pipe lit she would have moved out of the beam, but the act of dropping the smoldering bit of punk she had used into the clay dish by her side, of laying her arm across her chest, of stilling her entire body until she could feel her heart beating in the rush mat against her back, had made movement impossible. She was wood, like the floor beneath her.

The beam fell through the gap in the rush roof where her pipe smoke crowded before slipping out, and she squinted to watch it swirl, drew deeply and let the gentle plume rise from between her lips. It was an unladylike habit, and when she was still living at home she had only indulged in private. Since her leaving, the pipe had rarely left her hand; the smoke deadened the pain in her body and mind alike.

Her pipe was similar in shape to the one that had been clenched between her mother's teeth whenever she sat outside the kitchen door, cross-legged and rocklike, waiting for her daughter to appear. What Medora had then taken for apathy on her mother's part she now realized was a pained patience, a willingness to wait forever so long as she might catch a glimpse of her child. Smoking helped with that sort of waiting, offered a calmness, made her feel loose and far away from her body—her burns had healed to a waxy smoothness and no longer troubled her, but her bones still ached where joints had been wrenched out of place and breaks knitted roughly and it had taken her some time to adjust to having the use of only one eye.

She had learned recently that there had always been Indian women living in the marshes on the edge of Accomack Island, trading herbs and advice to the sharecroppers and smallholders too poor for a doctor. Like the Shore was part of Virginia, the Accawmacke were part—or had been part—of the Powhatan Confederation, spoke Algonquin and offered yearly tribute to their emperor across the water. But the Chesapeake was so large and the island so remote that the Powhatan left the Accawmacke mostly to their own governance, just as the rest of Virginia left the farmers and tradesmen to their marshy backwater.

They had called her "ma'am" before, and the title had never felt comfortable to her; now they called her "Aunty," and that felt more right. Even when they had called her ma'am she had had a reputation, had known much, occupied herself with herbs and simples. Her cook had joked that the poor folk already thought her half a witch. Then her husband had made her over to look the part. It was Nittawasew, though, who had completed the transformation, who had found her wandering in the marsh and knitted her back together, taught her the use of the local plants that she didn't recognize, helped her make a place for herself.

Over the sound of the wind through the marsh grass she could hear tentative, sucking footsteps, and she gathered her faculties. She felt too young, too inexperienced, for the trust that people put in her—at twenty-seven she guessed that she was the youngest healer they had ever had—and she compensated for her self-doubt by playing the role as best she could, by imitating Nittawasew. It wasn't so hard; she already felt old. The scars bothered people, she knew, and even though she hated them she liked how they kept her visitors off-balance, unsure whether they should avert their eyes or pretend that she looked normal. As the footsteps drew closer she let herself sink more leadenly into the mat: Nittawasew never jumped for anyone.

"Aunt Medora? You t'home?" Ruby knew she was there; it was just a politeness to ask. Medora opened her eye and looked up at the girl who was sticking her head through the door of the hut and slapping at mosquitoes.

"No, child, I'm swimming with the pelicans. I just left my body behind to mind the house."

"Yes, Aunty." The hut was on stilts to raise it above high tide, and barely large enough to fit both of them. Ruby pulled herself up onto its warped board floor and crouched in the doorway, the old horse blanket pinned across the opening draping over her shoulders like a cape.

"You're needing something, then?"

"I'm late again, Aunt Medora. Just a few days, but I can't take no chances right now."

Medora clenched the pipe in her teeth and sat up. Ruby's husband owned a tiny patch of boggy land out near Greenbackville, on the northwest coast, where, from the look of things, they raised weeds and babies. The woman wasn't many years younger than herself, Medora guessed, but she had seven children, spaced like porch steps, each running up the heels of the one before. She was a pretty girl, her light eyes shocking in contrast with her rich reddish-brown skin, short body curved like a classical Venus: Medora had heard comment to the effect that if Ruby's husband hadn't kept her pregnant there'd have been no shortage of volunteers to do so.

She could reach her medicine chest from where she sat, but stretching for it would have been undignified. Instead she pulled herself painfully to her feet, with only a little exaggeration, and knelt in front of it with her back squarely to Ruby. It was made of dark wood, the only real furniture in the hut. Her sleeping mat and gathering basket she had woven herself out of rushes, her one iron pot sat on its stubby legs in a corner with her knife and spoon and horn cup inside it, and the two clay dishes she'd gotten in trade stacked next to it. If she looked down she could see between the boards to where the fiddler crabs scuttled across the black mud, and the walls were woven of green switches; it was more an inverted basket than a house. But it was only meant for summer residence, a place for her to be private. She had bargained the stilts and platform out of some of the freeholders, an afternoon's work, and built up the walls and covered the roof herself.

"How old's the youngest?" she asked as she sorted through the contents of the chest. *M. piperita*, *Hypericum perforatum*, *Hydrastis canadensis*. She was running low on ramson bulbs. Dried herbs were kept bundled and wrapped in greased paper in muslin pouches, tinctures in corked black bottles, salves in small pots. Much of it had come with her, first from her father's house and then again from the wide plantation house that Andrew had built for them, overlooking the creeks and the sea; recently she had added preparations of indigenous plants that her books had not taught her about, preparations specific to women's medicine.

"Not quite a year, ma'am. Milk dried up two months ago—my sister's been fostering her since."

Medora grumbled to herself as she rifled through the chest. You'd think men would learn to be a little more circumspect, at the very least keep their hands to themselves if they wouldn't shoulder more of the housework. Near the bottom she found what she was looking for, twisted up in brown paper and wrapped in unbleached muslin.

"Listen close, then, and do exactly what I tell you. This—" she turned the woman's left hand palm-up and closed it around one of the packets—"is the last of my pennyroyal. Make a tea of it, and drink four cups a day for five days, spaced out even as you can." She put a similar packet in the woman's other hand. "This is cotton-root bark. Boil what I've given you in a pot so big—" she indicated with her hands—"until the liquid is halved, then sip a small cup, warm, every hour. Get up in the night if you can. Those two together should do the trick. If your blood doesn't come in five days, come back to me and I'll see what else we can do."

Ruby nodded, and slipped the packets into the pockets of her skirt.

"Is there anything else I can do, to help it along?" she asked.

"Pick some raspberry leaves as you're walking home, and when the blood comes make a tea of them. Nettle tea is good too. Take what I've given you as regular as possible, but don't get nervous and take more than I've said."

Medora had her repeat back the instructions twice, to be sure. She'd been told about girls, mostly scared, unmarried girls, who had died from taking more than they'd been told to.

"I haven't got no money, Aunt Medora," Ruby admitted at the end of the second recitation.

"Didn't think you did," Medora conceded.

"Got some potatoes and collards I can bring tomorrow."

"I can get all the greens and potatoes I need myself, thank you." Medora settled cross-legged on her mat, tucked the fraying ends of her blue skirt around her, and sucked her pipe. This was the part she didn't like. She needed the payment, but she hated bargaining for it.

"Yes, ma'am, didn't mean to offend. I can bring half a pound of salt pork without my man noticing, or I've got a petticoat from my sister what's too long. And I've got news about Mister Day you'd most likely want to hear."

Medora's stomach knotted at the name, but she sat still as a rock.

"All right then. What's this news?"

"People's been saying he's set to marry his girl, Gracie Cole."

"Not if he's got a wife, he isn't," she snapped.

"If a judge says his wife is dead, then he's got no wife." Ruby was hesitant, as if she expected to have the herbs taken from her if Medora didn't like the news. "And with his money, if he wanted he could have the whole of Virginia saying the sky was green by dinnertime. They might probably be waiting till end of harvest—girl like that's going to want an awful lot of lace in her married clothes."

"Thank you, Ruby. If I can, I'll come for that bit of pork tomorrow." She lay back again, ramrod stiff, and drew deeply on her pipe. The woman mumbled a goodbye, and Medora listened to her slow, sucking footsteps as she made her way carefully to drier ground.

Rage was boiling her stomach, and she breathed deeply to calm it. She had underestimated Andrew Day, perhaps, and she was lucky to have survived the mistake. They had invested the money well, built up their farm until Andrew was one of the richest men on the island, and she had to admit that she wouldn't have been able to do so on her own, a woman and half-Indian besides. But it was her cunning that had gotten the money in the first place, and even though he called himself her husband, played the part quite well in public, it was only the bit of paper with their signatures on it that permitted him to manage her money. She would laugh if their marriage were ever exposed as a sham, but he would never lift his face again. Without her, he would have ended in prison, a two-bit con man without the sense to put together a passable story.

She would not let him get away with this.

She still dreamed, nearly a year later, of the intense heat, saw leaping flames and cried out in her sleep, smelled her hair and her skirts burning. The left side of her face and neck, her ear and a large patch of her hair had burned. Her corset had saved her breasts and belly, but her legs had been scorched and blistered in patches, and what of her left sleeve had not burned entirely had adhered itself to the raw flesh.

She had thought that she was going to die, felt that she was still burning as she fled the house. She had no doubt that he had, in the moment, fully intended to kill her, to hold her there in the fire until she stopped breathing. Fear mobilized her, pain blinded her, and when she finally collapsed she was lost on the edge of the marsh.

And there Nittawasew had found her.

Her nation had long been fractured, their numbers reduced by illness and the violence of invaders, their remaining members integrated with the settlers or living privately in the places where no one else dared go. No one knew how old she was, but Nittawasew reigned over a tribe of children and grandchildren, and had the trust of the poor and the laborers. One of her granddaughters worked in Medora's kitchen, had heard their shouting and had seen her run from the house, had tracked her on her erratic path through the marsh, and had brought the old woman to tend her when she fell. Medora did not know this; to her, Nittawasew had found her through magic.

She had woken eight days later, in a longhouse on one of the barrier islands, and wondered why she couldn't open her left eye. At first she had assumed that she was dreaming, or had died and rejoined her mother: she was surrounded by native and half-native women, speaking quietly in a language she did not understand, feeding infants and doing handwork, their talk not quite drowning out the rattle of rain on the woven rush roof.

The burns, once treated, had healed cleanly, though her left eye had sealed with scar tissue and could not be opened; the wrist that had broken when she caught herself falling, the shoulder that had come out of its socket, took longer. Her mind had taken longest of all.

At first she had sat with them, not speaking and not responding, barely thinking even, lost in a pain that she couldn't identify as being in her body or in her head. The old woman had pulled her out of herself, given her a mortar and commanded her to grind the herbs for her own poultices, showed her catnip and cannabis leaves and told her what they could be used for, took her out into the marsh to search for plants to stock her pharmacopeia. Medora was interested in spite of herself; most of her knowledge came from European texts, written by men, and focused on European plants and the illnesses and ailments of men. Calley had added to her knowledge somewhat, but many of the plants on the Shore she had not seen used before, and she knew only the basics of women's medicine. She watched as three babies were birthed that fall, and as dozens of others were prevented, and learned all that the older woman was willing to teach her.

The other women came and went as they pleased, sometimes returning with news for her. Andrew had called in the doctor for his scorched hand, told the man that it had happened in pulling her from the flames, showed him the patch of floor on which she'd extinguished her clothing. His wife had thrown herself into the fire during an argument, had run from the house so badly burned that she could not survive, and when they searched but found no body, she had been declared dead. She gritted her teeth at this; in fighting against him she had given the man exactly what he wanted, both her fortune and the opportunity to marry someone more appropriate, to go back to the mainland and high society with a suitable wife on his arm.

When spring came and her body was mostly healed, one of the granddaughters smuggled her chest and papers out of the house and brought it to her, and her interest in life returned; if only the girl could have brought her children as well. They thought her dead, and dead she wished to remain for the moment, at least to the gentry of the island. The poor knew how to keep a secret, knew that their loyalty would be better invested in a healer than a rich man, and they were all perhaps a bit frightened of her, believed that, somehow, she had died and come back to life.

She had no plan at that point. She had come to respect and love Nittawasew in the time that she had spent flat on her back in the woman's lodge, but the privacy of the marsh appealed to her, after so many years of sharing a house with men that she despised. As her petticoats frayed and she grew better at scavenging wild food and spotting useful plants with her remaining eye she felt her selfness increase. She passed the time quietly, losing track of the days, sitting cross-legged at her doorway at high tide dangling a line for the fish and crabs that never seemed to fill her, digging roots, lying for long hours stretched on her mat, pipe clenched in her teeth, counting the breaths as the pain in her bones ebbed and swelled. Her arms ached for her children in the night. Still, she had not decided what to do, had thought that she would have more time to determine a course of action.

Now, with the mosquitoes slipping through the cracks in her hut walls and the incessant rustle of the wind in the reeds and her searing anger at the man who was not her husband, she wished for something to distract her. The pipe was almost empty, the crusting ash giving nothing but a dry, papery taste. She sat up and knocked it out against the floor so that the detritus sifted through the cracks in the floorboards, cleaned it carefully with a bit of twig, then fished a small percussion-cap box from her skirt pocket, filled half with moist, local tobacco and half with

fat sage-colored buds, and began shredding a fragrant bud into
the lid so she could have a pipe while she went searching for
ramsons. No sense wasting away the entire day, no matter the
heat. There were things to be done.

Stiffly, she took up the gathering basket, wrapped herself
against the mosquitoes, strapped the broad, flat oval marsh
shoes that hung from the frame outside her doorway to her bare
feet, and ducked out into the sun. In the light she could see the
dirt ingrained into her skin, and her hair hung heavy and thick
about her face; she couldn't remember ever having been this
dirty before. Her father had given her the limp, Calley had told
her, by knocking her down the front stairs when she was small.
The woman had interposed herself that time, gathered her up
and taken her away to the kitchen and pushed the heavy sideboard against the door, then carefully forced her partially dis-
located thighbone back into the hip socket while she screamed.
After that he had been more careful with her, no matter how
angry he was.

Absently she tracked through the marsh, skirts tucked high,
the black mud oozing silkily up through the gaps in her woven
shoes and between her bare toes. If her father could see her
now . . . Andrew had never spoken it directly, but she knew he
despised her for her wildness, even though it was the quality
that had made him trust her in the first place. He was softer at
core, more timid than her father, less brutal not from kindness
but from an inherent callowness that he would never rise above.
Calley had been right: there was nothing worse than sleeping
with the enemy.

She passed onto solid ground, into the trees, unstrapped her
shoes, and wiped her feet clean on pine needles. Her pipe had

gone out, and she stopped to relight it, then began to cast about in the undergrowth. Glossy green leaves; it was too late in the spring for flowers. She bent down and took a leaf between her fingers, crushed the springy greenness, and lifted it to her nose. It did not give off the strong scent of ramson, but instead the smell was innocuous, vegetal. She studied the flowerless stalks a moment. *Convallaria majalis.* Lily of the valley. She considered the little plant, then carefully dug up six, roots and leaves, and bundled them into her gathering basket.

Back in her hut, she crushed the leaves and roots carefully in her cooking pot, and covered them with fresh water. As they steeped, she considered the concoction. It would be more than enough, she knew, though it was a comparatively gentle poison. Thoughtfully, she sorted through the cloth bags and sealed bottles in her chest. It had always been hers, and when she was small she'd put her dolls to bed in it, or hidden away the silver paper from candies, when she had them. When her grandfather's books caught her interest, she had turned out the trash she had gathered into it and begun squirreling away herbs, sewing her own pouches for the dry ones, kidnapping bottles from the kitchen for the tinctures. Calley had encouraged her, taught her all that she knew of healing, of brewing, of the half-magic that couldn't quite be called medicine, but that worked nonetheless.

She found it, never used and fallen to the bottom of the chest: a small, sealed vial of dried Quaker buttons. She wasn't certain when she had gathered them, perhaps during her adolescence, when death was most on her mind. They didn't give a gentle death, but a certain one.

As the sun touched the tree line, Medora gathered up her

bottles and basket and set out. It was a long walk for a woman with a bad hip. She went slowly, the basket bouncing with every step, liquid sloshing in the bottle.

The sky was changing color by the time she approached the lodge, but even so she had to stand for a moment inside the door to allow her eyes to adjust to the dimness. She quickly picked out Nittawasew, her pipe in her mouth, the smoke blending with the thin trail from the firepit in the middle of the room, and went to kneel in front of her.

"Grandmother." Medora did not speak Algonquin, did not know the proper respects to offer, but did as best she could and hoped that it was good enough. Belatedly, she realized that she had come without a gift, and felt guilty.

"You haven't simply come for a visit, have you?"

"No, Grandmother, I haven't," she admitted with embarrassment. "I was told today that my husband plans to put me off—I am going to take my revenge. I wanted to say goodbye, in case I don't come back."

Nittawasew said nothing, gave no indication that she was listening besides cocking an eyebrow and exhaling a thin streamer of smoke. It was this immovability that Medora had tried to project whenever someone came to see her; it was also the quality that most unnerved her.

"And I wanted to say thank you, for what you've done for me."

"Revenge isn't going to get you what you want," Nittawasew said finally, slowly, as Medora was gathering her feet beneath her to stand up.

"But revenge is what I want," Medora answered.

"Revenge is what everyone thinks they want, but it's a bitter dish. Listen to me, find some other way."

"There is no other way. I'm sorry."

Medora left quickly, ashamed, conscious of the older woman's eyes on her back, of her silent disapproval.

Nittawasew waited until she heard the rustle of the marsh shoes through the grass, then motioned to the clutch of young people on the other side of the fire. One of her grandsons—or nephews, she couldn't keep them straight—detached himself from the group of talking cousins and came to her. Grandson, she remembered now. His name was Thomas; his mother had married a white man. Not a boy for many years, but still unmarried. It was always difficult for the storm bringers to find wives.

"Follow her. Keep her from doing anything foolish. I've brought her back from the edge of death once, I'm not going to go to all of that trouble again."

Her home loomed darkly against the star-shot sky, and she stopped to rest for a moment. There was silence except for the rustle of trees in the wind, and the distant throb of breakers crashing on the barrier islands. She considered. Not her home, anymore, just another rich man's house. Gingerly, she entered by the cellar door, which was never locked, passed silently through the rooms and up the stairs. They did not keep dogs, and now she was glad of Andrew's aversion to them.

She passed through the heavy shadows to the nursery. Their beds lay side by side, but Ruth had slipped in with James, as she always did, her chubby toddler body wedged in almost underneath his. She stood and watched them, motionless in sleep. She wanted to catch them up, bundle them to her, eat them whole the way she playfully threatened to when they were younger. Maybe there was another way ... No. She would not become her mother, watching at the window. There was no other way.

Gently, she woke James, and he started and clung to her.

"Hush, hush, baby. I'm here."

He did not question her presence, her existence, the horrible scars. He mumbled at her, rubbed his face against her chest, and fell back asleep with his arms around her neck.

She could not do it.

She had wanted to leave Andrew childless, to end his line once and for all. But she could not. They were hers.

She settled between them, feet hanging off the end of the bed, and gathered them to her. They curled instinctively against her, settled their heads on her chest, nestled into her and clung. She stroked their backs for a moment, felt the softness of their breathing, and then gently disentangled herself and stood up. She would have her revenge, but she would not hurt them to get it.

She tucked them back in, smoothed their hair away from their faces, then took up her basket again.

His bedroom was across the hall. She paused before the massive door and placed her basket on the carpet. How often had she listened to him talk about family, honor, his name, while she sat before the fire or lay in the bed in that room? He knew the money was hers; all he had left to take pride in was his bloodline. If it meant so much to him that he would break faith with her, then she would deprive him of the means for continuing it. Perhaps it would be better to leave him with his children, reminders that he did not have and never would have pure descendants.

A breeze touched her as she opened the door, and she stole over to the bed, shivering. Their bed. He was always hot in his sleep, and he lay naked across it, arms and legs flung out as though he had never shared it with her. Ridiculous in his nudity, snoring and defenseless. The knife was in her hand; she could just kill him. But it would be better for him to live with the memory of what he had lost. If she could be fast enough. If.

She played out the motions in her mind, watching him from the corner of the bed like a snake. It would be like gutting a fish, like cutting Mercury. It would be cleaner, and easier: he couldn't kick or trample her, couldn't smell her fear like a horse could, didn't know what was coming. Before she realized she was ready, she sprang. Soft in her hand, one quick moment, and it was done.

He started up, screaming, gushing, but she had them in her hand. Too late, she realized he might bleed to death, or go into shock, that he was a man, not a horse. Never mind, she had them. She stumbled back from the bed, dropped the knife, and ran. His screams followed her from the house.

The boat was there at the end of the dock, the small one that Andrew used to hunt ducks in the marsh. It rocked beneath her as she stepped into it, and in the first minutes she felt as though it and she were hovering in midair, though she paddled as hard as she could. When she looked back she could see the faint lights of the house, diminishing and flickering through the branches of the trees. She wondered for a moment what would happen in the morning, when someone came to her hut looking for a cure for toothache or earache or a cock that wouldn't stiffen when it was wanted, wondered if they would find her chest, what they would do with it. Probably bring it to Andrew, if she guessed right. What he would do with it she didn't bother thinking about, and for a moment she wished that she'd sunk it in the mud herself, rather than let him touch the one thing that in her whole life had ever truly been hers.

The velvet mud slipped by beneath her, by the yard and then by the mile, until the grasses turned to sand and marsh to brackish stream. She was on the barrier islands now, nothing before her except for the wide, wide ocean, and she drove the nose of the boat into the sand and stepped out. The wind off the water was cold, but the soft curves of the dunes retained the day's heat, and reflected it back into the soles of her feet, and then into her back as she lay down in the hollow between two gently rising hills.

Slowly she plucked at the folds of her skirt, drew out the bottle of dried Quaker buttons, picked at the seal with her ragged fingernails before finally prying it off with her teeth. She looked at the mound of seeds behind the glass, considered, then fished out her pipe and tobacco tin. It would make the journey easier.

For a moment she lay there, watching the stars turn above her, tasting the soft bitterness of the pipe, enjoying the sharp burn in her lungs. As her eyes began to close on their own she thought she could feel her children on either side of her, their heads nestled beneath her breasts, their fingers buried deep in the folds of her tattered skirt. Her fingers found the bottle beside her, and she shook three of the seeds into her palm. They felt like riverwashed pebbles; she rolled them around, enjoying their smoothness. She would see her mother again soon, just as soon as she finished her pipe.

There were footsteps on the sand, the soft sound of the grains grating on each other as they were compacted almost beyond the edge of hearing. She slipped one of the seeds into her mouth, but did not bite down; if someone was coming she wanted to know who it was.

A face appeared upside down above her, and for a moment she thought that the poison had already worked, that she was seeing her mother as she had been on that last night, a dark face and long black hair.

"Give them to me."

Not a woman, but a man. She clutched the seeds, but still did not bite.

"This is not what you want. Give them to me."

His voice was warm and smooth and so certain of itself; the seed slid from between her lips and into her palm before she knew that she was spitting it out, and he knelt down and took them out of her hand.

"Are you so hopeless?"

"Look at what I have become," she answered.

"But think of what you can become again. What revenge is this, removing the only thorn in your husband's side?"

"He isn't my husband," she spat.

"Then let the world know. Shame him, expose him, cast him out. But don't do this."

"They would take his side—he has everyone in the palm of his hand."

"There is no one from his past that would take your revenge for you?"

He was kneeling above her, looking down at her, and was at the best vantage point to see the smile that spread slowly across her face, crinkling even the permanently closed left eye, and in that moment he knew why his grandmother had chosen him to be the one to go after the woman. He stepped over her and pulled her to her feet. She tried to stand on her own but stumbled into him instead; her hip had gone stiff and cold from lying still. He bent to gather up her basket, her bottles.

"Leave them," she said. "I don't have a use for poisons anymore."

"Better to take them with us than risk fools finding them and coming to grief," he said, and settled her in the nose of the boat next to the detritus of her aborted revenge.

She would remember those minutes as a turning point, another rebirth in a life full of rebirths. But as she sat in her boat, waiting for him to come back, to row her to his grandmother's lodge, she did not feel as though she were being reborn. All she felt was an odd little flutter in her stomach, a jumping in her chest, a warm prickle beneath her skin every time she looked at him.

CHAPTER IX

1981

SOMETIMES IT HURTS

I found them half-naked in the forsythia bushes the spring after Mom died, a guy I didn't know on top of my sister Mo, with his big, loose mouth all over her neck. Was expecting to find a rabbit, from the noise I'd heard. At first I thought he was hurting her; her face was all twisted up in a grimace, and the way she was laying couldn't have been comfortable. Didn't even think, just hauled him up by the collar and whaled away at him, his jeans all bunched up around his ankles and his skinny white legs trying to kick out at me in spite of them. Mo didn't make a noise, just fumbled her skirt back down and her shirt back up and stayed right in that spot where the heat and weight of them had pressed the grass down.

After I finished with him I threw him toward the driveway, and he stumbled a few feet before he went over in the grass.

"You stay the fuck away from my sister, you fucking degenerate!" He curled up like he expected me to kick him, started blubbering but the only word I caught was "sir" repeated over and over. I realized then that he wasn't anything but a stupid little kid playing at being grown up the only way he knew how, but even if he hadn't meant to hurt her didn't mean that he hadn't managed to. When I turned around Mo shrunk down like she expected me to start whaling away on her too, but I scooped her up around the middle and hauled her back inside; she was sixteen and too old for me to be throwing her around like a little kid, but for once she didn't fight me.

No one else was home. I plunked her down in one of the kitchen chairs, and she watched me like a cat as I dug up two of Mom's cut-glass tumblers, threw ice into them, and nearly filled them with Dad's whiskey. All the wheels were clicking in my head right then, but I didn't say anything until I'd set her glass down in front of her and taken a long drink.

"What the hell were you two doing?"

It took half her glass for her to tell me that Johnny was just a sometimes thing. As was Stevo, and Roddy, and Chick, and a whole bunch of other names I'd never heard before. It didn't really feel good in her body but it made her feel better in her head, how she was all they were thinking about for the ten or fifteen minutes they took, and most of the time the five or six days she strung them along beforehand. I just sat there, rubbing my forehead and slugging down booze, and feeling a hundred years old and more like a dad than I ever wanted to. I'd never felt that way about people, never wanted to get my bits all up in theirs like that, didn't know how to talk to her about this because it made me sick just thinking about it but knowing that I had to because no one else was going to do it. But I was glad in a weird way that I knew, because it made sense now how she was never home. Why she didn't talk to me anymore.

"And what exactly are you doing to keep from finding out one day that you've got some peach-fuzzed boy's baby coming without any idea who it belongs to?" I finally had to ask.

"I'm not letting them squirt it inside me. Nothing bad's happened yet." She sulked a little when she said it.

"Well, thank God it hasn't. Jesus Christ, Mo . . ." I couldn't think of what to say after that, so we sat at the table, sipping whiskey, until she'd had enough to start filling in the details on the boys, telling me who had a car of his own and who was working on getting into college someday and who was really sweet, down deep. I couldn't give any advice like I thought I should be able to, but I could shut up and listen, and I was so glad that she was finally talking again that that's what I did.

Mom died when I was nineteen, in February of '65. It happened fast; one day she didn't feel so good, the next she was in a casket. It shocked us all, but more than anyone it shook up Mo. I'd been finished with high school and doing tig welding for my Uncle Benjamin at his shop just outside Parksley for a year by then, so I spent just as much time as I could working, and went clamming and fishing off the barrier islands when the work ran out. Dad barely acknowledged we were there, which wasn't much of a change. Bo and Lester were twelve; Bo, of course, handled it by punching kids and making trouble, and Lester followed right along with him. Mo was almost fifteen, and it made her go crazy.

We were buddies up till then, just like we'd been when she was two and would scream whenever I went to school. The day Mom died, she went to her room and screamed at the ceiling for a good solid hour. No words, just noise, until her voice was nothing but the squeak of air. That was the last sound she made for months. We wove around each other for that silent time, like ships in fog, blind and confused.

She started talking again when she went back to school in the fall, and I figured that meant she was better. Then I started noticing the little things, and if I'd been home more, like I should've been, I probably would've noticed it all sooner. She stayed out too late at night, left the house too early in the morning, changed the way she dressed and moved. The thing that bothered me most, though, was that she wouldn't say a word about it to me. She was always "fine," when I asked, not going anywhere or doing anything or broke out with much to say. Most people would've thought that she was just mellowing out, growing up, calming down. But something wasn't right.

After our whiskey talk she clammed up again, but once I knew what was going on I noticed it when she came home with her skirt all wrinkled, grass stains on her knees, or her makeup half rubbed off. Turns out I worried too much about her getting pregnant, but I had no way of knowing it then. She gave me these sideways looks, knowing I noticed, daring me to make an issue of it or tell Dad, and after a few months I couldn't do it anymore. I threw everything I owned into the bed of the baby-blue Ford pickup I'd fixed myself and drove south until I ran out of land, crossed the bay, and took the first job I could find, in the shipyards in Norfolk. That trip was my last time on the ferry; in April of '67 they finished building the bridge across the bay.

I found a way to be all right with it, in my head. She lived her life and I lived mine and when we saw each other we caught up on things and acted happy, and when she had rough patches I helped her out. But I missed the way we'd been.

It was a day in November '81 that Pony, the foreman that I answered to, came and told me that Mo had called the shipyard looking for me. It had been nine months, maybe a little more, since I'd last seen her, and we hadn't talked much in that time— so of course my first thought was, "Someone's dead." She'd told him it was a family issue, not life or death, but I needed to come home, and could I haul ass to her place as soon as I got off work? Maybe I'm a bastard, but the call made me relieved in a sick kind of way, not that she needed me but that she'd still look for me when she needed something.

I had the time saved up, so Pony let me finish the bead I was on and take off, not bothering with a shower but stopping for a pack of smokes because you don't ride into battle unarmed.

When I was a kid the ferry was the only way you could get to the mainland from the south end of the island, and the ninety-minute crossing wasn't something you did on a whim unless you were a bit crazy. I loved watching the marshy rim of the island get thinner and thinner and the mainland with all its buildings grow and solidify, and the tankers and the ships and the little sailboats moving in and out of the bay. Going home, at the end of a day of shopping or visiting or reporting to the draft, I used to imagine I was King Arthur going to Avalon, and none of the city mess could follow me. It wasn't just the trip away in reverse. The stink of the city faded and that ribbon of life resolved magically out of the haze on the water. It was all soft and green, and no one could tell me the Shore wasn't the most beautiful place on the face of God's earth.

The bridge is beautiful in its own way, I guess. I've had fourteen years to get used to it, and when I'm in a hurry I like how it's shaved more than an hour off the travel time. Considering how much easier the trip is now than when I was a kid, I really should visit home more than I do, but it's never been an easy thing for me to take time off. There's not much to go back to, now. Ma's dead, and Dad's rotting with dementia in an old folks' home outside Onancock—he was near forty when I was born, and lived hard ever since. We're not sure where Lester's gotten to, and Bo grew up to be nothing but mean. So there's no one left but Mo. I would have gone back to see her, but her husband Grant is such a prick that I don't really get around to it. He probably feels the same way about me, so having us both in the house would only make things worse for her.

The radio goes all to static halfway across the bridge, then I'm beyond the range of the signal and for a few moments it's silent. Not many people are making the crossing—late afternoon isn't a popular travel time—and I have the road all to myself. The water glints to the horizon and the voice in my head says, "Jump!" because the voice in my head is an asshole like that, and then the radio comes back to life, out of tune, with the afternoon's weather forecast for the islands. The last stretch of the bridge arcs up high, so smaller boats can get under it, and it gives me a good view of Fisherman's Island, where the bridge touches down. It's all swampy and marshy, but that doesn't matter because it's been set aside as a wildlife sanctuary. It doesn't look promising up close, and it makes you wonder what kind of people crossed the bay, hit a marsh, and decided that that was the perfect place to set up camp, way back when pilgrims were doing that sort of thing. My tires hit solid ground, then a few minutes later I smell it: not quite as bad as hogs, but it makes you want to never face a bowl of chicken soup again. The smell hangs with me for a few miles once I'm past the first chicken plant, and every bit of me knows I'm home.

Norfolk ain't home, though I've been there since I was twenty-one. Growing up I thought I'd never get off the Shore, and the way all us kids talked about how we wanted to go west, see mountains and cowboys and hunt down Reds, only made it worse. At the same time I was in love with the place, with the sand and the sun and the greenness, and the little critters in the creeks and the wild ponies, and didn't ever want to leave it behind.

Once I'm over the bridge it's just one straight shot up to Belle Haven, about eighty or ninety miles, and pretty much the dullest drive I've been on. The land's flat like a pancake, and even though there's water on both sides you can't see it from Route 13, which runs straight up the center of the island like a backbone. There are cornfields and potato fields and tomato fields, and every now and again a house set back from the road near a stand of trees, or a cluster of gravestones, wind-scrubbed and bleached like an old set of teeth left too long on a window-sill. You slow down and speed up as you pass through the little towns, but not by much. They've got names which I now real-ize are funny sounding, to someone not from here: Assawoman, Modest Town and Helltown, Onancock, Belle Haven, Horsey.

I drove through those towns as a teen, from just before I got a license till just before Ma died, when I thought life was shit because I was bored. Slumped down behind the wheel of the pickup, sucking on the end of a bummed cigarette, burning gas just for the sake of not being at home. Mo used to ride shotgun, feet up on the dash and giving me puppy eyes for a puff of what she called "our cigarette." She tagged along everywhere, before she stopped talking to me.

We drove, stopped sometimes to poke around in the little villages—most of them no more than a cluster of cheap one-floor houses around a post office—but more often we'd find the abandoned places, trespass to see what others had left behind. Our favorites were the health spa on the sea side near Wacha-preague, where rich people used to come so the women could go sea bathing and the men could shoot our quail and pheasants, because it had only been empty a few years and the buildings were still in good shape; and the village on Assateague Island just below the lighthouse, which was a pain in the ass to get to because you had to go through the village on Chincoteague Island, cross the channel, then hike through the woods, but it had been empty since the thirties and it gave us both the shivers all over to stand in the ruined foundations of what had once been family homes.

Three years after Mo and Grant got married, she'd gotten a funny letter from the bank. Their savings account was cleared out, and checking was overdrawn. They'd been squirreling cash away toward a house, one of the really nice ones on Chin-coteague, so it wasn't just some pocket change that was missing. She'd stormed into the bank, furious, and they'd had to tell her that Grant had been slowly cleaning out the account. Later she found out that he'd been going up to Atlantic City whenever he was in Maryland overnight for roofing jobs, playing the slots, poker, roulette, anything that could pay off big or clear him out fast. Mostly it was the second one. He'd been covering his tracks well, expecting to hit it big and put everything back in the account before she found out, so when she came home and started crying and screaming at him, he denied it at first. She threw some clothes in a bag, took his car, and showed up at my apartment, so mad she was shaking.

The first few days she did almost nothing but sleep; when I went to work she was passed out on the couch, and when I got back she was pretty much in the same position. She didn't tell me right off what had happened, and I probably would have gone after him if she had. After a week to sort her head out she started looking through the paper for jobs, and that's when he started calling. The first few times he begged like a wimp, and we just hung up on him. Then he called to say that he'd straightened out the account, gotten their bank balance back to zero even if he couldn't save the apartment they were renting in Onancock, and she decided to listen. He had enrolled in a twelve-step program, had taken on more hours at work, promised to earn back all the money he had lost and never go near a casino again. He didn't deserve her but they had said for richer or poorer and he swore that she wouldn't regret it if she didn't walk out on him. She'd found a job at a greasy spoon by then, and told him to prove it to her. My housemates didn't mind her, since she bought her share of beer, so she'd stayed around for six months, working double shifts and acting like one of the guys again, until she figured Grant had learned his lesson and she was ready to go back and give him a second chance.

I'd been glad when Mo got married, since she was so happy about it, but even from the start I hadn't liked her husband. He'd struck me as a spineless bastard, the sort that was always trying to weasel himself into or out of something, the sort you really shouldn't trust. He'd been chasing after her for years, and at first I'd thought he'd go the way of her other boyfriends. But he'd started talking kids and a future at some point, and before I knew it she was shopping around for a gown. When she showed up at my door that time I'd halfway hoped she'd just stick around, but even then I'd known that she wouldn't leave him so easily. When she'd told me that she was going back to try again I'd cleaned out my savings, gone up to Belle Haven on my day off, and bought their little shoebox house. I'd been welding ships for about eight years, through the Vietnam War when most of the guys I knew had been drafted, and I'd never gone on a bender or chased after women or even really taken a vacation in all that time. It wasn't like I was saving the money for anything; they'd lost their apartment when she left, and Grant had been sleeping on people's couches. The house and the half-acre it sat on I kept deeded in my name, wrote up a lease with an annual rent of a penny. I was worried that if I gave her the place outright he'd get himself up to the eyeballs in debt again, and it would go toward bailing him out. Going back to him was her choice to make, but even if it turned out to be the wrong choice, I wanted her to still have a place to live.

Mo and Grant's house is just outside of Belle Haven on the bay side, far enough south of Onancock that you think you can walk it but you probably won't be able to; you can see the marshes as a smudge of green and gold from their kitchen window. It's a little house, not much more than a trailer really, but with a poured foundation, and green fake-vinyl shutters to make it look homelike, and I'm relieved to see it still standing. After spending the drive mulling over the message she gave Pony, I'm about ready for any emergency.

Mo answers before I can knock; she must have been watching from the front window. She looks a hundred years old. Her face is creased up one side from napping, and there's kid spit down the front of her shirt. Charlie is dangling from her arm, giving me that toothless, vacant baby grin that most people go nuts over, and playing with his feet. Mo doesn't say anything when she opens the door; she just leans forward and smacks her face into my chest like she used to do when I came home from school.

"Hey, it's all right now. What's going on?"

Instead of answering she straightens up and goes back inside, and I follow her into the kitchen, where she pops Charlie into a playpen full of chewing toys. It took them nine years together to come up with him, and as far as I know it wasn't from lack of trying. There are some girls who get knocked up from being in the same room as their men, and Mo just isn't one of those girls. Ma wasn't one of them either; Mo and I are four years apart, so she should have guessed that it would take some trying. She told me the doctor had said it was about time to give up and start looking at adopting when they suddenly found out that Charlie was coming. Kid was born skinny and blue, but she didn't care; ask Mo it was the prettiest baby in the world. He's filled out since I last saw him, looks like a bologna loaf with a head on top, and I guess most people would say he's cute.

"I am so fucking glad you're here," she says flatly, and pours herself a cup of lukewarm coffee from the stained glass pot on the table. "I seriously don't know what to do anymore. Want some?"

"Nah, looks like you need it more than me." Charlie has pulled himself up and begun flinging his toys out onto the floor, one at a time, and she gathers them and dumps them back in.

"Remember when I was a kid and I said I wanted triplets?" she asks.

"You also wanted to name them after the bunnies in *Peter Rabbit*," I snort.

"Thank God we don't always get what we want." She sinks down into one of the wooden kitchen chairs and slings her feet up onto a second. I sit down across from her, gingerly.

The kitchen is a wreck. Every surface within three feet of the ground has a sticky patina to it, dishes litter the tiny counter, and toast crumbs dust the table. Mo was the kind of kid that sorted her blocks by size, shape, and color, and called it playing, so I can only imagine how worn out she has to be to leave things like this.

She takes a slow gulp of coffee. "Can I get you something?"

"No, really, I'm good. Just tell me what's up," I say. I'm not going to tell her, but her call scared the putty out of me.

"Well, now that you're here, I really don't know where to begin," she says and sets her cup down so that she can run her finger around its lip.

"You can start by telling me you haven't lost it and killed Grant and now need me to do something about the body."

She laughs. "No, though sometimes I wish I had. It is about Grant though, mostly. You remember his gambling thing, don't you?"

"He's gone back to it, I'm guessing?" I ask.

"I really wish that was it," she says. "Sure you don't want some coffee?"

"I'm good, but let me make you another pot. That shit looks rancid. Then tell me what's going on, OK?" I get up and dump the pot before she can answer; the dregs are full of grounds.

"He went back to it a few years ago, only he tried to be smart about it. When he started losing money, he borrowed instead of pulling it out of our account. And when he couldn't pay it back in cash, he started paying it back in work, a bit at a time."

"Not roofing work, I guess?"

"Nope. He said that they told him everything was all right—he was in good and had an unlimited line of credit. Except last month they decided he'd had enough credit and it was time for him to start paying it back."

"Back up, Mo, how much did he owe?"

"He wouldn't tell me, but the guys that came by the house looking for him said it was almost a million dollars."

I'm shuffling through the cupboard for the coffee filters, and nearly pull the shelf down on myself. "How the fuck do you lose a million dollars?"

"That's what I'm wondering. He's been borrowing it from some dealers, he told me, guys that run cocaine up the coast and have money to burn. Every time he lost they just gave him more cash, had him do them a favor or three, and told him that he could pay it off later. Then the coast guard found one of their buddies floating in the bay, a whole bunch of cocaine was missing, and suddenly it was 'later.' He wasn't going to tell me about it, he thought he could pay them back without me finding out, take care of it all himself, but then guys started showing up here."

"Where is he now?" I'm still fiddling with the coffee, to avoid turning around.

"In jail in Parksley, only until they can move him to the mainland. Police caught him with marked bills. It's probably a good thing; if he weren't in jail he'd probably be floating in the bay too. I thought it was going to be OK, since they couldn't get to him there, but this morning—well, two of them showed up here looking for him, and now I'm wondering . . ."

"If they might do something to the two of you," I finish for her. "Whatcha reckon you should do about it?"

"Really? I don't got the foggiest." She stares at me for a few minutes, like she's just woken up. Charlie starts up a wail like a siren because his cage is empty, and I scoop toys back in with him. "I haven't got a million dollars," she says. "And I can't really tell the police anything. If I sell the car and Mom's jewelry, that's not even going to begin to cover it."

She starts drawing in the puddle of cold coffee that's formed under her cup. We just sit there for a few moments, not talking, looking at the dirty tabletop, marinating in the mess of it all.

"Starting over isn't so hard," I say. I take her cup, dump it, and refill it with hot coffee. "New name, new address, part-time job, and until we sort that out you'll stay with me again. Before you know it the past won't exist anymore."

"The past always exists," she says. "I think I'm really fucked this time."

"Hear anything from Lester lately?" she asks. I'm not sure if she's completely changing the subject or bringing it around to something important.

"Nope. Last I heard he was going to try his luck in California."

"One of my old boyfriends, he's a construction foreman round here, works with Bo. Told me that Bo'd gotten a girl what they work with knocked up, married her at the courthouse last month."

"I'm guessing he didn't invite you either," I say.

"How'd our family fall apart?" she asks. "And is it bad that I don't want to put it back together, that I don't want to go track his sorry ass down and bring his knocked-up shotgun wife a cake or something?"

"Some families just don't work out, I guess," I say.

She's quiet for a bit, sipping at her coffee.

"Gone to see Dad lately?" she asks, and my head whips up on its own.

"What kind of question is that?"

"I was just thinking, wondering, if he and Mom had problems like this along the way," she answers. Charlie's started to fuss, and she pulls him out of his pen so he can bounce on her lap. He laughs as she bounces him, so he sounds like a machine gun with the hiccups.

"You just wonder? Dad wasn't much of a man even before his brain started rotting out," I answer. "I'm guessing he had a girlfriend or two on the side, at least when I was little. He drank like he was about to go in front of a firing squad, he never came home when he said he was going to, he had tempers and smashed up furniture and shouted, or pulled out that 'king of my castle' shit whenever she asked him to do anything."

"And Mom never said or did anything about it."

"Nope. She didn't have much of a choice, though. It wasn't like she could leave, with a kid, no education, and no job prospects."

"If she were still here, what do you think she'd say?" Mo asks me.

"Ditch the bastard, pack up, start over somewhere else."

"No, that's what you'd say. What do you think Mom would say?"

I have to think on that one longer than I would like. "I don't rightly know. It's been too long, I think, since she passed."

We sit in silence for a second, except for Charlie gurgling as he gums her fingers, then she says, "You stopped talking to me after she died. Don't think I ever forgave you for that."

"What? You're the one that stopped talking!" My voice comes out louder than I intended.

"Who was I supposed to talk to?" she responds, voice rising to meet mine. "You never came home except to shower and sleep. It was like if you'd stopped working for even a minute the world was going to end." She's almost shouting now, the kid looking up at her with big, startled eyes, and I try to shush her just so that we won't have to add crying to the mix. "And don't you 'shush' me, I've had enough of being shushed!"

"I'm sorry, Mo, but for the love of God, please don't start the baby off."

She pulls a yellow pacifier out of her pocket and crams it in his mouth. "There. He'll stay quiet. Now answer me."

"What do you want me to say?" I ask.

"Anything! Everything you didn't say. At the funeral, when you were off with Uncle Ben or fishing or any of those places you went while I was stuck at home with Dad and the twins screaming at each other and trying to keep the house in one piece because nobody else was about to."

"Geeze, Mo. I was just trying to stay busy, to not think about it. It's not like it would have done any good if I'd said anything to you—you didn't say a goddamned thing for months after she died."

"And did you ever try and talk to me?" she asks, her voice like a needle. I think backward, to the brown-gray days after the funeral, with strange-tasting casseroles and people we hardly knew in and out of our house.

"I figured you needed to be left alone," I finally say, and she smacks her hand down on the table.

"Exactly!" she shouts, and Charlie's pacifier pops out onto the floor. He looks confused for a second, then starts screaming, but she shouts over him. "You just left me there, in that fucking house with no one sane to talk to, dumped me like a three-legged puppy by the side of the highway. You found your own way to deal with things and left me to take care of myself. Then you had the balls to get pissed at me when you found out just how I was dealing with it. Remember that?" She ducks down to retrieve the pacifier, but he turns his head away from it and bawls louder. She chucks it at the sink, leans back in the chair far enough to reach the refrigerator, and pulls out a nipple-ended bottle of apple juice.

"I figured when you were ready to talk, you'd find me and start talking," I answer lamely.

"Really? When I hurt myself or got in a fight you didn't wait for me to ask you for help, you just took care of things." She's still angry, but she's quieting down some. "When Grant was being an ass the last time and I needed a place to live you didn't make me ask you to take care of it, you just bought a house. So how come the one time I really needed you to just step in and be there, you stepped out?"

I rock back in my chair, then get up and dig through the cabinet for a clean mug, fill it with coffee, and slug it down all at once.

"Look, Mo. I'm sorry. You're right, I fix things. I like to fix things. I know how to fix things. But back then, I didn't know how to fix you. It felt like you'd stopped talking to me, 'cause you never had much to say to the rest of them anyway. I thought that if I let you alone you'd just start back up when you felt like it."

"Guess you were wrong then," she spits.

"Not quite. You're talking now, aren't you?" She grins a little at this, and settles back in the chair more comfortably, resets the bottle in the baby's mouth so he gets more juice in with his air bubbles.

"You want me to fix things?" I say, and she nods sharp. "OK, I'm here to fix things. Get a divorce. He doesn't have any kind of claim on the house, so no one can touch it for his debts. I took out insurance on it and kept it paid up, so if they burn it down there's no big loss there. Come to Norfolk with me, change your name, stay there till the kid's in school, the divorce goes through, and these guys are off your back, then come back if you want to or go explore the rest of the world if you don't. You got money troubles, I got that. If you want to work, great, we'll get someone in to watch Charlie. If you don't want to work, fine, stay home with him till you do. I'll take care of it. Life looks a bit like shit right now, but it seems to me like Grant just freed you up. You can do just about anything you want to now and he can't say boo about it."

"Will you come back to the Shore with us?" she asks.

"Now?"

"No, later maybe. When Charlie's older. I don't want him growing up without a man around."

"Mo, are you just trying to get me to come home?"

"No, it's a legitimate concern." She sounds hurt. "And besides, can you fault me for wanting you to be close, for not wanting to leave home?"

"The work is in Norfolk. But I'll think about coming back, sometime. It's more important to figure out where to put you right now, anyway."

We can probably do everything from Norfolk, pack them both into my truck right now, see a lawyer in the morning. It would be safer in the city, with people around.

"So I'm starting over, all over again." She blows out air hard. "Guess there could be way worse things going on."

We're quiet for a bit.

"I gave it a shot, you remember, the day I caught you and your boyfriend in Mom's flower bushes. Talking, I mean. About what happened after Mom."

"Yeah, you did, I guess. I could've made it easier for you. But after that I couldn't talk about it, couldn't tell you about it, really. I was doing shit that you'd never done. Don't think you'd ever really thought about then. For the first time in my life there was stuff you hadn't tried out first and couldn't tell me anything about."

There isn't much I can say to that, so I start scraping up the toast crumbs on the table in front of me, building them up in ridges and making little ant-sized mazes out of them.

"Benny, have you ever had a girlfriend?" she asks finally.

When she says "girlfriend" I know she means "sex."

"I mean, I know that you didn't ever when you were home,

but I thought then that it was because you were working too hard, that you'd spent too much time with Mom and me and thought all women were too much crazy to deal with."

"Women are too much crazy to deal with," I answer.

"So no then?"

"Yeah. I haven't really met anyone I'd want to sit and chat with."

"What about just kiss and have a good time with?"

"Mo, you got a point here?"

She shifts around on her chair, hooks her arm around Charlie's middle, stands up, and gets down two squat, heavy glasses. "You did make me talk to you, but when you did it was so all-fired weird that I didn't want to ever do it again. It was like we were speaking two different languages, or like I'd just stopped being human and it was some Martian that was talking to you." She kicks a stool out from under the table and reaches up to the highest cupboard. "Get out the ice, will you? I can't do it with one hand."

She sets a half-full bottle of Jim Beam on the table and plunks back down, then laughs a little. "But the look on your face when I told you about sucking off Roddy at the drive-in—"

"You make me throw up, I'm not the one that's going to be cleaning it," I cut in, and put ice in the glasses. We'd first found a bottle of Dad's Wild Turkey when I was seventeen, and shared sips back and forth on the porch while watching the Fourth of July fireworks over the bay. At some point we'd grown up enough to drink it out of glasses, but I couldn't remember the last time we'd sat down with it together.

"Never understood why that bothered you so much," she says as she opens the bottle.

"It's disgusting. It's all disgusting. People are disgusting, nothing more than meat and blood sloshing around in a bag of skin, and when they start oozing their fluids all over each other—"

"OK, OK, stop! I'm sorry I said anything," she cuts me off fast. "You don't have to be graphic, just say you're not into it or something."

"Like that would make you leave it alone," I answer.

The whiskey splashing into the glasses looks like iced tea, like our childhood from both ends, and she makes me clink glasses with her before I can have a sip.

CHAPTER X

1919

WAKE

J ackie watched the church float away while sitting on the top of the hill where the Assateague Lighthouse stood, a dull heaviness in the pit of his stomach. Elijah Binney had bought it with the intention of taking it to Chincoteague and turning it into a house, and Jackie had climbed to the base of the lighthouse early that morning and settled in the dust near the shed where the kerosene for the light was kept to watch the entire process of jacking up the building, rolling it down to the water, and settling it on the barge. A small, square, white wooden building with a rough steeple and oversized windows, it wasn't the prettiest church, but it was the only one on Assateague Island. He'd never liked going to church, in fact he was quite happy that he wouldn't have to sit on the hard pew next to his mother not swinging his legs all through the sermon, but it was the principle of the thing. It was their church. They were proud to finally have one. The village had only built it three years before, when their population was still growing, when Assateague was becoming a place you could be proud to come from.

Eighteen months after the church was built, a gentleman farmer called Sam Fields had come from the mainland, looking to buy growing land. None of the locals would have sold, but the island had been the property of the county, and the county was willing to sell. Apart from the village and the lighthouse, most of the southern part of the island now belonged to him, and the arable part was planted in corn and beans. This wouldn't have mattered as much if the land didn't include Tom's Hook, the long, sandy arm that cradled the quiet bay, the clam and oyster beds, and the best fishing and crabbing. Fields had a strict "No Trespassing" policy, and it was his right to do so, but not being able to cross his land made fishing and trapping difficult, if not impossible, and the harder it became to eke out a living on the island, the more people bought lots on Chincoteague and jacked up and floated their houses across to town.

The church had been used for a single wedding, and no christenings. They'd make do; before the church had been built they'd met in the schoolhouse, or taken skiffs across the channel to Chincoteague.

Below Jackie the square of packed white sand that had so recently been the building's foundation stood out brightly among the roofs and gardens of his village. From Lighthouse Hill he could see it all laid out like a map: the soft curve of the little bay cutting into the land like a bite out of a cookie, the cluster of houses and kitchen gardens, the schoolhouse and the place where the church had been, all ringed by the communal fields where larger crops like oats and corn were planted, the village and the fields surrounded by the dense thickets and forests where the wild ponies—and often their goats and chickens—foraged. They were little houses, handmade of raw wood, one or two rooms with perhaps a single window, front steps leading up to packed-dirt floors. The gardens were riotous, bordered and divided by swaths of long grass that the sheep and goats never cropped short all at once, and the dusty oyster-shell paths shone out between the fronds, trailing from house to house like string. Neighbors were bent over in their gardens with their hands in the rich, dark earth, and he could pick them out even at that distance. His mother was not there; he had seen her leave earlier that morning, while the church was still being rolled toward the water, walk down to the dock, and row herself across to Chincoteague. She would not be back for hours yet, would not know that he'd spent his morning and a good portion of the afternoon bone idle, but still he felt a tinge of guilt. At eleven he was the man of the family. He ought to have been helping her, working the garden or going after fish and clams down by Tom's Hook, but he didn't have the heart for it, not today.

Every village and hamlet on the Shore had its own steepled building—except Tasley, but that had gambling, vice, and a train depot instead—and several had more than one. There were only twenty-odd families left in Assateague village, not counting the lighthouse keepers, not enough to warrant a church of its own anymore. By the end of the spring term the school had dropped below forty pupils, the number required by the county to receive its own teacher, and in the fall the children who could manage would be skiffing across the channel for school or staying with relatives on Chincoteague. Even with the difficulty he had often had at school, knowing that he would not be one of those children made him feel sick in the stomach, like a pie had gone moldy in the cupboard before he'd even known it was there.

He heard the door of the kerosene hut slam closed behind him, and the crunch of Graeme Quillen's boots on the oyster shells. The assistant lighthouse keeper came up to stand beside him, his hands deep in his pockets, and they watched the church drifting away for some moments in silence.

"Sad sight, ain't it?" the man asked, and Jackie nodded.

Three families lived in the lighthouse keepers' mansion: the head keeper John Anderton, and the assistants Graeme Quillen and Warren Jones, each of the three with his wife and children. The locals called it a mansion half-seriously: it wasn't much bigger than any of the houses on Chincoteague, and barely held the three families comfortably, but compared to the one- and two-room cottages below it was a palace. The offspring of these unions was impressive, a massing brood of daughters between the age of thirteen and birth, with one or two long-haired, coddled sons somewhere in the mess, whom their sisters treated more as living dolls than siblings. They were part and not part of the village. Paid in cash, they didn't have to keep gardens, pigs, and goats, or worry especially about being shot for trespassing on Sam Fields's land while fishing, or freezing through the winter. Some of the villagers avoided them, for class reasons, but Jackie had long been a playmate of the daughters. He'd caught baby rabbits and birds for them to keep as pets in summertime, wove them baskets out of rushes, and was occasionally dragooned into serving as the pack mule or dragon or other beast for their private pretends. Graeme Quillen was a young, friendly man, and Jackie liked him especially. Anderton was solemn, but kind, and Jones was sour-faced, but none of them chased him off the hill, though other boys often were when caught near the kerosene shed.

As the barge neared the far shore, Quillen pointed out a

small scow moving toward them across the channel, a large man propelling it with strong strokes of his oars.

"Ain't that your uncle Leo?" he asked.

Jackie supposed it was. Leonidas Wallace, his father's only brother, was a massive man, nearly six and a half feet tall and so broad in the shoulders that he went through doorways side-on. He owned one of the general stores on Chincoteague; as a service to Assateague village he would row across weekly to deliver groceries and take orders, but he'd already been that week, and his boat appeared empty.

"No use moping up here, better get down and meet him." Quillen smacked the seat of his pants and turned back toward the kerosene shed. "It's not as bad as it looks, boy. They can take the church, but they can't take the whole village."

As he picked his way down the nearly vertical hill to meet his uncle, Jackie considered those words. He suspected that it wasn't so much "can't take the whole village" as "won't take the whole village"—no one would want the cottages, they'd just be left behind when everyone eventually moved to Chincoteague or Accomack Island.

Jackie's father, John Wallace, had drowned in the storm of 1911 while fishing out on the bay; his body never washed up. He had left behind next to nothing: the two-room house with a single window that he had built for his wife Maude, three sheep, a garden, a nine-year-old daughter named Alice, and a two-year-old son. Uncle Leo helped as much as he was permitted, and Maude had briefly considered searching for a second husband, which wouldn't have been easy with two small children. On the rare occasions that a suitor had shown his hopeful face, there was Alice. Fiercely loyal to her father, she drove off each one with inspiring displays of temper, bad behavior, and cunning. After several years of this Maude gave up. Alice had only gotten more willful, more difficult, as she grew, and when she was sixteen Maude allowed her to move to Chincoteague. She now lived in one of the back rooms of Uncle Leo's store, worked cleaning houses and doing laundry, and seemed to find the arrangement far superior to Assateague village, but Jackie and Maude stayed put. Jackie wanted it to be because of a loyalty to his father, to the home that he had left them, but he couldn't fool himself into thinking that his mother wouldn't have left, if they could afford to: at the end of every year they barely had enough money squirreled away to make it through to the next.

At the bottom of the hill Jackie turned along the oyster-shell path, wove through gardens and around cottages, and trotted across the long stretch of rough grass and sand down to the dock. It was a solid structure, built by the county, and he dangled his feet above the water while waiting for his uncle to finish the crossing. Uncle Leo's shirt stretched and gleamed in the sunlight, like it was painted onto him, and his battered straw hat bobbed in time to his rowing. The water of the channel felt satiny as Jackie dipped his feet to wash off the dust, and he caught the rope his uncle threw and tied it off on one of the posts.

"Your mama around?" Uncle Leo asked as he stepped out of the skiff.

"No, sir, she rowed across just before noon to see Alice and run some errands. Not rightly certain when she'll be getting home," Jackie answered.

"Alice said she was coming across, I just wanted to be sure.

I was expecting to have to come searching for you—I've got something to say that I'm pretty sure she wouldn't want to be hearing about."

They walked to the edge of the village in companionable silence; Jackie knew better than to press his uncle to tell before he was ready. It was a warm day, midafternoon, and not much was stirring apart from the goats and the greenhead flies. Jackie poured his uncle a glass of tea and gave him a damp cloth to wipe the sweat from his face before settling on the front step, so as to get the benefit of the breeze. Mal, the oldest of their three sheep, stared fixedly at them from across the fence, their only company except for the chickens which scratched between the rows of their garden; chickens barely counted.

"Awful nice day for a boy to spend doing nothing," Uncle Leo observed as he sipped the tea.

"Wanted to watch them float the church away. Going egging in the dunes," Jackie replied, and pulled on one of the long strands of grass that sprang up around the steps to give his fingers something to do.

"Going to skiff across for school come fall?"

"No, sir, don't think so. There's work to be done here . . ." Jackie began to shred the grass, picking it smaller and smaller, the juice gumming his skin.

"Well, that's a pity. What grade you in now?"

"Should be fifth, but I got held back 'cause I can't spell. Not sure what it would be now, I've forgot so much."

"No shame in that." He took a long drink, and glanced up at Lighthouse Hill. "I've got some work I need done, and I'm thinking you're the only boy I trust to do it right and do it well.

Your mama don't like charity, and neither do I, so I'm going to insist on paying you fair for it, but I won't be able to until everything's said and done, and you won't be able to tell her what's going on, hear?"

Jackie nodded. Uncle Leo sat silent for a moment, looking at him, before continuing.

"Well then. I've got a man wants some good apple brandy. Since Virginia went dry a few years back it's all been coming in from Maryland, but with all this Prohibition nonsense it looks like that's going to be mighty short-lived. Chincoteague's stem to stern houses, so there's no place safe and private there to let it work, but I figure if I set up an operation in the woods a few miles north of here, no one will ever find it. Unfortunately, if I up tent pegs and leave myself people are likely to get suspicious."

"So you need someone to watch it for you?"

He nodded over his glass. "Want to move the equipment across in the next few days. The apples will more or less take care of themselves for the first couple of months; the distilling I need someone to watch pretty closely. It's a tedious job. You'll have to keep after it like you were watching a newborn, but when it's finished I'll pay you fair for it. Probably be enough to get a lot in town and barge your ma across, could go back to school and have your sister living t'home again."

"I don't think Mama would like it much . . ."

"Well, it's your choice whether you do it, but I'd ask you not to mention it to her either way."

"Yes, sir."

"There's a good boy. You take your time thinking, though

I'd be mighty obliged if you'd throw in a hand moving it all—
it's a fair pull across and every back's appreciated."

"Anyone else helping?" Jackie asked.

"The lighthouse keepers are, Anderton and Jones, though
the young one's to be kept out of it." He drained his glass and
set it down. "We're going to fix up some of the old cellars,
where they used to keep fish oil for the light, and use that to
stow things. Makes a snug little hiding place for it to age, before
we ship it out."

"I'll have to think on it some. Mama wouldn't like me doing
it if she found out." Jackie dropped the shreds of grass and
plucked another stem. "When do you want to start moving
things?"

"As soon as we can. I'd want you to come across tomorrow
and fetch a few barrels of apples; you should be able to get away
without your ma seeing."

Jackie put the end of the stem in his mouth and chewed,
tasting the deep greenness of it. "How's Alice getting on?" he
asked.

His uncle plucked his own stem, changed his mind, and
pulled a stubby clay pipe out of his shirt pocket and began to fill
it. "To be fair, I couldn't rightly say. She's gotten quiet of late.
Keeps to herself." He took a long draw at the pipe, scowled at
it, and drew again. "Think there might be a young man at fault,
but if so, that's for your mother to deal with. A bachelor such as
myself has no call to be messing in a young girl's affairs." The
flame took, and he blew out a thin gust of smoke. "You'd do
well to remember that."

"I won't forget."

After his uncle had gone, Jackie took a basket through the woods and over to the dunes, to search for plover's eggs. The small birds themselves were also tasty, but it was their nesting season, and he knew they would be just as good when there was less food to be found. Though they needed the eggs he liked taking his time about it, and so instead of choosing the fast but risky cut across Sam Fields's property he set off north through the woods and bogs.

Assateague Island was nearly forty miles long, and a good part of the southern end was too marshy to plant. The village itself had first sprung up as a resting place for men that worked the water or ran the rescue station on Tom's Hook, and for a long while that was all that it had been, a place to tie up and repair, perhaps eat and catch a few hours' sleep. Then the men began bringing their wives across, buying up plots of land from the county and building their own snug homes. Though they could still row out into the bay or trap squirrels and muskrats in the marsh, the loss of the oyster beds and fishing grounds of the Hook had been too much for the community. Chincoteague offered an easier life for the people who could afford to leave, but even though he understood the logic of it the loss of the church, the loss of the neighbors who he'd grown up around, felt like abandonment.

As he trekked through the marsh, eyes peeled for copperheads and cottonmouths, Jackie considered his uncle's offer. It had pained him sorely to hear that the school would not reopen in the fall; he had enjoyed learning, the routine of it, the full feeling he got when he'd just learned something interesting. He could go work at the oyster-packing factory on Chincoteague, or for one of the fishermen, but his mother wouldn't like the idea of him out on the water; she'd made him promise over and over that if he died young he'd leave her a body to bury. But he didn't want to spend the rest of his life shucking oysters or digging clams. He wanted to be like Uncle Leo and do business with people.

He passed out of the forest and onto marshier ground. The water between the hummocks of grass was thick and greasy, and he hopped from tuft to tuft to avoid sinking into it. Elsewhere the trees were in full leaf, but because of all the salt in this low-lying patch the few trees were spiny, gnarled, nearly choked to death. Even this part of the island had its own wild beauty, the sunlight reflecting off the slick surface of the mud, the twisted shape of the trees, the blueness of the sky above it all.

A flash of brown caught his eye, and he crouched low in the grass. A small herd of ponies shifted in a stand of twisted evergreens, cropping at the salty grass and stomping to dislodge the greenhead flies that nipped at them. No one knew where the ponies had come from, just that they were as much a part of the island as the greenheads and the cottonmouths. Jackie settled in to watch them. They weren't especially noble, not like racehorses or the riding horses the local landowners kept. The ponies were short, stubby, compact animals, much like the fishermen he knew, that avoided people unless there was food at stake; the little sods loved apples. When he was five, he'd been having a picnic with the lighthouse keeper's daughters when a pony had come out of the woods and taken the apple right from his hand. It had terrified him then, and he still stayed well away from the horses, but he loved watching them.

The wind shifted, and a sorrel raised its head, scenting him. The way they moved reminded him of deer in a way, more alert and timid than tame horses. They made breathy sounds to each other, stamped their feet impatiently, and he stood back up and moved on. No sense in riling them needlessly.

The ground firmed and then grew sandy, and the trees thickened and then thinned until he was out among the dunes. He stopped for a moment to fall back onto the sand and enjoy the sea breeze, then sat up and began looking for eggs. The nests, shallow depressions in the sand like tea saucers, usually held four eggs, and out of respect for the birds and hope for future dinners he always left two behind. They blended well with the sand and the sparse shining grasses, as did the small birds, but he had practice and rarely missed a nest. The eggs themselves were pale and speckled brown, and felt warm and smooth in his palm.

Jackie loved eggs. He loved them boiled, he loved them fried, he loved them deviled or scrambled with brains or baked into cakes or puddings or pickled and put away for winter. He loved the richness of them, like meat without bones, or fresh butter, and the soft custard-like texture when they were cooked just right. Even if he were rich, he thought, he would eat eggs every day, as many ways as possible. The eggs their chickens laid were good on winter days, but the plover eggs, which he could collect by the basketful, were better if only for their quantity.

As he searched he wondered about his sister. Alice was not an easy person to get along with, and the part of him that hoped that they would move to Chincoteague dreaded sharing space with her once again. Nevertheless, she was his sister, and if

Uncle Leo was worried he supposed he should be too. Alice had a raging temper, and it was not natural for her to be quiet. As he thought about it, he realized that she had been quiet on her last visit back to the village, as well. He had been fuming at the news that the church was to be sold, and so hadn't taken as much notice as he might have. He doubted that it was a young man, as his uncle thought. If it had been, she would have been crowing and showing off and planning the wedding and making Mama crazy. Alice was only quiet when something was wrong.

He sometimes wondered what home would be like if his father was still alive. To hear other boys talk, their fathers were the bosses of their homes, but Jackie had learned early that he was at the mercy of the moods of the women he lived with. The best thing he could do was to tiptoe around his sister's tempers and cheer up his mother when the gloom settled down on her. Alice, he had been told, had inherited every spark of their father's temperament, and he couldn't imagine a moment's peace with two people as moody as her in the house. He liked to think that when he grew up he would be just like the father his mother told him about, and wouldn't stand for fuss or tantrums from anyone, but he suspected, especially when Alice was home for a visit, that he'd gotten too deep into the habit of placating women to do any different. The older boys spoke loftily about taking a firm hand with women, the way you took a firm hand with horses, but he couldn't imagine anyone taking a firm hand with Alice and getting anything out of it besides a kick in the pants.

When his basket was full, Jackie stripped naked and ran into the water, diving below the breakers to pop back to the surface like a cork and float, belly-up, in the shallows. The bottom of the channel was thick with muck, and the edges sharp with oysters, so he only swam in the ocean, though other boys he knew didn't mind the slower-moving water. His mother swore by scalding hot baths, and forced him into one every Saturday night, but nothing made Jackie feel as clean as the cold salt of the Atlantic, even if it found every cut and scrape on his body.

The walk back to the village dried him gently, and the thought of the eggs he had gathered made him feel hollow from the inside out. Smoke wafting from their chimney showed that his mother had returned and put on the obligatory pot for evening tea, and he readied his face before going inside. He had a very honest face, people told him, which meant he had a face that wasn't very good at lying. He still wasn't sure if he would take his uncle's offer, but he wasn't about to squeal to his mother and ruin everything.

The next day Jackie skiffed over to Chincoteague at first light, though he figured he should have been fishing, clamming, oystering, patching the roof, fixing the fence, weeding the bean patch, or doing any number of things at home. A promise was a promise, after all, and if it meant putting off work, well, the work would still be there when he got back. The town was busy for a Wednesday, and he darted around people and jumped mud puddles in the rutted dirt road between the dock and his uncle's store. He knew most of the town people, but not well enough to talk to, so he got by with a nod.

As he turned onto Maddox Boulevard he caught sight of a familiar pair of shoulders retreating down an alley. Without giving it much thought, he followed after. Alice wasn't the kind of sister you ran up to and hugged hello, even if you hadn't seen her in a few weeks, but he still felt an odd closeness to her, a curiosity to see what she was up to without necessarily being seen himself. He tailed her quietly down the alley, around the corner of Thompson's Rooming House, and along the outside of their back fence to the wash house. She had been helping Mrs. Thompson recently so there was nothing odd in this, but the hunched way in which she held her shoulders, the quickness of her step, made him wonder if this errand was part of that "helping." She looked around before going inside the small wooden outbuilding, and he ducked down behind the fence before she could see him.

The wash house was roughly built, the boards knotted and warped, and it took him only a few seconds of looking to find a crack that gave him a decent view of the copper kettle, his sister standing behind it, and the young man of middling height who had her firmly by both arms. They kept their voices low, and strain as he might Jackie couldn't make out a word they said, but he could tell from long experience that his sister was on the edge of crying. The man was well dressed, sporting a carefully waxed mustache that Jackie figured he was just barely capable of growing, and looked both regal and nervous. He did most of the talking, looking down at her, and Jackie realized that, though she wasn't a tall woman, he'd never seen a man looking down at her; normally they were cringing away and asking if she wouldn't mind not making a scene in front of everyone. Alice was looking down also, appearing not to notice how tight his hands were on her arms; Jackie could see the worn cloth creasing where his fingers pressed. Her lips were pressed together even tighter, except for when she spoke in short, quick bursts. The man took a hand off her arm, touched her neck, fished out a string, and held something up on the end of it in front of her, and it sparkled in the dim light of the wash house. It was a ring. That seemed to be too much for Alice. She shook her head and began to cry, without making a noise but with lots of tears, which Jackie had never seen before. Shaken, he pulled away from the peephole and scurried back out to the main road.

He turned the moment over in his mind as he made his way to his uncle's store. It was unfathomable to him, his sister's distress, the man's firm and yet unsure response, the way in which the two appeared somehow connected. He realized as he walked that, though he had spent a lot of time with old married couples like the Meers, who owned the next house over, and old people on their own like his mother and Uncle Leo, and young people like the lighthouse keepers' daughters and his friends from school, he had never spent much time around young men and women together. Perhaps that was just how they acted, and when he got to be of an age to grow a mustache the girls who threw apples at him and said that he smelled would look up at him in the way that the island ponies did. It was a curious thought, and he didn't know if he liked it.

Uncle Leo was at the counter with a handful of farmers when he got to the store, so he perched on one of the half-barrels by the cold wood stove and waited to be noticed. He liked spending time in the store, listening to the farmers and fishermen talk about past storms and fires and seeing who could tell the tallest tale. They'd offered to take him snipe hunting, when he got bigger, but so far they'd only gone mistletoe hunting. Uncle Leo had skiffed over to the island in the early light two Decembers before, a flask of Kentucky bourbon in his pocket and a shotgun on his lap. Mama had made them a large jug of sweet, hot tea, and he'd emptied the flask into it when her back was turned, then told Jackie and his cousins—who Jackie never spent much time with and didn't trust as far as he could throw because they were town boys—to drink up in order to keep warm. Then they'd set out into the thickest part of the woods, heads craned back, looking for the heavy clumps of green mistletoe at the tops of the winter-bare trees. Every sighting was announced by a shout, at which point Uncle Leo, who had consumed a fair amount of the tea, would gather them behind him like a mother quail before sighting along the gun and firing. He usually missed the first shot, but the second felled great clumps of the parasitic plant, which they gathered up and dragged back with them to decorate for the holiday.

Eventually Jackie was noticed, but not before an older man had given him a handful of raisins, which he'd lined up in rows along the barrel top beside him and eaten in pairs, and a second had offered him a chaw of tobacco, which he'd politely declined. His uncle hailed him over and went into the back room, and Jackie followed him.

"Glad you've come over, I have enough apples to feed every herd on Assateague. Anderton will be waiting to show you where to unload; there's a gut that runs up to the clearing I want to use for the first fermentation, the press is already there. What you need to do, now, is load up with apples and cart them over. Anderton's readied the clearing. You can just beach the skiff and leave them covered, so the ponies can't get at 'em. Once everything's moved we can get to pressing."

Jackie hung in the doorway. "What happens if someone finds the clearing?"

His uncle considered this a moment.

"Nothing against the law about pressing apples, or having barrels of juice, or making vinegar. It's only when it turns alcoholic instead of running to vinegar that you get into trouble, and that won't be for more than a month. You'll have till then to decide how much of a hand you want to have in it, and whether you want some of the profits when it's sold."

After some minutes of deliberation, Jackie nodded his assent. "Where are all these apples at?"

Loading the skiff took more effort than Jackie had imagined. The store backed onto one of the canals that had been cut to let the low-lying island drain properly in the rainy season, and for that he was grateful. First he'd run back down to the dock and rowed around the island and up the network of canals so as to be as close to the store as possible, then carried the apples down a bushel at a time and wedged them into the skiff before covering them with canvas. Uncle Leo then set him on one of the barrel seats in the shop and gave him cheese and apples and let him listen to the old men chew the fat while he shook the soreness out of his arms. He considered telling his uncle about what he had seen in the wash house, but thought better of it. Alice would skin him like a deer if she found out that he'd followed her; he didn't even want to think about what she'd do if he told on her.

The skiff sat low in the water on the row back, and to Jackie the trip felt as though it took twice as long. He was used to rowing; he'd known the rock of a boat since before he could walk, but they'd rarely had heavy or large loads to take across, and his shoulders were aching by the time he found the gut that his uncle had described to him. It was a little narrower than a creek, and wound tightly the farther into the island it went, but it was surprisingly deep, and he managed to avoid getting hung up on waterweed or the bottom itself. He was slightly dreading meeting Anderton, having to keep up with the man while unloading the skiff, and the uncomfortable silence that he knew there would be throughout, so he was disproportionately relieved to see Anderton's eldest daughter Hannah waiting for him on the bank instead, plaiting marsh grass into a basket and kicking her bare feet into the dirt. Hannah was younger than him by a few months, and they'd sledged down Lighthouse Hill and stalked rabbits together for years, though he hadn't seen much of her since Alice had left and more of the daily chores had fallen to him. He felt a little shy now; he couldn't put his finger on why, but proud too. She helped him beach the skiff, and they began unloading the bushels of apples, not hurrying because there wasn't anyone watching, their feet sinking slightly in the soft black mud.

"You know what they plan on doing with these?" he asked her loftily, in a tone meant to convey that he knew well enough.

"Course I do," she scoffed in reply. "What kind of fool drags this many apples out to the middle of nowhere to make vinegar?"

Jackie felt embarrassed. Maybe it was only a big secret to him and Mama, and the whole village knew that Leonidas Wallace and the lighthouse keepers were making brandy in the woods.

"They're gonna build a lean-to to keep the rain and things out of it. Pa said I could help if I promised not to get my fool neck broke," she continued.

"Well, Uncle Leo asked me to watch the still when the time comes," Jackie answered. "Bet you don't get to do that."

"Naw." She made a face. "Ma'd miss me if I were gone all night, and anyway, I don't want to be stuck watching some fire for hours and hours with no one to talk to and nothing to do. You can keep it."

"You don't mind not talking and not having anything to do, if your job's important," he answered. He knew by the look she gave him just how much she didn't believe him, a one-quirked-eyebrow look that he knew she'd practiced, but he was glad that she didn't say anything.

As they unloaded the skiff they played that they were soldiers on the front lines in France, carrying wounded comrades out of the trenches to be treated by beautiful nurses who wore red lipstick and spoke in high, breathless voices. Hannah provided the dialogue because she'd seen movies on the mainland and knew what they would say. They each took a handle of a bushel, lifted on three, and carried the load to the edge of the clearing, where they set it down carefully and determined what kind of wound it had suffered, and whether it would survive. The clearing was small, and overhung with deciduous trees, and Jackie half-wished he had found it first so that they could keep it to themselves.

The game made the work go faster, though bodies felt no lighter than apples, until every last basket was arranged square to its neighbor in an edge of the clearing and carefully tucked under the canvas. Hannah dug out an apple for each of them before helping Jackie push the skiff off the muddy bank and climbing in opposite him. As he backpaddled them out of the gut she took a large, juicy bite of hers, and he refused to continue on until she'd held up his apple so he could have a bite as well.

It was late in the afternoon when she helped him tie off at the dock and they washed the marsh mud from their feet, but they took their time walking up the path to the village. Jackie paused at the trail off to his house, unsure. Reacquainting himself with Hannah was proving to be quite enjoyable.

"Want to come up and see the hiding place? Pa's been working on it, here and there," Hannah offered, sensing his reluctance to return home, and he followed her along the path to the lighthouse.

The hill was steep and thick with shrubs, with the shell path the only safe way up on the village side, and then only when the weather was good. It would have made for a deadly sledding hill, but the scrubby grasses and hardy bushes kept the hard-packed earth from washing down with every storm. The lighthouse could be seen from any point on the south end of the island, and cast a cool light down on them all through the night; Jackie had never slept in complete darkness. When the lighthouse was built it had been lit with fish oil, which had been kept in brick-lined vaults beneath it. The switch to kerosene had required that an above-ground fuel hut be built in case of explosions, and the vaults had fallen into disrepair. They'd been warned away from them as children, and so of course developed a fascination with them. The roofs had caved in, and Jackie could still trace most of his more serious lickings back to being caught in, around, or near the vaults, or else having thrown one of the girls' dolls in to make them go down after it.

He expected Hannah to take him to the top of the hill, to one of the vaults that they had played in, but instead she stopped halfway up and struck out laterally across the hill, clinging to the twisted bushes to keep from slipping. Behind a particularly dense patch of brush she stopped and waited for him to catch up, which he did with considerably less dignity than he would have liked. When he was close enough he realized that she was standing on a narrow shelf cut into the bank, and a segment of the hill was draped in dusty burlap and scattered with plants. She knelt down and twitched aside a corner so he could see.

The room was larger than he'd expected, nearly as large as his kitchen, except with a lower ceiling. They had salvaged bricks from one of the vaults and laid a tight, neat, level floor, and he could tell that they were in the middle of building up the walls and digging back deeper into the hill. The ceiling was supported by a thick pine scaffolding, but Jackie doubted it was necessary; the whole room looked as solid as the hill itself. Two bulbous shapes huddled in the corner near the picks and shovels. Wrapped in muslin and tied off with sisal cord, they looked like overly large gourds, but Jackie knew that they had to be the stills, already bought and carefully hidden for when they would be needed.

"They sure done that quick," he observed and slid back out into the sunlight.

"Been working on it for weeks now. Sometimes I come down and look out," Hannah answered, and Jackie decided not to mention that he'd only just found out about the plan. It galled him that she was so in the know.

"Would make a nice little house, wouldn't it?" he said, trying to steer the conversation elsewhere.

"Get awful crowded though, once you started having babies," she said, and sat down with her legs dangling. They could see boats moving across the bay below them, and the dun smudges of the barrier islands and the marsh. It was a comforting sight, so peaceful and so alive at once. He supposed he could forgive his uncle for letting Hannah know before him. She had just found out because she happened to be around. He had been asked to help, to be a partner in it all. Below them he saw his mother, moving slowly through the garden, scattering the chickens, and he realized how low the sun had sunk in the sky. With a wave and an "I'll be seeing you," he turned and started off down the hill.

Smoke drifted from their chimney, and as he stepped toward the house he could see her in silhouette in the doorway, bent over the fire. They would be having the eggs that he'd collected the day before for dinner, he knew, and they would probably still be hungry afterward but neither of them would say anything, and tomorrow he would work the garden or fish, and the same the day after and the day after until winter, when they would be hungry and cold and still not say anything. His mother's face was seamed from the sun and the salt and the worrying, though she wasn't that old. There was no way out for them, and when all the other islanders finally left for Chincoteague, for town life and sociability, they would be left alone, with no company but the lighthouse keepers. The sale of the church had been a simple declaration of defeat for the village: they would not stay, could not stay, any longer. The only thing worse, Jackie thought, than leaving the island was being left behind on it.

He paused in the doorway, watching his mother moving slowly, stiffly, between the sideboard and the table, and behind her was Alice sitting in one of the rush-bottomed chairs against the far wall, hands motionless in her lap, eyes pinked with crying. His mother's mouth was pinched tight, and he scraped his feet on the top step without a word and sat down at the table. The sight of their faces made his stomach go cold; he wanted to ask what had happened and at the same time wanted to linger in that space of not-knowing, where everything was still all right. Then the weight of his secret fell on him.

When they'd been playing in the clearing it had felt so simple, a game on a grander scale, with adults involved. But he knew—he just didn't want to consider it—that if he or any of them were caught with the fermented mash, or tending a still, or in any way in connection with the finished bottles of brandy, they would be going to prison. He didn't want to imagine what his mother would say to that, having the sheriffs show up on the doorstep of their tiny house and take him away.

His mother glanced at him as she set a cup down in front of him, and in that moment he knew that there would be no more games over baskets of apples. She needed him to be an adult now.

"Are you all right, Alice?" he asked quietly, timidly.

"Your sister is just home for a visit," his mother said quickly. "She's all right, just a little tired."

"There's no sense in lying to him, Mother," Alice snapped back. To Jackie, she said, "I'm ashamed of it, but that doesn't make it not true. I was dismissed from Mrs. Thompson's, for engaging in a romantic relationship with one of the guests." Her face had gone red with embarrassment, and her eyes remained fixed on the table, but her voice was steady. "He's promised to marry me, but if his parents will not consent we will have to wait. And I will have to find other work."

"It isn't the end of the world, Alice. Someone is bound to want you as a shop assistant—"

"After they know why I was dismissed?"

"That won't bother everyone," Jackie interjected. "You could work at the oyster factory and they wouldn't care. Maybe Uncle Leo knows someone that would give you a job—he sent you to Mrs. Thompson in the first place."

"Shh, Jackie!" said his mother.

"No, he's right," said Alice. "I can shuck oysters if I can't do anything else. There are just as many women as men working there, I shouldn't think I'm above it."

That grim pronouncement was followed by a few moments' silence as they bent their heads over the dishes and their mother quietly intoned the usual prayer. Jackie had guessed correctly: eggs, and peas from the garden, over thick slabs of dark bread and under a satiny sauce.

"What's his name?" he asked after the first bite.

"Liam Fields." She was trying to keep a straight face, but couldn't help the smug way one corner of her mouth quirked upward.

"Should we know who that is?" her mother asked.

"Sam Fields's son."

Jackie choked on a chunk of bread; his mother only fared better because she took smaller mouthfuls.

"I was ashamed of being caught and dismissed, not ashamed of the romance itself."

"Well, that's good news, I suppose," their mother replied. "A pity the satisfaction won't keep us in food over the winter."

"Ma," Jackie cut in. "I spoke with Uncle Leo yesterday, while you were away. He might have work for me, later in the year." He grasped for a reason, a task that would logically call him away for the right time, at the right time. "The train brings his stock early in the morning or late at night, and he says he's getting too old to unload it at all hours. I didn't want to leave, but if Alice—I shouldn't pass up the opportunity."

His mother cocked an eyebrow at him. "And why didn't he mention this to me?"

"He didn't think you'd want me away for so long, so often. But it doesn't sound like I have a choice now." Jackie hated to lie to her, but he had to remove the worry lines from her face, to ensure that they would have food when winter came. If Father had been there, he would have agreed.

"Well. It seems you're both leaping out of my hands. Not that that is entirely a bad thing. You could be turning to rum running, to smuggling, to worse things entirely."

The guilt that Jackie felt at his mother's words would not be the last in connection to his uncle's plan. It will return in flashes as he minds the fermenting apple pomace, as he leaves the house in the evenings to relieve one of the lighthouse keepers in tending the still, and will nearly overwhelm him in the days after a local smuggler is caught, when his uncle is certain that they will be next. Prohibition will continue until he is nearly twenty-five years old, and in that time, though he will work for fishermen, for oystermen, in the factory and in his uncle's shop, he will continue to throw in his lot with the bootleggers, saving the money while his mother refuses to leave Assateague, finally moving her to a cottage near Uncle Leo's shop when a stroke paralyzes the right side of her body. A few years after the end of Prohibition they will abandon their setup in favor of honest work, leaving any equipment that they cannot sell carefully hidden on the island, in case the government changes its mind. Jackie will be an uncle by then, and his sister, after much labor and a quiet charge of breach of contract, will have changed her name to Fields.

But that is yet to come.

CHAPTER XI

2037

TALISMANS

S ome days it is hard to remember that she isn't the only one left, that no matter how long it has been since she's seen another soul, today could always be the day that someone comes wandering down the road, picking their way around the potholes and rogue stalks of corn, calling out to see if anyone is around. When she lies with her back cool against the slick green cement and looks up through the gaping hole in the rotting roof to watch the clouds roiling above as the pills that she's taken tilt and dip her she pretends that even she doesn't exist, that the world is devoid of life, that she's the ground and the grass and the trees and every growing thing.

She first found the little house when she was in middle school, two rooms upstairs and one room downstairs and a porch on both floors, long abandoned with the marsh encroaching up its front yard. Usually her school friends came exploring with her, but she was the only one that had been willing to trespass on the Lumsden farm. People said they did black magic, but Tamara laughed at that. Her grandpa was a Lumsden; if he could do magic then she was the true king of Scotland. You couldn't see the shack from the big house anyway. She'd used it as a private place to smoke up when she had the good stuff and didn't want to share. It had never had electricity or septic, probably hadn't ever been much more than a farm office, but black magic aside there were weird stories about that corner of the world. People had been murdered there, been buried there; a girl went crazy and knifed her dad. Place had been empty since.

When the epidemic started looking serious she'd dragged Willie out to see the place. The door was solid enough still to be barred against predators of the two- and four-legged variety, and Willie had figured that no one would come looking this far out on the edge of solid land, but just to be safe they'd dragged boards from the nearest abandoned houses to reinforce the walls and cover up the broad window of the lower floor. The hole in the roof let in enough light, pouring down the stairwell and through the moss-rimmed hole in the upper floor. Now that Willie's gone she has the candles he squirreled away to get her through the sleepless nights.

It had happened quickly. They'd all been drinking and dancing and blazing up on the beach like every autumn night she could remember, then two weeks later half the people she knew were in the clinic, and by Thanksgiving most of them were dead. She'd gone to the clinic too, more out of caution since she felt OK, but they thought that it was sexually transmitted and that kind of thing didn't always give you a warning. The test had been uncomfortable, embarrassing, and she almost blushed when the nurse asked her how many partners she'd had in the past five years, not because of the number but because she'd had to ask how they defined "partners" and then tally them up on her fingers. The woman had tightened her mouth in disapproval when Tamara had finally told her to call it a round three hundred. Which sounded like a lot, but if you divided it out it only meant that she got with one or two new people a week, on average. A lot of them were from the Shore, people she'd gone to school with, but when she was bored of the same old she'd drive over to the mainland and meet guys from Internet hookup sites for a one-off. Three hundred was probably a conservative estimate, but she wasn't going to call the prune-mouthed nurse back into the exam room to tell her it was more. She liked sex, it didn't matter so much who with, and unless you could afford to be on something all the time there was fuck all else to do on the Shore.

There had been no traffic on the drive back to the clinic to get her results, but she'd had to yield to two funeral processions. The news articles she'd skimmed when people she knew started getting sick had assumed that the disease would wipe out the less desirable elements of society, the young and promiscuous and those too poor to afford care. By the time the deaths began it was already too late: just as many bored housewives and middle-aged husbands were packed away in urns and pine boxes as irresponsible teenagers and neo-hippies with vague opinions about free love.

Tamara had resigned herself to the diagnosis she knew was coming: they didn't make you come in person to tell you that you're clean, and she'd screwed more people than anyone she knew. So when the nurse took her in the back room and told her that her reproductive organs were not going to rot painfully out of her body, poison her blood, and kill her quickly, she had to ask the woman to repeat herself. She wasn't clean by any stretch of the imagination, but she wasn't among the doomed: she was an asymptomatic carrier, possibly one of the first vectors of the disease, and she was going to be contained and tested in the hopes of developing a cure. The nurse had gone to get the forms, and Tamara had walked out as quickly as she could, head down: there was no way in hell she was being anyone's guinea pig, no matter what kind of disease she had.

At first it had been like all the zombie movies she'd ever watched: fewer and fewer people walking the streets, until Onancock looked like the set of a ghost town for something ridiculously low-budget: *Attack of the Killer Ovaries from Space*. They'd moved to the shack by then; Willie had wanted to go to ground before things got too bad, but they still went out during the day, looked around. This was before Christmas. She'd waited for the day that even the gray-uniformed worker failed to open the post office, then went over to the alley behind Runninger's pharmacy and smashed a back window. No alarm went off, no one came to stop her. There wasn't anyone left to care. She loaded up three of the backpacks from the back-to-school aisle with uppers and downers and weight-loss pills and prenatal vitamins and everything she could imagine wanting, chucking in bottles of things she didn't know the use of, but figured she could find out. Willie had shook his head at her, but helped line the pill bottles up alphabetically, and look them up by shape and color on the Internet—while there still was Internet.

Willie didn't know that his older brother Scott had been Tamara's boyfriend before him. Kind-of boyfriend. Scott was a wild one. Had been a wild one. She'd wanted him since they were in middle school, but she'd never expected him to notice her, anticipated his on-again, off-again attention. When she'd gotten pregnant they'd been off again, and she hadn't had the guts to tell him. For three months she'd nursed the idea of the baby growing inside her, its teeny face and fingers—even if it had been legal anymore to get rid of it, she couldn't bear the idea of ousting such a little person from her womb. It had devastated her when she started bleeding. She'd decided immediately she wanted another, got Scott to go parking with her by promising him head, and was doubly devastated to find the bruise-colored mottling on his skin when she unbuttoned his Levi's. He hadn't lasted much longer than that, and when she had cried at the funeral it had been just as much for the baby she wouldn't have to remember him by as for the loss of him.

Willie hadn't known that, but he probably would have still gone with her if he had. He was the quiet middle brother, the plotter, who didn't care if he got the scraps so long as he wound up with more scraps than everyone else. He liked living in the little shack with her on the edge of the marsh, when everything was going crazy everywhere else. He was the one who stole the backhoe and dug the well; he knew that the freshwater recharge spine, the strip of underground river that lay between Route 13 and the railroad tracks, was the only groundwater that wouldn't poison them with salt seep, and he knew how to find it. He was the one who had jerry-rigged the stolen generator, gotten them Internet when no one else had it, Internet that they'd used together to look up the pills she'd stolen, even as he was shaking his head over her lack of method. Sure, morphine and MDMA were fun, but when they weren't feeling well they'd be wanting the boxes and boxes of ibuprofen and decongestant she'd left behind.

He'd gone back to Runninger's after dark, plundered the painkillers, fever-reducers, first-aid kits and spray bandages, and the entire case of condoms. Ribbed, nubbed, extra-thin, lambskin, he'd nabbed them all before someone else got them.

They always made love in the light, and it hadn't escaped Tamara how he watched her, deciding whether he was seeing her natural skin color or something trending more sinister before he progressed. Willie didn't expect fidelity any more than he expected honesty from her, but she hadn't been running around on him. There wasn't anyone left to run around with.

She thought what the nurse had said about her being an asymptomatic carrier was bullshit. You either had a sickness, or you didn't. The way meat was either rotten or it wasn't. She was perfectly fine, and it annoyed her how careful Willie was with the condoms, with the checking, with her. He looked a lot like Scott, in the face and coloring, even if he was narrower in the shoulders, more rangy. He'd give her a pretty baby.

This time she did it smart. She broke into one of the upscale houses, came back with six bottles of wine. After he'd half-finished the first, she handed him one of the special condoms to use, one that felt warm or tingled or something like that. The extra-fine needle she'd stolen from the upscale house too, and he hadn't even noticed the tiny holes as he ripped the foil packet open.

The morning sickness started the same day Willie noticed the purpling on his cock. He was convinced she'd given it to him, and she'd screamed that he'd been bringing his whores to her house while she was out. He'd punched, and she'd bit, and in the end he'd run out of the house, leaving her clutching her middle, where he'd kicked her. The bleeding had started almost immediately, and two weeks later she'd found him lying on his back in one of the fallow potato fields, staring at the sky with empty eye sockets, stomach ripped open and guts trailing away where the feral dogs had taken chunks out of him. She'd cried then, mostly from frustration and disgust—she was still angry that he'd killed her baby. The flies and the smell were too awful, and she left him for the sun and the dogs to take care of. It was better than burying him anyway.

So here she is, alone and babyless, walled into the cottage while the world outside goes crazy. Maybe there is something to being a carrier. But if she has a baby, then it will be a carrier too, like she has blue eyes because her mother has blue eyes. But every time she thinks "baby" she sees Scott, the pictures of him when he was still tiny that his mother had shown her one afternoon when she'd knocked on the door of his parents' trailer and only the older woman had been home. She wants his baby, but Willie's would have been close enough. And that asshole Willie had kept her from even having that.

There is a third brother, but if she remembers right he's barely thirteen. Yeah, boys are all horny at that age, but the idea makes her sick, even though her dad had been ten years older than her mom.

She lets the cold of the cement soak into her back as she lies still, head lolling from side to side to make the sound of the birds outside strobe in and out, like the Dopplering of passing ambulance sirens that she remembers from when she was a kid. It isn't a bad place to live, even with the hole rotted through the roof that lets the rain drip in, turning the edges of the hole in the floor above a soft, mossy green and crumbling the gypsum-board ceiling.

It had been pretty easy to steal anything she wanted that first winter, after so many had died but so few of the living had figured out how to respond. Houses were empty, stores were empty, people left each other alone. She'd stocked up on canned food and bottled water and beef jerky, hoarding it the way she'd hid cans of SpaghettiOs under her bed every time she found spare change when she was a kid, planning ahead for the days her mom stayed on the couch with the lights off instead of going to work and she and her little brother had to feed themselves. She felt bad for her mom now, just a little. It hadn't been hard to leave. Her mom and her brother had been sitting on the couch, dazed and vacant with television; Tamara had said that she was running out to pick up a pack of cigarettes and had taken her clothes with her, headed to the shack and never returned home. Part of her wants to go back to their trailer outside Belle Haven, but she doesn't want to find the woman dead in the living room almost as much as she doesn't want to find her alive, whining and pathetic, prematurely wrinkled and yellowed by nicotine.

When she first started plundering the abandoned buildings she'd been careful, sidling into places expecting to be stopped, but as more and more people died and the survivors fled to the mainland by the busload she'd grown more confident, until she was smashing the lower windows of the nicer houses in the middle of the day and taking a turn around to see if anything caught her eye. But no matter how brash she'd gotten, it had taken Dutch courage to break into the Lumsden farmhouse.

She didn't believe the bullshit about magic, but the house unnerved her. Grandpa Pierce had grown up there, and one of his favorite things to bitch about, drunk or sober, was how it should have been his. He was the eldest, he should have inherited the farm, he would have been smart and turned it into a shopping center so people would have something to do of a Friday night. When he was really in a mood he added an X-rated multiplex and topless bar to the fantasy, a casino to put Accomack Island on the map, and even she had been able to see how ridiculous that was. But his whore of a sister had gotten everything, and contesting the will had burned through what money he had inherited. He'd decided that if he couldn't have it, no one would, but when he'd gone to torch the farmhouse he'd used vodka as an accelerant. There had been prison for that, followed by a restraining order, and while she couldn't blame her great-aunt for that she couldn't shake the image her grandfather had put in her head, of a violent, grasping, witchlike old crone, bitter because she'd never gotten a man, holed away distilling poisons and collecting rent from her tenants.

There had been rumors, when the disease was first spreading, that her Great-Aunt Sally had taken a shotgun and her grown-up children and a chest full of medicine and lost herself in the woods and marshes of Assateague Island, but she knew that she couldn't trust rumor. Rumor also had it that the slasher girl, the one who had lived in Tamara's own shack, was still alive, had come back, in fact, with some man from the mainland she put under her power, had sucked the blood from a dozen throats and dug up the daddy that she'd killed to desecrate his body—that part Tamara really didn't believe—and seduced a dozen men before also losing herself on Assateague and the barrier islands, where the Indians and the healers and the weather mages had once hidden themselves.

Tamara wasn't going to trust rumors; she was going to trust common sense, and her own eyes.

She perched on the shack roof to watch the farmhouse: two weeks, nearly three rolled by and she saw no movement, no lights, no one coming or going. The windows weren't boarded, the blinds hadn't even been pulled, so she'd taken a machete and a fifth of Captain Morgan, and hiked across the cornfield. Even with a pull of the rum, she hadn't wanted to go up the front steps. Around the back was a greenhouse, and she'd shattered a pane with her machete to get in, freezing after the patter of glass to listen for any movement inside the building.

There were benches set up along the walls with pots and sprouting trays, with larger plants and bushes growing out of beds in the ground. Cement paths were laid out between them, and she walked carefully down to the sitting area in the middle. Most of the potted plants were dead, the planted ones dying, but they had been trimmed back before they were left. The cluster of wicker chairs and loungers in the center of the greenhouse had been squared off with each other, the magazines on the little table aligned with the corners. She'd looked through the magazines, but there weren't any worth taking back with her; they were all about medicine and genetics.

The back door was unlocked, and she took another drink before she went in. She didn't like being startled; running into a dead body would be just as bad as running into a live one, and it didn't seem like the last person in the house had left in a hurry.

The first door on the left led to a little bathroom, and she used the toilet before moving on. That was one thing that sucked about the shack: no real toilet. There had been an out-house at the end of the yard, but she didn't like to risk leaving the building at night. Willie had never found a good solution for that, so she used an old cooking pot and threw her waste off the upper porch into the bushes.

The door opposite led into what had been a large farm kitchen, stone floored. The metal countertops remained, but had been taken over by a proliferation of beakers and Bunsen burners, lab equipment in organized ranks, now coated in dust.

She passed through the rest of the rooms on the lower floor: no bodies, or people jumping out at her, everything coated in dust but put neatly away, as if crazy Great-Aunt Sally had an-ticipated her death and prepared for it by tidying, or else left the house months before. Tamara went through the drawers and shelves, but didn't find anything that she really wanted; while in the other houses she snatched anything that took her fancy, here she found herself touching books, money, ornaments, but leaving them where they stood.

Upstairs she expected to find a body, perhaps laid out on the bed with its arms crossed on its chest, or slumped over a desk with blood spatter on the wall and a handgun hanging from the limp fingers, but she found nothing. The bed in the master bed-room was neatly made, the bedrooms of a son and a daughter showing the half-grown state of children just gone to college, expected back any day, everything in its place as though it was a show house and potential buyers were about to come through. The drawers in the bedrooms she let alone. A lot of the furni-ture was under dustsheets, but instead of pulling them off the way she would have in any other house, she passed those rooms by. She couldn't say why; maybe she did half-believe the stories people told about the house.

When she'd gone through the whole house once and found no bodies, no notes of any kind, no sign that the inhabitants had died but rather that they had packed carefully, left intentionally, she went through the house again, stuffing canned food from the pantry and the alcohol burners from the kitchen into a pillowcase. It was hers now; the rumors were probably right and even if they weren't, the old bat wasn't coming back.

There were bookshelves all over the house, crammed with kids' books and teen books and fat sci-fi and fantasy novels and romance novels and every single damned classical book she'd not read in high school, and all of those she left alone, but when she saw the high-up shelf behind the desk in the living room, she knew that she'd struck gold. At the best of times Tamara wasn't a reader, she didn't even really enjoy movies unless she had someone to make out with during the talking parts, but the part of her that jumped at the sight of a sexy body jumped at the sight of that shelf. There was *New Gray's Anatomy*, *Fertility and Conception*, *Physicians' Desk Reference*, *Home Remedies for Young Mothers*, books that weren't meant to be read for entertainment but in order to make things happen. She pawed through, picked out the volumes on fertility and genetics, *What to Expect When You're Expecting*, guides to women's health printed on thick stapled paper and neat gilt-edged pages alike. She left behind the pillowcase of food, choosing to carry the books back first: they were her inheritance, would help her get the baby that she wanted.

⌒

Now the plundering is over. The last time she went out she was chased by a gang of survivors, shot at, nearly killed, and she has hunkered down in the shack to wait until all the idiots kill each other off. She has food, she has medicine, she has anything she could need.

One of the pluses of having the marsh right up on her doorstep was how easy it had made bringing things around by boat. If she could get it into the boat, she could usually get it out of the boat, and she'd smuggled loads of pressure-treated wood, nails and hardware, food and clothing and pretty, useless junk from the expensive waterfront houses and rowed them practically to her front door with barely a sweat broken. Willie had taken over from there, when he'd still been alive. It's a good thing she doesn't mind bats, cats, and the occasional really stupid bird, as they are the only animals that can still get in, but sometimes she sits and watches through the cracks in the boards as deer graze by the foundation of the shack.

Even the pretty, useless junk has its purpose now. She is waiting for something, she doesn't know what. An army of scientists, with needles to shoot everyone up with a cure or something to prevent the disease, so they can all come out of hiding and go back to living life. Or an army of do-gooders, come to get the survivors off the island and to someplace that still functions, that still has cities with corner stores that you can go to anytime to buy a pack of cigarettes and a chocolate bar, not because you need it but because you feel like it. Or maybe just an army, to gun down the bands of survivors who have gone feral and violent. But they won't shoot her, she's unarmed, she's not like the gun-waving crazies who chased her. They will take her to the mainland, to hot showers and fresh food. When she starts wondering if the only thing she is waiting for is her own death, that's when all the stuff comes in handy.

Willie made her keep it neat, stacked the chests he'd made for her against the north wall of the shack, two deep, so that she had the whole of the slick, green floor to spread out across. Now that she's bored of watching the oak leaves flicker above the hole in the roof she gets up and begins rifling about in the chests. Willie is gone, but she still keeps things neat, not so much in memory of him but more because the floor gets damp sometimes.

There are silk dresses in some of the chests, and even though she prefers jeans Tamara slides them on, one at a time, twirling in front of the cracked full-length mirror taken from an abandoned clothing store, like she is five and dressing up as a princess again. She could go outside, but the chances of getting bitten by a copperhead or a cottonmouth are pretty high, or stepping on something or getting cut on a piece of rusting farm equipment half-buried where the field hand left it, and since she isn't sure which type of antivenin goes with which snake, or what exactly to do for tetanus, she stays inside unless she's going scrounging, refilling her water barrels or adding to the stack of canned and dried food against the wall opposite her collection of trunks.

Her bones have surfaced beneath her skin, and a lot of the dresses are far too big. She smooths her hands over her belly muscles and wonders if this could help her get the baby she wants: she looks like she belongs on the cover of one of the supermarket magazines from before, at least with clothes on—it makes her sick to look at herself naked, it reminds her too much of a girl she knew in high school that died of anorexia. Probably she should eat more, but it's hard to get excited over the same food day in and day out, and a lot of times she doesn't eat just because the taste is boring.

But back to the baby—men like skinny, don't they? Maybe it depended on the man, but who would care if she is hip-bones-like-elbows skinny when there is no one else around? One of the things that Willie told her, in the long afternoons spread out on their triple-high stack of mattresses, was that his daddy had had a plan for years, for what to do if everything went tits-up. That's how he'd known where to dig the well, because his daddy had figured it out, had started stocking up on ammo and batteries when his girlfriend got pregnant with Scott. Willie had laughed at his dad, even as he lay there with his head on her arm in their own little bunker, surrounded by their canned food and drums of well water, but now it makes Tamara wonder if his daddy—Mr. Todd to her—isn't still out there, hunkered down in a camouflage hole in the ground with a generator and chocolate bars and all the things she and Willie hadn't quite gotten around to finishing before he left her.

Willie's dad was a big man, she remembers, and she's always had a thing for big men. Tall men with broad, deep chests, and perhaps more fuzz on those chests than strictly necessary, and hands like spades. Sure, when she was younger she'd go with any boy, even if they did look more like girls and do nothing but whine because no one understood them, and girls too because most girls were damn cute and really grateful if you actually knew what you were doing, but really if she had her druthers, she'd always preferred her fellows on the manly side.

And more importantly, Scott had been a carbon copy of his daddy.

As she slips the cold silk over her head she thinks about this.

It has to get awful lonely, sitting in a hole in the ground, even if you have a generator and lights and everything. Real lonely, seeing as how Scott's mama and her on-the-side boyfriend had been among the first to go. Among his other familial revelations, Willie had mentioned that his daddy and mama hadn't touched each other since before his baby brother was born, so Tamara had no worry that Mr. Todd had gotten the disease from his wife and died. There was still someone out there who could give her Scott's baby, or close enough to Scott's baby that it didn't matter.

Her thoughts speed up as she shuffles through the chests. Just being alive is more or less proof that she doesn't have the disease, but even so a man that plans that far ahead would want to be careful. She can get around that, though. Seduction isn't hard. It's the getting-pregnant part that she's more concerned about.

The impulsive part of her wants to pop open a bottle of fertility pills, down it, and head out, but the part that really wants the baby makes her sort through the chests, find the one crammed with books on women's health and the female body, that she'd taken from her great-aunt's house. She sits cross-legged on the double bed that she once shared with Willie. She begins to slowly read, stumbling a bit over the Latin names for common weeds, but mostly comprehending.

It takes Tamara days to wade through the books, mostly because she finds herself rereading things that don't make sense. Women's health was once about preventing pregnancy as much as encouraging it, and she can't believe that it had all more or less been common knowledge, that women shared cures around and tended to their own insides, and only went to a doctor when something was really wrong. But then, many of the books had been published when abortions were still legal, before the country had gotten right with God again. Perhaps they had only escaped pulping because no one had read them, because her crazy Great-Aunt Sally had kept them in her crazy old house, waiting for Tamara to find them.

As she reads the books, Tamara begins marshaling pills, lining the bottles up in neat rows across the floor. Antibiotics, just in case she has something that will hurt the baby. Vitamin C, but not too much because it can cause a miscarriage. Pills to stimulate ovulation, and extra-strong vitamins, and a whole bunch of things that she doesn't really understand but figures are good because she remembers them being given to pregnant women when she and Willie looked them up online. Halfway through her reading she goes out again, breaks into a CVS out along the highway that has already been raided, and takes the morning-sickness pills and iron pills, and a couple of other kinds of pills she figures might be useful, and adds them to her ranks of amber bottles across the floor. She starts with Clomid, because she wants it to take the first time, but then she starts worrying, since she's not gotten pregnant by accident nearly as much as most girls seemed to, that it will be especially hard. So she adds Heparin, then doubles the amount she's taking, just in case. Also just in case, even though she knows it's silly, she hangs the charm around her neck, the one her grandmother had made her mother wear when she'd wanted a son after three miscarriages. It was carved out of a tooth that her grandmother had found on top of a mountain, years before, and even though Tamara doesn't believe in that sort of thing, her mom had had a baby boy, and it never hurt to try. As the days pass she feels more and more confident that she is doing the right thing, even though the pills make her nauseous. She has to have a baby. She deserves to have a baby.

When the day comes, Tamara knows it. She dresses slowly, playing with clothes and makeup until she feels, not like herself, but like a woman again, at least. A handle of whiskey goes into her favorite backpack, along with condoms that she's carefully pricked full of holes, and a bottle of water. It's strange, a woman showing up at his doorstep offering whiskey and demanding sex, but she hopes that Mr. Todd won't find it so strange that he turns her away.

Willie had told her where to find the hidden entrance to his dad's bunker, and to get to it she hikes across the sunburned potato fields, now gone to overgrown grass, past the creek and toward the highway. It's nice being out in the daylight, even if it is weak spring daylight and the slanting sun is in her face. It's been weeks since she left the shack in daylight. Something feral in her likes the dark corners, the hidden places, doesn't take risks and doesn't go out in full sun. And besides, she doesn't need any more than what she already has in the shack, except for a baby.

As she draws near the place, Tamara begins to wonder if Mr. Todd is dead. His trailer still stands underneath the pecan trees like she remembers, but it leans in on itself in the drunken way that shows no one lives there, much less the kind of handy man that would still be alive in such circumstances. She wanders around in circles for a bit, calling out softly, looking for some indication that he is still around. Maybe he's dead, of the rot or something else, and she'll never have Scott's baby.

Then a potato sack comes down over her face.

The bunker is underground, just the way Willie said it would be. She expected a hole covered with a tarp, a dirty sleeping bag, dampness and spiders, but when Mr. Todd takes the bag off her face she sees that she is only correct about the dampness.

It's larger than she'd expected, perhaps sixteen feet cubed, with concrete floor, walls, and ceiling. He brags that he'd had it made special by a company that did septic tanks and burial vaults. There is a second one too, just full of canned fish and long-life milk and boxes of water-purification tablets, even though he has his own well, off in one corner of the floor, that taps directly into the freshwater recharge spine. But she had guessed right in one regard: the single biggest thing that he hadn't thought to stockpile was booze.

He insists on making her dinner before uncapping the bottle, and she sits on the edge of his bed while he fries canned meat over a camp stove. It's neat and comfortable, with the bed up against one wall and a cooking area against the other, surveillance equipment and a radio dominating the space. There isn't much in the way of entertainment, though, or any signs of company, but as he adds vegetables to the frying pan he regales her with stories of sneaking through the abandoned villages in broad daylight, finding what he needs while hiding from the bands of survivors. They've fortified the villages, made war on each other in a perfunctory but brutal way for food and medicine, and women that aren't tainted with disease; the largest group was isolated on Chincoteague and Assateague Islands, since a storm destroyed the causeway. He's traded a bit with some of them, shot those who tried to steal from him; he's surprised that she's still making it on her own.

The food is good. The whiskey is better. As it slides down Mr. Todd gets more and more friendly, inviting her to cuddle up next to him on the bed, running his hand over her back and shoulders, his laugh getting louder and more boisterous. He does look just like Scott, Tamara thinks, and it's Scott's face that she has in her mind's eye when she leans in and kisses him.

It takes three weeks for the purple rash to begin showing in Mr. Todd's groin, but that is more than long enough for Tamara. They barely leave the bed in that time, sliding out from under the sheet only for necessities. If it's been a while for Tamara, it's been even longer for Mr. Todd, and she doubts that even if he noticed the purpling he would let her leave. She slips out, sans backpack, while he's passed out asleep after a particularly vigorous session.

She has no doubt that she's pregnant. She can feel it in her middle, a pressure, or maybe just a hope, slowly building. Her baby is growing inside her. Scott's baby. Their baby.

Summer comes and goes, and Tamara barricades herself inside her house. Being alone doesn't bother her anymore, because she isn't alone. She moves sluggishly around the shack, following the sunshine, lazing, as her belly slowly grows firm, then starts to expand. As summer moves into fall, and then to winter, she piles on clothing and spreads a clear plastic tarp across the hole in the roof. There is a little frost inside in the mornings, but it doesn't get bitterly cold. She is safe and warm enough.

The pregnancy book from her great-aunt's library says she'll be hungry, but she finds that even with a reason to eat she simply can't stomach one more can of creamed corn. She takes pills instead; the prenatal vitamins and the anti-nausea pills and anything that seems like it will help her feel better or the baby grow faster. Some of them space her out, leave her watching the patterns on the walls as the light changes, and even though she uses them sparingly they are her favorite ones.

She doesn't know what happened to Mr. Todd after she left. Maybe she'd been mistaken about the purpling, about hav-ing given him the disease. Maybe he was just bruised from all they'd gotten up to, and she could have stayed. He could have taken care of her. They could have had the baby together. But then it would have been Mr. Todd's baby, not Scott's baby. Mr. Todd had only been the sperm donor, she reasons. This baby is Scott's. It will look just like him. She knows it.

She also knows that there is nothing, besides this, to wait for. Mr. Todd had told her there was no army of humanitarians coming with a cure to rescue them. Most of the country is dead, not just the Shore; the straggling handfuls of people left quaran-tined by ocean on either side, Canada and Mexico to the north and south. Everyone is suspected as a vector, and anyone who tries to get out is shot, women especially because it is harder to tell if they have the disease at a glance. He'd said it was only a matter of time before the plague spread, nowhere was immune, and nowhere was far enough away. It was like Noah's flood, like smallpox, like bubonic plague, and maybe humanity would rise up again after it, but not in her lifetime.

As her belly swells Tamara begins to wonder just how her little boy will get out of her. Or little girl, she reminds herself, but her first thought is always boy. She wants a boy. She knows how it works when there aren't doctors around to put you under in a clean hospital bed and take the baby out the way it was meant to be done, like picking a fruit, but she hadn't thought when she'd gotten pregnant that she'd actually be pushing the baby out on her own. She hadn't assumed that some doctor would show up with a scalpel and anesthesia and get it out for her, of course, she just hadn't thought much about it. She counts the weeks anxiously, reads the pregnancy book, and wonders what to do.

When it happens, it's completely unexpected. At first she thinks it's a stomachache, dull and cramping, but the feeling is too regular, too persistent. It doubles her up on the cool cement floor, moaning quietly because that seems to make it feel better, swallowing painkillers with long-life milk. Then she feels wetness between her thighs, and realizes what is happening. And panics.

It's too soon, nearly a month too soon. The aching and tearing feeling that lightning-bolts through her and makes her want to throw up with pain, can't be the beginnings of childbirth. It's a nice thing, a natural thing, it can't feel like this. She counts the weeks again, tallied in permanent marker on the white plaster wall, and swallows handfuls of pills to deal with the pain. She paces the floor, doubling up with the contractions, trying and failing to think of a solution, a fix, a way out.

Gradually the pain fades, or not so much fades as becomes

too much to think about, and she begins to focus on the patterns on the walls, the tiny ridges the brush has left in the paint. Her body isn't hers anymore, but something she is only vaguely attached to, like her clothes or her third-grade report card.

She doesn't know how long she stays in that state, floating just outside her body, quiet and preoccupied while it moans and rocks and does God-knows-what on the cement floor. She comes back to it with a snap, a heaviness, and the urge to push back against it. Senses dulled, she does. At the last moment she realizes that the baby is coming out, finds its head with her hands, then its shoulders as it slides free. Everything is blood, and pain, but she lays it on the mound of clean towels she keeps just for this eventuality.

It had gotten dark at some point; her baby is just a shape on the towels. It's supposed to start crying now, isn't it? She knows that much. She holds her own breath until she hears its echo, then a tiny, kittenish mewl. Close enough.

Exhausted, she fumbles for the pack of matches by her bed, for the emergency candles, and kills three matches before she manages to get a taper lit. She is still connected to the baby, it looks like—the book mentioned "umbilical cord," but it hadn't registered with her that she'd have to find a way to cut it, that there is still a placenta to come and be dealt with and hopefully disposed of where it won't attract the larger predators. That can be taken care of in a minute. She raises the candle high, and looks at her child for the first time.

He—and it is a he—is red with her blood, but when she wipes it away his skin is tight and shiny, like wax. That's all right, she guesses, maybe it's because he's early. But his eyes . . . They look like skinned plums, bright red and oozing and painful, not eyes at all. As he kicks and mewls louder, she notices that he has a third leg, bent up and wasted between the healthy two, and two sets of genitalia, one in the crotch of each pair of legs.

She's beyond horror, beyond pain. A few hours earlier she might have screamed, or cried, or done something. Now she just sits there, if only for a moment, looking at what she has borne. His mouth opens wider, the mewl turns nearly to a wail, and her breasts begin to ache. Carefully, she picks him up, pulls him to her body, and lets him eat.

CHAPTER XII

2010

———

MISSING PIECES

I t isn't until I get to Matthew's—or rather, flash by it and catch the sign in the rearview mirror—that I realize that I'm There. You'd think a place would get more crowded in fifteen years, people and stores and all the crap they call civilization popping up like a rash. Instead the Shore's emptied out a lot. The whole drive north from the bridge I've passed houses with boarded windows, post offices that have closed for good, churches with roofs that are caving in and lightning-struck steeples that no one's bothered to fix. Granted, when I was last here there were too many post offices, too many churches, for the number of people that live the year through on the Shore. But there's something about buildings with their windows painted over, parking lots cracked with weeds and the entrance chained off, that makes you believe a place might be dying.

Everything looks familiar now, and at the same time not familiar, and I pull onto the shoulder and lean my forehead on the wheel of the car, because I'm crying tears that I can't feel, that aren't coming from me, just coming from my body. I feel guilty when I do that, because Seth gets worried when I cry, and buzzes around to try and make it better and I want to scream at him that there's nothing to make better, that I don't feel whatever it is that people feel when they cry but it just happens like a runny nose when you have a cold, so I sit still and let him do what he wants to because there's no point in both of us crying.

Seth was excited when I told him that I felt like I was ready to go back. Dr. McKenna was too, in a more professional way; told me I needed closure in a lot of areas and this trip might help me move on. They had wanted me to do a lot of preparation beforehand, phone people and gather information that way, but I hadn't wanted to wait. On Wednesday I'd decided to go back, on Thursday I'd packed, and on Friday I'd taken off on the eighteen-hour drive from Cairo, Georgia, to the island. Seth was the practical one; he'd Googled the few names and addresses I remembered and read up on the Shore while I was stuffing my overnight bag, finding out things about it that I'd never known to think about. It's been dying slowly, he told me, and that was a surprise. The big boom was in the thirties, when the resort was up and running. I didn't know that we'd had a resort. Now parents come with their kids to the beach, or rich people retire to Onancock so they can keep their yachts tied up behind their million-dollar homes, but the old families are dying out, their kids leaving it behind as soon as they're old enough to go. No one that has a choice wants to work in the chicken plants.

I breathe deep, then start the car again and turn around. I hate driving, and I suck at it, but it's the only way to get here and I didn't want Seth to come. I wanted to do this by myself.

It's weird, going down that gravel road in a car. The first-thing-in-the-morning light streams through the trees, the dust rises up in a cloud around me, and I can hear dogs barking but for once I'm safe from them. Then the long smooth curve around the cornfield and I can see the farmhouse with the columns, but the white shell road through the cornfield is overgrown. Not that I want to go down there anyway.

No dog barks when I pull onto the grass in front of the farmhouse, and I would wonder if anyone still lives here if it weren't for the scatter of kids' toys on the front lawn. My first knock goes unanswered, but at the second the door inches open wide enough to show a thin, sun-cooked face that's mostly sharp nose, with a bony body hidden behind it in the shadow of the house.

"I'm not buying any," she snaps at me.

"Good thing I'm not selling any, then."

"I like my church and I don't keep cans around." She begins to shut the door, but I stick my boot in the space.

"Sorry to bother you, ma'am. I'm looking for somebody that used to live around here."

She doesn't open the door, but she doesn't try to close it farther.

"Mr. Thomas Lumsden used to own this farm? I need to talk to someone that has access to his tenancy records." My birth certificate and driver's license are in a plastic sleeve in my pocket, and I pull it out and slide it through the gap in the door. She takes it rather than letting it fall. I didn't expect anyone to recognize me, and I'm glad that she doesn't.

The door opens a bit more as she reads, but I'm massively relieved. She only acts old, I realize now that I can see her. Her hair is smooth and straight and streaked heavily with white, but that's premature, she can't be quite forty. Her face hasn't softened much, though. She looks like the absolute last person

I'd expect to be a mom; I hope for the kids' sakes that the toys on the lawn are from babysitting, and don't belong to her own children.

"I do have his tenancy records, as it happens. I'm his grand-daughter, Sally Lumsden. What were you looking for, exactly?"

All the words that I'd been over in my head the whole drive up from Georgia are gone.

"I . . . My parents used to rent the little house out on the edge of the marsh, and I was hoping that—I'm looking for someone they used to work with."

The woman's face blooms with recognition.

"The little house? Then you're—I remember when your parents moved in." She opens the door and steps back, but I'm waiting for her to remember the rest of it. "Come in."

I follow her down a hallway, through a kitchen and living room and out the back door into what I think is a garden—less cluttered with kids' toys than the front yard, but they're peeking between the leaves—until I see the ceiling: she's built a massive greenhouse onto the back of the farmhouse, crammed it with plants. She pushes me into a wicker chair near the middle of the room and disappears back inside, saying something about tea. I hadn't expected this kind of reception.

When it happened I'd been a minor, so the newspaper hadn't been allowed to publish my name, and then Social Services decided that it was self-defense and made sure I stayed right out of the brouhaha. They hadn't let us see the papers then, and even though I'd been curious in a weird, sick, self-torturing way, even after I was old enough to make my own choices I hadn't been able to make myself look. I'd figured that a Lumsden, at least, would have known a little better, wouldn't have even let me in until she'd made sure that I wasn't there to murder her. It's strange that people can look at me and not know right away what happened.

She comes back with two glasses of iced tea with mint sprigs in, and I sip mine to be polite; my stomach is still nervous. The other wicker chairs are covered in mounds of books and magazines—mostly plant- and drug-related, though one of the top magazines has a picture of a DNA strand on the cover, with a headline about chromosome substitution—but she shoves them off onto the cement floor and settles in.

"Now, you're going to have to pardon me if I put my foot in it, but I'm going to at some point." She takes a sip of tea. "You're the . . . younger one?"

"Older one."

"I used to see you walking down the road to Matthew's. Was so upset that my mother wouldn't let me go and visit you when you were born—baby cuddling was my favorite sport. How's your little sister?"

"I don't rightly know. I don't know where she is. We got split up in foster care."

"Now that's awful. They really should make more of an effort to keep families together."

"You've got children yourself?"

"Twins, boy and a girl, six years old next month." She says it in a cadence that sounds like she says it all the time, and I hope she keeps talking about them instead of asking about my family. "They're visiting their daddy on the mainland for two weeks. I can't imagine anyone splitting the two of them up."

Next subject.

"Was the greenhouse always here?"

"No, I added that when I inherited the house."

"I wasn't half-surprised to find you still here, thought you'd have sold it off for condos years ago."

She shakes her head with a big grin. "Conditions of the will. Whoever got the farm had to keep the family name and stay put, no selling out to developers and shipping off to the city. My older brother is still pissed as hell that they wouldn't let him cut it up. Built the greenhouse as a birthday present to myself."

"Do you take them to flower shows?" I don't know how to talk to someone about her gardening; it's the first thing that comes to me.

"I'm not really that type of gardener." She reaches out and snaps a leaf off a bush nearby. "What they can be used for is more interesting to me. Do you recognize this?"

The smell is familiar and the shape is familiar, but I don't know it.

"Catnip. Besides getting cats stoned you can use it for colds, fevers, stomachaches, migraines, to stop bleeding, or to start uterine contractions. Every plant in this building grows wild on the Shore, and every one has a medical use."

"If you can just go for a walk and pick them, why do you have them all gathered up here?"

"I'm writing a guide to emergency field medicine for rural hikers, for when there isn't anything available but the native plants. Don't want to put anything in that I can't test and make work myself."

"So you'd be the person to come to when the apocalypse hits and all the drugs run out."

"You could say that . . ."

I was joking, but she's looking into space thoughtfully, and I feel like I'm missing something important. I don't want to keep talking, but I don't want to come right out with what I'm there for; I gulp tea and wait for her to say something.

"Now, what were you hoping to find in the tenancy records?"

"I'm trying to find family, or people that knew them. My parents. They worked together before they got married, so I thought that if the lease mentions who their employer was back then, I can go find him and maybe get someone to tell me . . . anything, really."

She nods at me, then gets up and goes back into the house, taking my empty glass with her. I'm not sure if I'm supposed to follow her or stay put, but she doesn't tell me to come with her so I stay in the greenhouse, looking at the plants.

We had decided that leaving it vague was the way to go, that anything I dug up about anyone I was related to would be welcome. My grandmother cut ties with her family before my mother was born, so the full extent of our relations that I'd known growing up were my mom's sister, Aunt Olivia. She'd been the fun kind of aunt, who lived in a little prefab in Belle Haven with a succession of roommates I'd only recently realized were probably her girlfriends, but she'd died of bone cancer when I was a kid.

When Sally Lumsden comes back she's carrying a dark brown hanging file folder, not as thick as I'd hoped it would be, but still pretty thick. My hands are itching for it, but she sits down and opens it up on her knees.

"Can you just remind me real quick when you were born, Chloe?"

"February 1982."

"This is it, then." She pulls a Manila folder out of the big brown file, with the dates 1981–1995 penciled on the tab. I had been hoping that the whole file was on us, but this is better than nothing.

Their pictures are stapled to the first page of the rental application. I freeze when I see them. They didn't let me take anything with me, when they took us out of the house. I haven't seen Mama's face in so long.

"Let me get you some more tea," Sally says, and I mumble a thank-you as she gets up and leaves. We both know that I don't need tea, that she's leaving me alone on purpose. I don't look at his picture.

Their full names are written out under their signatures: Eloise Fitzgerald and Boris Gordy. I flip through the pages slowly, skimming because I'm not sure what I'm looking for, stop for a moment when I see the place where monthly rent has been written in: twenty dollars. Mr. Lumsden rented the little house to a down-and-out couple with a baby on the way for twenty dollars a month, just enough to keep them from feeling like they were taking charity, not so much that they couldn't still afford to eat. I don't know what to say.

I find it eventually, a page that lists my father's places of employ. There's a bunch of them: Perdue and Tyson and the battery farm up the road, but the very first one, from 1978 to 1983, is "Lovett Renovation, LLC." There is a signature along with Bo's, verifying that he was employed and drew a paycheck: Charles Morgan, with his address given as Temperanceville. I pull out that page and, as the sound of footsteps gets closer, begin copying down the information onto the pocket notepad I brought with me.

"Found what you were looking for?"

"Thank you, ma'am, I did," I say all chirpy, and hand the folder back to her. She tucks it into the file while giving me a studying look.

"Congratulations," she says.

"I'm sorry?"

"On the engagement."

"Oh!" I had forgotten about the ring, wondered now if I should have left it behind. "Thank you."

"Is that why you're looking now?"

I want to tell her to fuck off and mind her own business, but I'm too flustered. I hadn't thought that anyone would care why I'd decided to come back.

"It's just the right time, is all. Thank you for the help."

"Well, I'd be very curious to know if you succeed. Drop by before you leave, I'll give you some food for the road."

I make polite sounds until her front door closes with her on the inside and me on the outside. It feels like she's watching me from behind the curtains, so I don't put my hand in my pocket until I get back in the car, and even then I don't look down. The photograph is stiff, the corners sharp, and feeling it there makes a warm spot in my belly. I have my mama's face again.

I told Sally Lumsden that Renee and I got split up in foster care. That's basically what happened.

The police wanted to think that it was one of his meth buddies that cut his throat, or that he'd gone crazy on the drug and cut his own throat, but I kept confessing and confessing until they finally had to admit that maybe I'd done it, and even then they didn't put me in handcuffs like I thought they should; instead they wrapped me in another blanket and had a doctor dope me.

I went to family and juvenile court but I didn't get a jury; I remember being a bit annoyed that it wasn't a real trial, that if they were going to put me through that I wasn't going to get all the bells and whistles like they showed on the TV we got to watch in the detention center. They decided that it was self-defense, manslaughter instead of murder even though manslaughter sounds nastier. It was a lady judge, who might not have been a judge, just a social worker. I don't remember that time very well. They sent me to a juvenile psychiatric hospital where I had four different therapists, plus group time with a bunch of sociopaths that killed cats and tried to light shit on fire. Bo was wrong: nobody beat my ass in there, even though some of the other kids did whisper about the freaky shit they would do to me if they got the chance.

I'd been fine in our little house with him smoking up and losing his temper, not knowing if he was going to kill us or forget to feed us one day to the next, but once I got to the hospital I started having screaming nightmares, cried for no reason, hid in closets because I felt like I had to. The doctors weren't worried about that, though; being wrong in the head in ways that just hurt me didn't matter as much as being wrong in the head in ways that could hurt other people. Even after I'd convinced them all that I wasn't going to kill again, that I did have empathy and loved cats and was scared of fire, it took six years and a court order to get me out.

I didn't see Renee at all at first, but we wrote letters back and forth. Hers were mostly pictures in the beginning, but by the time I was put in the hospital she could tell me what was going down. She got placed with a family right away, one that had been taking foster kids for years and knew how to help her. At first she had nightmares, wet the bed, and begged them to bring me to her, and when we both started getting better they did bring her to visit me at the hospital a few times. Then she cut all of her hair off and started blaming me for everything, and wouldn't talk to me or see me anymore, but I still wrote her foster mom to know how she was doing. Just before she turned eighteen she ran away with her boyfriend; at first they thought that she'd been kidnapped, but she left a letter in her foster mom's purse saying that she was choosing to go. I haven't heard from her since.

I drive back down the gravel path and park in front of Matthew's before I call Seth. It's a Saturday, so he's free and, from the speed with which he picks up, watching his phone. I remember that I promised I'd call him when I got to the island, and I feel guilty. He won't call me when he thinks I'll be driving because I can't resist picking up, even on the freeway at ninety miles an hour. When I'm late getting in at night he gets scared, not that I'm fooling around with someone else like a lot of the guys I've known would think, but that I'm dead somehow. Can't fault him for it: I wake up in the middle of the night sometimes and put my ear to his ribs to hear his heart beat, just to make sure he's still alive. Even the people you can depend on, you can't depend on to never die.

"You got there OK?"

"Yeah, sorry I didn't check in when I did. It kinda threw me, being back here."

"Found anything yet?"

"One of our landlord's daughters still lives in their house— she was around when it all happened. She found me the name of someone they used to work with. Could you look him up for me real quick, baby?"

He wakes up his computer, and I give him the name and address that I've copied down. I lean back and put my feet up on the dash while he searches through hits, and wonder how the hell I would have done this before the Internet. Charles Morgan goes by Chick; he's about sixty-three now and listed as being a resident of the Tasley Assisted Living Facility and Rest Home; the local paper has a brief story about his car accident in 2007. Seth gives me that address, and I start gearing myself up to being the old man's missing niece or whatever I have to do to get them to let me see him. I'm about to hang up when I hear Seth shouting for me to wait a moment.

"I almost forgot. So I've been going through old tax records and shit, since you left. I think I found one of your aunts."

"Really?" I can't tell if the fizzing in my stomach is excitement or dread. Strangers that used to know my parents are one thing, actual family is another.

"It took a bit of looking. Bo Gordy had an older sister, and I haven't found an obituary for her or anything like that, so it looks like there's a good chance that she's still alive. Do you know where Belle Haven is?"

He talks slowly as I scribble down the name and address, but doesn't try to keep me on for long afterward.

"Call me tonight, OK? I want to know how you're doing."

"I will, I promise," I tell him, even though I know I'll forget again.

I'm grateful that he doesn't try and talk for longer. Seth likes to talk, likes to hear me talk, but right now I don't know what might come spilling out of my mouth. He thinks he knows everything, that there's nothing else that I could possibly spring on him. I didn't think there was, either, but now that I'm here I wonder if there is any statute of limitations on the human conscience.

I flip a coin: heads, I should go talk to Charles Morgan in the old folks' home. Which makes me instantly want to go find Bo's family instead, so I turn south onto the highway and head down to Belle Haven.

I drive by it three times before I decide that it's the right house—the plastic number by the door has fallen down, and the green shutters have moss growing on them in places. I screw up my courage, get out, and rap on the door: no one answers. No one answers the second knock, or the third, but I can hear a dog barking in the house next door. After a few minutes of standing there like an idiot, not knowing what to do, I go back to the car and find my notebook again. It's a straight shot up the highway to Tasley, and I remember where the assisted living facility is. Instead of going anywhere I sit there in the front seat, feet up on the dash again, staring into space and thinking about not much of anything. Seth had told me to do it all from home, contact people by email instead of showing up on their doorsteps. I told him that I didn't want to wait, but in reality I didn't want to be at the mercy of strangers. I didn't want them to know who I was, where I lived, to be able to find me. I hadn't really considered how much door-knocking it might involve, how many agonizing, polite conversations would be necessary.

As I sit, an older woman in jeans and a plaid jacket comes down the street toward me, carrying a sack of groceries; I only register her when she puts the sack down on the top step of the green-shuttered house and fumbles in her jacket pocket for her keys. My body falls out of the car and sprints across the street while my brain is still getting into gear, so when she looks up at me I don't know exactly what to say. So the truth comes out.

"Miss Maureen Gordy?"

"Yes?"

"I'm sorry to just turn up like this, but I'm your niece."

She doesn't gasp or faint or anything like that, but her eyes narrow a bit, and I can see that she doesn't believe me.

"Are you, now?"

At least this much I've planned for. The birth certificate and driver's license come out. She looks them over twice before handing them back.

"Well, I haven't got any money and the family as a collective, as small as it may be, doesn't have anything worth taking, so if you are a con artist you might as well give up now and try someone else. But if you're really Chloe, you may as well come in."

I follow her into a small kitchen, where she begins unpacking the grocery sack. She nods me into a chair.

"I'm not really surprised that you're back—everyone and his brother is obsessed with genealogy these days. Pointless waste of time, is my opinion. Finding out you're descended from a prince just gives a person jumped-up notions of himself. Coffee?"

I don't want it, but I'm scared of annoying her, so I nod.

"But you didn't have to come all this way from Georgia for a copy of the family tree." She dumps twice as many grounds into the filter basket as necessary, fills up the reservoir, and sits down opposite me; the power button on the machine is taped in a permanent "on" position.

"I got a couple of reasons, and none of them's money, so don't worry about that."

"If you want me to tell you how wonderful your dad was when we were kids, then you're out of luck, I'm afraid."

"No, I know that. I grew up with him, didn't I?"

That makes her smile a bit.

"One of the big ones, I guess, is my sister. Renee. She was nine when we left, so as she got older she forgot some things about how it was. She ran away a while back, and I haven't heard anything from her." I pull a picture out of my wallet, now years out of date. "I was hoping she'd taken her rose-colored glasses back here, tried to find our family maybe."

Maureen looks at the picture, and I know that she's seeing Bo. What on him were thick slug lips are on Renee a plump, kissable mouth; his bleary bug eyes her large, clear ones. Her skin is bone white like his, her hair gingering up in the picture but still curly. Maureen looks up at me, then back down.

"Haven't seen her, I'm sorry to say. Can't believe he made something so pretty." She hands the picture back to me. My stomach sinks, but I wasn't expecting to find her, anyway.

"I guess the other thing is really why I came, though. I called him Daddy, but when they did the DNA test, after they took us away, he and I didn't match. At all. And there wasn't anybody left around to tell me why that was. So I hoped, if I came back here and found people that knew them, back then, I might find someone with a fair guess of who my dad is. Or was."

Maureen pours herself more coffee and stands, staring into her mug for a few minutes, sloshing the liquid in small circles as if she's seeing the future in the reflections on the surface.

"After Mom died, Benny and I got tired of his shit pretty quick. Lester might have known, but he died in California a few years before Bo." She sloshes some more, then gulps down the coffee and pours another cup. "Benny might know something, but I really doubt it. He left the Shore in the sixties and didn't come back for good until he retired from the shipyard, and I know that he didn't talk to Bo or Lester in all that time. Hell, he barely talked to me for most of it. But if you're out of leads it won't hurt to ask him. He's quiet but he'll probably talk to you."

I push my half-drunk coffee away and get slowly to my feet. "Thank you for your time, ma'am. Sorry to have bothered you like this."

"No, wait. Wait." She waves me back down into the chair. "I've got something to say first." I sit back down, nervous that she's about to chew me out, but instead she sips on her coffee for a while.

"Bo and I never got along," she finally begins. "Sometimes families just don't work out. I stopped talking to him when he was still a teenager. Rumors get around quick out here, but all I really knew was that he'd found a wife and had a few kids, not quite in that order, until a cop came knocking on my door to tell me that he was dead. And I don't want you to think that we didn't care—I asked them to let me take you. You'd never met me, I'd not made an effort to be a part of your lives as far as they could see, it was no surprise that they said no. I tried to visit you, they wouldn't let me do that either. And maybe I shouldn't have, but eventually I stopped trying."

"I don't blame you for not talking to him," I finally say. "Didn't talk to him myself if I could help it."

She cracks a smile at that.

"None of the rest of it is any of your fault either—it was just a messy situation. We all did what the cops and the social workers told us to. Maybe Renee had the right idea."

She lets out a big sigh then. "Well, I know you've got other people to talk to probably. But I want a chance to start over." She holds out her hand, and I shake it, a little bewildered. "Hi. I'm your Aunt Mo. Screw whether you're my actual niece or not—everybody is a step-something these days. I've got a son named Charlie, who's maybe a year or two older than you, I'm divorced and I've lived on Accomack Island my whole life."

"Hi, Aunt Mo," I say. "I'm your niece Chloe. I've lived in a psych ward for a long time but I'm mostly not crazy. I manage payroll for the county where I live and I'm getting married next year."

After they discharged me from the hospital they couldn't just drop me back into normal life again, so they sent me to a residential rehab facility. It sounds like another hospital, but it was just a set of apartments owned by the government, where people could learn to lead a normal life with someone watching over their shoulder. I had nightmares still, but I didn't let anyone know. They helped me find a job delivering newspapers and got me signed up for classes at the local community college, but I felt like I had a normal-person disguise on.

I didn't tell my first boyfriend why I lived in a rehab community, or even that it was one. Some of the other kids at the hospital had gotten together and broken up and gotten together with other people while they were in, but I had a hard time getting all romantic feeling about anyone that might want to light me on fire or rape me in the mouth with steak knives, so he really was my first boyfriend. It lasted until he found out about what happened to my stepdad.

When Seth moved in below me I was still trying to date guys I'd met at school or work. If they didn't leave when they found out on their own what had happened to me, they left when I told them. The ones that weren't around long enough to find out I dumped when they made fun of my neighbors, asked me to score them some psych pills, said that they loved fucking crazy chicks, or did things that reminded me of Bo.

Seth came to introduce himself while I was playing *Resident Evil 2*, and stayed to backseat game until I had to leave for class. When I asked him if the scars down his arms were on purpose or on stupid, he casually told me that his mom had lit him on fire.

I find the Tasley Assisted Living Facility from memory, without having to look at the map. It's prettier than I expected, with a pond and little cottages and apartments for the more independent older people. I don't expect them to let me see Charles Morgan since I'm not related, but the receptionist doesn't seem to care when I tell her that he's my godfather and that I'm there to surprise him; I stopped at the Food Lion to pick up some flowers on the way. She shows me on a paper map of the campus which cottage he lives in, and I skip off with my visitor's badge like I know who I'm looking for.

No one answers his door, but I'm less nervous now, less off-balance because nobody's shouted at me yet today, so I ask the first person I run into, an older woman stepping slowly from her door down the path to the main building, if she's seen him. She shakes her head, because she couldn't hear me or she doesn't know who he is or both. I wonder if they've got an indoor rec room, if his real goddaughter would know that he sits there and plays pinochle with his friends every day at a quarter past one, but it's sunny and cool and I'm hoping that someone who spent his entire life working construction will be out in it, somewhere private-public where I can talk to him.

There are two men ensconced on a bench, feeding ducks, and when I ask them the blue-shirted one points across the water, to a red motorized wheelchair that's tootling along the asphalt path that rings the pond.

"Chick likes to go for a spin after lunch," he says. "Used to try to go into Tasley with it, but the deputies kept picking him up."

When I get close enough to make out his face clearly my stomach knots. He and Mama would have known each other at the right time, and he and I have features in common: dark eyes, and the white of his thick, curly hair makes his tanned skin look even darker. He's still muscular under his clothes, sits bolt upright in the wheelchair; his braced and wasted legs look like they belong to someone else. I wonder, like I have since I found out about blue eyes and brown eyes, if I'll recognize my dad the moment I see him, if I've seen him without recognizing him.

He rolls by me with a nod.

"Mr. Morgan?" I unstick my feet and trot after him. "Are you Mr. Morgan?"

I pop around to face him. He stops now, and it looks like his stomach is knotting in the same way mine just did.

"You knew my mother?"

"If your mother is who I think she was," he says. "She worked for me. Your dad too."

I hand him the flowers, for lack of anything better to do.

"I'm sorry for springing up on you of a sudden like this, but I didn't really plan things in advance. They died when I was pretty young, and I want to know more about who they were."

He's quiet for a minute, thinking back, then starts up his wheelchair again, but slower this time, so I can walk along beside him.

"I didn't know them as well as you'd probably hoped I did," he says finally, slowly. "I was the foreman, had to keep from getting too friendly with everyone. Felt real awful when all that happened. Of course, didn't hold a candle to how you felt . . ."

I wave the sympathy away.

"He was loud, and she was quiet. He liked to rag on her, Tiny did too, and she was pretty easy to rile. Had tempers, both of them did. But they were dependable, and even when they were jabbing at each other they kept working. Ellie was a fair electrician too. Never expected them to get married, though."

"Who's Tiny?"

"He worked with us then, was a friend of your dad's growing up. Tiny recommended him to me. He'd be able to tell you more about your dad as a person, I'd reckon, if that's what you're after. Might be difficult to track down, though."

"Did they work with anyone else?"

He thinks on that for a moment before he answers, keeps rolling at a pace that is just a bit too slow.

"There was a young kid, apprentice for a while, got good at carpentry so I kept him on after your mother left. Name began with a K ... Kyle? Kevin? No, Jacob! Jake Potter. Why did I think it began with a K? After Lovett—our boss—closed up shop he started teaching wood shop at the Combined School on Chincoteague. He really had a thing for your ma, though, back then. Got a few drinks in him and he'd pretty much stare his eyes out at her."

I get my notebook out of my back pocket. "Could you just tell me again real quick what their names were?"

"Jacob Potter, spelled the normal way, he probably still lives on Chincoteague. Tiny ... Didn't keep up with Tiny after I didn't have to no more. He's a Bloxom, if I remember right, but I don't recall his full name."

I hear a fuzzy sound in my ears that might be all the blood rushing, and I put a hand on the back of the wheelchair, to make the world stop tilting.

"Bloxom?"

"Yep. Lived out near Modest Town, when I knew him. If you take the main road back, when you run out of paving you get to an auto shop. He had the apartment over it. Don't see why he would have moved on, would be worth it to check there."

My first urge is to chase up this info immediately, but I stay and hear about his grandkids as we slowly circle the pond in a way that reminds me of water circling a drain. I don't leave until he excuses himself to go back to the main building, not for pinochle but a painting class. As I walk back to my car I text Seth, asking him to look up Jacob Potter on Chincoteague, then head out for Modest Town before I can think about it too much.

I almost turn back when I see it: a tilting wooden building floating in a sea of long grass and derelict cars, out past a welding shop and one of the chicken plants. I haven't missed that smell at all; when I open my car door and step out into it I feel like a little girl again, dirty at the knees, just waiting for the wild dogs to get me.

There are two mechanics, monkeying around under dented cars up on lifts, but they both ignore me. The man at the desk in the office is on the phone, leaning back in the greasy yellow vinyl swivel chair, and he looks right through me when I stand in the open doorway. There's a wooden staircase that goes up to a tiny porch and a solid green door, so I pay them back in kind and go up. It's not really a porch, just enough of a platform to let someone stand safe while they find their keys, but I can see beyond the stunted treetops the green of the marsh, the gold of the barrier islands, and without meaning to I stay there for a bit, tasting the salt edge on the air and trying to see into tomorrow, the way I used to think I could.

I can hear a television humming on the other side of the door, so I knock loud. A moment's wait, then shuffling footsteps, and an interior bolt is drawn back.

He is tall and skinny, so the beer belly that he carries under his dirty undershirt doesn't look like it belongs to his body, like he's smuggling a basketball. His hair's mostly brown still, his eyes darker than Chick Morgan's, skin similarly tan but with a greenish undertone. He smells like booze.

"Well, hello there," he says.

"Are ... are you Tiny?" I can't make myself say his last name.

"Not if the ladies are telling the truth. Did the guys over at Shuckers send you to keep me company tonight?" He puts a hand on my elbow to draw me inside, but I lean back a bit. The porch rail presses against my back.

"No, I came on my own—"

"My reputation precedes me. Come inside, beautiful, we can't have no fun if you stay out here. I'll make you a drink." He's chuckling, but his voice makes my stomach go cold.

"Sir, I'm not here for that." I'm not sure I want to be here for my original purpose anymore. I try to remember what it is Jehovah's Witnesses say when they knock on your door on a Saturday afternoon, but I don't think I can even fake that right now. "A friend of yours said that you knew my parents."

He stops trying to guide me in, but he doesn't take his hand off my arm.

"Did you know Ellie Fitzgerald?"

For a bit he looks at me blank, and even though I don't want him touching it I pull out the picture I have of her. He studies it for a few moments before letting me take it back.

"Don't really remember the face, but I did work with one chick for a while, maybe a few years, back around 1980. Bit of a frigid bitch, if I'm honest. Pretty little tits but never let anyone touch them. Sure about that drink?"

"Just one more question, sir. Did you know her husband at all? Bo Gordy?"

"Bo? Still owes me a tenner. We was friends, for a long while, but after he got married he didn't want me coming around no more. He were jealous, thought everyone was out to con him out of his woman."

"Do you know if she was seeing anyone before him?"

"She probably got around a lot, girl like that. Didn't have a boyfriend when I knew her, just liked to show it off and leave 'em hanging. Fair tortured the poor kid we worked with, it was funny as hell. Surprised she didn't get knocked up sooner."

There are more questions I want to ask, that it sounds like he'd be able to answer, but I pull my arm away and take a few steps down the stairs.

"Thanks for talking to me, sorry if I bothered you."

"Don't have to be sorry, just come in for that drink and we're square," he smiles at me. I shake my head at him and smile back even though I don't want to, and walk quick back to my car. I pretend to not see him leering at me as I start it up and turn around in the tall grass.

Sometimes when I can't sleep I think about Cabel Bloxom.

That's not entirely true. A lot of times, for no reason that I can guess, I think about Cabel Bloxom. We knew each other when we were little; I was scared of him because he was bigger and liked to twist my arm behind my back, do things to see if they would make me cry.

Renee told the social worker about how he'd touched her, and when they asked me about it I thought that my number had been called. It was only a matter of time before they figured it out. I answered their questions, told them about finding him doing things to her, about how we hid in the woods a lot when Daddy was smoking up. And then they asked if Daddy had known that Cabel had touched her, if we'd told him about the threats—and Renee had said yes. She hadn't told him herself, she'd been too scared, so I'd done it alone. He'd told me that we should stay closer to the house, stay out of the woods if we're so scared, but Cabel didn't mean anything by it. But only I knew that; Renee had been hiding downstairs. So when the social worker asked me what my Daddy had said when I told him that a neighbor had threatened to hurt us, I answered, "I'll take care of it, baby."

They tested our guns, then asked me why my fingerprints were all over the .22. It didn't matter whether they liked it or not that I'd been target shooting, since the .22 didn't kill him, but I'd wiped down the .270 real good, so only Daddy's prints were on it. He'd only been shooting at deer in the yard, but they didn't know that. Our tracks were all through the marsh, mine and Renee's from when we'd hid out, Daddy's from when he'd come to find us or gone hunting a bit, Cabel's from lord knows what. They'd looked at me and looked at Renee and probably hadn't seen anything dangerous there, looked at Cabel and decided that there was no way he'd shot himself in the back of the head with our gun, looked at Daddy and decided that he was the easy answer, and charged him with it.

Maybe they asked Renee, when I wasn't there, if she thought that I could have done it. Probably not in those words, probably they asked if I ever left her alone, if she ever got lonely. And she would have said that I never gave her a moment's privacy, that I was always looking over her shoulder, that we even shared a bed and I took up all the space, forgetting the times that I'd gone to Matthew's and the library on my own, or when she'd wandered away from me while we were in the woods, all the little moments when I could have done something and she'd have no idea.

They asked us about gunshots, if we'd ever heard any, unexpected, in the woods. And we did, a lot, because deer are vermin, meat is expensive, and people do reckless things when they're hungry. Someone's always letting off a round or two, then pretending they didn't or hiding the evidence before the sheriffs turn up. And they weren't happy about us telling them that wide-scale poaching was just a cultural reality, but telling them something they didn't like wasn't an execution-worthy offense.

When I was a kid I had a lot of daydreams about what would happen if they found out. Sometimes it was a firing squad, sometimes the electric chair, sometimes they'd just leave me to rot in prison, let Renee come down every five years to see me but she'd never say a word, just give me the cold hard glare she did when I'd made her mad and she wasn't talking. For a few years I had a recurring daydream about lethal injections, which got more and more elaborate each time I thought of it. It made me feel sick and scared and prickle behind the eyes and down the throat, but I couldn't stop it, a lot like the sex daydreams I started having when I was older.

Now, though, I think about Cabel himself. What he would have looked like, whether he would have stuck with his girlfriend, if they would have had kids. If having kids would have made him . . . not nicer, more humane maybe. If he would have hurt those kids. If I was supposed to kill him to keep him from hurting more people. If he would have redeemed himself if I'd let him live.

I can't know what would have happened. I know two things: I killed him, and I'm the only one that knows I killed him.

⌒

As I head north to Chincoteague I count the little villages, the way I used to out the school-bus window, but I don't let myself think again until I get to the stoplight at T's Corner. Straight on another twenty miles and I'll hit the northern causeway, leave the island—and it is an island, even though it's so big most people forget—and be in Salisbury, Maryland, in an hour and change. Instead I turn right, down a winding road through thick brush, which opens up unexpectedly into marsh, flat green marsh and glossy dark water, the horizon left and right hidden by spits of land, clumps of trees, with nothing ahead but a shimmering black lump floating on the seam between blue sky and blue bay.

The causeway bunny-hops from island to island across the marsh, then arcs out over the bay and the oyster beds to touch down on Chincoteague, and I can pretend that I'm just a tourist as I drive slowly through, giving way to entitled ducks and children dripping ice cream on themselves and screaming at each other. It's quieter than I remember it from before: a lot of the big houses stand empty, and all of the hotels have their "vacancy" signs lit, even though they should be jampacked at this time of year. I remember an obnoxious crush of tourists, family vans with Pennsylvania license plates pulled over on the side of the road out to the refuge, little kids screeching about how they can see Black Beauty when they're really pointing to one of the villagers' goats, the real ponies stepping gingerly, camouflaged by their splattery markings and half-invisible, through the marsh, sipping the salt from the tips of the sharp-bladed grass.

I see the road where Jacob Potter lives and pass it, keep down the main road for another five minutes until I get to the bridge to Assateague, which used to cross a small bay. It's silted up in the past fifteen years, so if I wanted to I could get out and walk across on the wet mud under the bridge.

The traffic barriers on the other side of the bridge are missing, the little booths where rangers would collect your entrance fee untenanted; the asphalt is splitting. There is no one else on the road as I drive slowly out, but I keep to the speed limit anyway, in case they're still ticketing people. The lighthouse, the woods, the marshy parts in the middle: Assateague Island itself is exactly how I remember it, but when I get out to the beach I see what's changed.

There are still a few pilings where the visitor's center used to be, but the changing stalls and the outdoor toilets have been completely wiped away. Ragged-edged hunks of what used to be the parking lot sit half-buried in the mud and dunes. The beach itself, the long stretch of sand down to the water, has constricted to a narrow band, steep down to the breaking waves. The park service hadn't been able to keep replacing the sand that the yearly hurricanes wiped away, so they'd abandoned it. No more tourist beach, no more tourists.

I park the car off the end of the road, step out of my shoes and tuck them just behind one of the front tires like I used to do when Ma brought me out here, and go down to the water's edge. Something inside my chest feels cool and lonely, but in a good way. The sand is soft and hard at once, and I bury my feet just above the waterline, then kick it all away and start walking.

I used to skip school sometimes as a kid, get there for breakfast and stay for homeroom, then slip out when I wasn't being watched and hike down to the beach. Renee always got mad that I went without her, but she couldn't walk all the way there and all the way back in time to catch the bus. And I wanted to keep the ocean to myself, the whole Atlantic.

People used to live on Assateague, once. There had been a village, down below the lighthouse. I was jealous of them when I was a kid, being so close to the water all the time. I'm jealous again, now that I'm back here, and even though I want to go home to Seth in Georgia, to people that don't know me, another part of me is wondering if they'll let people settle here again, now that the National Park Service has pulled out. I think about making Seth move back here with me, building a little house hidden in the woods just off the road, being able to run down to the beach and skinny-dip whenever we want. The hurricanes wiped away the beach, but it would only take one really big one going at the right angle to give us back yards and yards of pure, clean sand.

I don't know how long I walk for, but when I get back to my car it's still before six. Seth texted while I was gone, asked if I'm getting along all right, and I text back that I'm doing OK but don't call him. I can't quite manage being relational right now.

Jacob Potter's house is small and neat, the house of a carpenter. The tiny lawn is thick and well kept, the window frames square and recently painted. I tell myself that this is the last house, the last stranger, and afterward I'll stop at the first place that looks good and eat whatever I want, find the motel Seth booked for me and take the longest hot shower, and figure out what happens next when I wake up. Even after this internal pep talk I sit in the front seat of my car for far too long, looking at the house, daring myself to go up and knock. Maybe I'm afraid that he'll be more aggressive even than Tiny.

At the first knock someone inside shouts out, "Just a second!" I can hear him coming and I want to sprint away. I've decided to do just that when the door opens.

He's over six feet tall; when he looks down at me he freezes, like Renee used to do when she saw a spider. I think for a moment that he's going to start whimpering too, like she used to.

"Ellie?" is what he says instead. His nails are digging into the door frame.

"I'm her daughter," I say. "I'm sorry, I didn't mean to upset you."

He's composing himself now, passes a hand over his eyes and puts on a smile, but a kind one, not like Tiny's. Deep in the chest and thick in the arms: he's not aged as well as he could have, but he's ruggedly good-looking, and I wonder if my mom thought so too.

"Can I help you?"

"I hope so," I answer. "I'm trying to find out some things about my parents. It sounds like you knew them."

He lets me in, leads the way through a cluttered house to a shaded back porch, pulls out a chair for me and sits down opposite. The look he keeps giving me is strange, even though he's gotten his face under control.

"What can I do you for?"

I'm tired of polite fictions, of not being straight up from the get-go.

"You knew my mother, didn't you?"

"We worked together for a while, saw each other from time

to time in a social setting. She was a private person, I don't know if you can say that many people knew her."

"You heard how they died? It was in the paper."

"I heard," he says. I'm grateful that he doesn't apologize, or tack anything on after that.

"I never got to know them as anything other than Mom and Dad. I don't know, really, where they came from, and I don't know who they were. But the thing that I wish I knew more, and I'm sorry but there's really no way to put this delicately, is whether or not Bo Gordy was my father. Well, he wasn't really any kind of 'father' to anyone, what I mean is our DNA doesn't match. So I've been asking around after people that knew them then, just in case someone knows who my biological father might have been."

If he looked startled in the doorway he looks positively sick now, crumpling in on himself and breathing in gulps through his mouth while trying to stay composed. He looks guilty as all hell, and I want to think that I know why.

He sits for a bit, sucking in air and not looking at me, thinking.

"I don't rightly know how to tell you what I need to tell you," he says slowly.

"If you're going to tell me that you're my father, I don't want to cause you any trouble. I just want to know."

"No, I wish I were telling you that. I also wish I didn't have to be sober for this, but that's how this all started." He sits still for a minute.

"Have you ever done something, and in the moment it felt like the only thing that you could do, but you regretted it for forever afterward?"

"Everyone does," I say.

"Not quite like this. I didn't do something, almost thirty years ago now, and I've regretted it. Which doesn't make it any better."

I only nod. I don't know if I want to know what he's about to tell me.

"When I knew your mother, I was eighteen, nineteen years old. Chick, the guy we worked for, took me on as a carpenter's helper, more out of pity than anything, I think now. Payday was Fridays, and once we got our pay we used to sometimes play poker and drink bourbon together; your mom played too. It was just another one of those card nights. It had been a tougher day than usual, but you get those sometimes. Chick had already gone home, so it was just the four of us then—me, Tiny, Bo, and your ma—but it was just the four of us a lot. And I don't know what had been going on between your ma and Bo outside of work, but he was angry at her for something private. So when she ran out of money to bet, they made her bet her clothes."

I feel sick already, but not quite as sick as Jacob Potter looks. He's talking quiet and slow, pausing at the ends of sentences or sometimes in the middle, so that I'm not sure if he's stopped altogether.

"I was drunk then. She didn't want to. I tried to say some-thing, but they said it was all good fun."

"How do you try and say something?" I ask.

"OK, then, I didn't say enough. I said whatever it was I said, it didn't change their minds. They made her bet her clothes. And when she'd run out of those," he breathes, "she tried to leave. But they wouldn't let her."

He stops there for a bit, but I don't tell him to go on.

"They did things to her, then. On the floor. I couldn't make them stop."

"Did you try?"

"Yes," he finally says, in not much more than a whisper.

"Did you really try, or did you just tell them to stop?" I can feel tears making my voice thick, but they won't come.

"I should have done more."

"Did you touch her?"

He doesn't answer, just stares at the floor, face like a clenched fist.

"Did you touch my mother?"

"No." When he says it his eyes close, tears bunching on the lashes.

I want to kill him. I want to punch him in his stupid face, scream at him that his crying isn't going to bring her back, isn't going to take her hurt away. But I sit still.

"When she found out she was pregnant," he finally says, "Bo offered to marry her. I thought she was safe with him. If I hadn't been so ashamed, I would have asked her myself."

"You ashamed?" There's iron in my voice, and he nods.

"I deserve that." He swallows. "Yes, ashamed. For not doing more. I don't know what she did after that night. She might have been with someone else soon after, but I don't think she was that kind of woman."

"So Tiny is my father." It comes out flat with disgust.

"It appears so."

"And you never touched her?" I ask.

"Never." He has more conviction now, but I know from the

way his eyes slide off me when he says it that he's holding something back. I want to beat it out of him, I want to scream and shout and hurt him, punish him for what he didn't do. But I remember Cabel Bloxom.

It's getting dark now. The sky has turned to indigo, and the light is heavy. I want to cry, but I can't.

"I've never told anyone what happened. I've kept it to myself for far too long. But it shouldn't weigh you down, now that you know."

"I won't let it," I say, though I don't know yet if I'm lying.

"Can I get you something to drink?" he offers.

"I'm good, thanks." I stand up slowly. "I've had a long day."

"When I saw you at the door I thought it was your mother come to settle things." I don't know if I'm supposed to laugh, so I don't, and somehow that's the right thing to do.

He sees me through the house and back out the front door, offers any kind of help I ever need before finally shutting it and leaving me on his front step, breathing in the cool night air as deep as I can. The tears don't come, though, until I get to the car, and these I feel. Relief, I think, just because the wondering is over. Later there will be anger, and fear, and bitter sadness, but now it is just relief and it aches like a sore throat.

I wait until I can breathe again, then call Seth.

"Hey, no, I'm all right, was just crying a little."

"Did you find out . . ."

"Yeah. I guess it's better than having a murderer for a father, but not by much," I say. "I met him earlier today, before I knew. He tried to get me to sleep with him." And then I'm laughing, loud and long and uncontrollably.

"It sounds like you're losing it, baby."

"I might be. I'll tell you about everything tomorrow. I'm going to spend the night and then drive back first thing, I think."

"I'll be watching for you. Text me before you go to sleep, all right?"

"I will."

I go straight to the motel—my stomach feels full of cement, and I know better than to try eating when it gets like that—check in without saying anything to the desk clerk, just hand over my reservation printout and ID when he asks for them, then lock and chain the room door and get in the shower. The hot water pouring down my back usually helps me think, usually helps me unwind, but right now my brain feels numb, half-thoughts pinballing around like they do right before I fall asleep.

There are lots of Bloxoms on the Shore, and if you go back far enough everyone that lives out here is related, but I don't want to interrogate the connection too closely: Cabel, Tiny, me. I want Jacob Potter to be lying, to be the source of half my DNA. When Tiny had opened the door I had seen Cabel in him, heard him in his words; I didn't want to see myself as well.

Dried off and in my pajamas in bed the thoughts come faster, looping and repeating, and I can't shut them off. This is the mental illness that they found: obsessive spiraling that keeps me awake for days at a time, not the serial killer's psychosis they expected but the normal human preoccupation of thought, taken to an unmanageable extreme.

It's still evening, more or less, when I give up and put my clothes back on. Usually my break point is around three in the morning, so maybe I knew already, maybe from when I got in the shower, that I'd be going back out.

Once I'm headed down Route 13 though, it feels like the middle of the night. It's only been truly dark, nighttime dark, for a little while, but there aren't more than one or two cars on the road: farmers, hunters, watermen all start their days early, and the chicken-plant workers that aren't on shift are probably sleeping. I keep it just below the speed limit, but still I get to Matthew's and the turnoff sooner than I would like. I consider wasting time, driving past and turning around after I've geared myself up some more, but I'm worried that if I wait too long Sally Lumsden will be asleep by the time I get there.

When I kill the ignition in her driveway the clock on the dashboard reads 10:57, but there's a light on in one of the upper rooms of the farmhouse. I knock, then step back to watch the lights flick off and on as she moves through the house, until the little frosted window above the door flashes sudden gold and the bolt is drawn back.

"I take it you found what you were looking for?" she asks me without preamble, but in a friendly way. She has her bathrobe on over her clothes, her thumb marking a page partway through a paperback book.

"I think so, but all of my answers just lead to more questions."

"Which is why you're back here."

She opens the door wider and lets me step inside, but I hesitate on the mat.

"As a rule, I try to avoid being helpful," she says. "But in this case it looks like I've already made an exception."

"I'm sorry it's so late—it's only a few quick things." I follow her into the house, not back to the greenhouse this time but instead into the kitchen. Or what had been the kitchen: the butcher-block counters and slate floor, the oven and refrigerator, remain, but the room has been proliferated by test tubes and beakers, spirit lamps, esoteric equipment; a battered chest made of worn dark wood sits next to the sink, and a small still crouches in the space where an appliance, probably an electric dishwasher, has been ripped out. She lights the stove and puts a kettle on, and I wonder how many drinks, hot and otherwise, I've consumed out of politeness over the course of the day; I've probably stopped to pee at every single gas station between Belle Haven and Chincoteague.

"You've lived here all your life, haven't you?" I begin when she turns back to me.

"I can count the times I've set foot on the mainland on my fingers, never been gone longer than a day." The kettle was hot already; steam streams from its spout and hangs in puffs behind her head.

"So you probably heard my parents shooting at deer from our porch."

"Probably. They ate our crops, though, and my dad figured your family could use the meat, so we pretended that nothing was happening. The police asked me the same thing, when they found that neighbor boy shot, but you get so used to the sound that you don't really pay attention."

She has her back turned to me, making tea, so she doesn't see me wince when she mentions the "neighbor boy."

"So you could hear my parents fighting too?"

"Not so much." She hands me a steaming mug, then takes

her own and perches on the countertop. "Voices don't carry like gunshot does, especially when the corn gets high. We didn't think them any different from any of our tenants—they paid the rent on time, you and your sister had good manners. Everything seemed normal."

"So you didn't notice, when my mother disappeared."

She doesn't answer right away, looks down into her tea like she's trying to see the future. It's got chamomile in it, I can tell by the smell.

"I remember right after it happened—after the police came, that is, and found out about your mom. None of us could believe it, that it had been just down the road, that no one saw anything or said anything. Afterward, there was a piece in the newspaper, about how your teachers should have noticed, about how someone should have noticed, about the responsibility of a community for its weakest members. But we all thought that your mother had left, that we shouldn't say anything because it would just hurt you and your sister, and her leaving fit with what we expected enough that no one wondered. You remember, don't you, how much people value privacy out here? And I watched you and your sister grow up—walking to the grocery store, on your bicycle up and down in the summer, waiting for the school bus. I didn't imagine that anything was wrong."

What I want to know is if she heard it, the night that Bo killed my mother. If anyone bore witness besides me. If someone could have stopped it, the way I still feel I should have been able to even though the therapist has told me that there was nothing I could do then. But I can't push that line of thought any farther.

"That's all I wanted to know, I guess. If there was any chance of things working out different."

"No one can tell you that, hon."

The silence starts to get uncomfortable, then she asks, "Did you find out about your dad, after all?"

"Yeah. I kinda wish I hadn't, though." I deliberate for a minute, then say, "It looks like the guy that my stepdad shot might have been my half-brother." It feels weird coming out of my mouth. "Won't know until I get home and look it up, though. There are a lot of Bloxoms out here."

"Same dad, then?"

"Possibly. Need to double-check, though. We could be cousins, or no relation."

She holds the rim of the cup against her bottom lip for a moment, thinking.

"It happened on our land, as I recall. Our records are pretty damn thorough—would you like me to take a look? We probably hung onto a copy of the police report, maybe the obit or the newspaper article too."

"You don't have to bother with that, I can do it just as well when I get back to Georgia."

"No bother, really."

"Well, I'm also not sure that I want to know just yet."

"Fair enough."

She watches me and I watch her while I drink the tea. I'm trying to think of how to get out of here, politely, but she looks like she's going to say something, so I don't make straight for the door, but wait.

"You've probably been thinking about coming back here for a while," she finally says.

"Not really."

"Ever thought about coming back to live?"

I can't answer right away, instead pretend there's more tea in the empty cup.

"Not till today." When I say it I realize that I have been thinking about it, have been easing back into the landscape like putting on a favorite coat. I hate this place and I love this place and I don't know if I want to go as far away as possible or never leave.

"It's a pain in the ass to get out to, isn't it? Just forever away from anywhere."

"That's one of the nice things about it."

"I'm glad we agree on that." She smiles at me, but it's a crafty smile. "Good place to be when the world ends, don't you think?"

"Sure, if you're the kind of person that thinks the end of humanity means the end of the world. If the world were really ending, the best place to be would probably be Mars or somewhere. Species go extinct, what's the big tragedy in one of those species being humans?"

"But still, where would you go if it looked like humanity was going to end?"

I think for a moment.

"You're right, I'd probably come out here. There's food, there's water, I know how to get by. Why do you ask?"

She breathes in before she answers, and I know she's getting to the part that she really wants to tell me about.

"It's a fact that when a population gets too numerous for its environment, something happens to reduce it. Bacteria, ants, cheetahs, every living thing. It's perfectly natural, and very necessary, but every time it happens to human beings we all go utterly to pieces. Bubonic plague in Europe, syphilis in the

Americas, contagion that we could only assume to be the hand of God, because we didn't understand what was happening. Now that we have germ theory and hazmat suits we think that we're immune to that kind of event, that we'll be able to prevent it. So when it happens again, as it inevitably will, and our doctors and our scientists cannot control the spread, the world is going to panic. And if the goal is, in that panic, the preservation of the individual, then they'd have a very good reason to panic. But if the goal is the preservation of humanity, then there is some hope."

"So you're planning on preserving humanity?" I'm wondering now if she's got a cellar full of women of childbearing age and plans to repopulate the planet after the apocalypse, or similar craziness.

"Not in so many words. This is an isolated community, a remote place. It's fertile, it's temperate, and it can be very difficult to get to. And it might not happen in this decade, or even in my lifetime, but the next great plague is coming. And I think that it is coming quickly.

"This is my land. I am responsible for it. I promised to stay. So I've spent my time learning what can be done with what is at our disposal here. I know how to use the plants, how to make the medicines we won't be able to buy if the world as we know it ends. Other people that are close to me and also believe that something is coming have designed ways to make shelter with what is readily available. Some have worked with animal husbandry, horticulture. We're planning, and learning, and experimenting now, so that if and when it all goes sour, our children will have a place to go."

"How are you going to keep it off the Shore, if it's a disease you think is going to kill us all?"

"We can't." She grins at me. "And we're not. Accomack Island is too big, more than we need. But Chincoteague and Assateague, we could manage those. Without the causeway—all it would take is one big storm, one perfect hurricane—we would be unreachable. Isolated. Safe."

"You're crazy," I say.

"Do you think so? What would you do if you woke up one morning, and swine flu was plastered all over the papers?"

"It was," I say.

"But what if you woke up a week later and half the people you knew were dead?"

I think a bit before I answer. "I'd go somewhere isolated and wait it out."

"And that's what I'm planning. Just on a bigger scale. More long-term. Genetic mutations might become a problem, but if we set it up well, we could outlast the disease."

"I still think you're a little crazy."

"Just a little, maybe," she concedes. "But being bound to this place for life would make anyone a little crazy, don't you think?"

I don't know what to say to her. I wonder what I would have been like, if I'd stayed until I was her age, in the same house, on the same land, alone.

"Are you trying to recruit me for this?" I ask.

"Only if you want to. Genetic variety is never a bad thing, and your husband won't be from around here." She grins at me. "A secret is a secret, remember. Don't tell anyone.

"I've kept up with repairs on the house you lived in," she says as she walks me to the front door, and I think she's trying to be gentle. "In case someone ever came back."

"You shouldn't have."

"It's a cement-slab building with a cedar roof—it's mostly continued to exist in spite of human action," she says. "If you want to go and see it before you leave, the keys are still under the whelk shell on the front porch."

I shrug at her and step out the front door.

"I might do, in the morning," I say.

"No one's been killed around here in fifteen years, so you should be safe."

She could mean my mom or Bo, but for a moment I get a stab of fear in my stomach that she means Cabel Bloxom. That she knows.

The door shuts behind me for a second time. I look up at the moon for a moment, huge with balancing on the horizon, and I remember sitting on the upstairs porch at night when I was younger, watching the reflection on the marsh. The stars are smeared across the sky, not the pretty scatter that most people imagine, but a crush of millions in the beautiful, pure darkness. I'd forgotten how big the sky is out here, how black it gets at night, how far it feels from the rest of the world.

My feet start walking, past my car, across the gravel road, to the cornfield, and the remains of the oyster-shell road gleam up at me through the stalks, pearlescent in the moonlight. I'm going to go back to my house, and I'm going to watch the stars from my porch again, and I'm going to pretend that Renee is already in bed asleep, that Mama has just stepped inside to get us glasses of soda, that Daddy isn't someone to be scared of, because he wasn't always. And when I get back to Georgia I might tell Seth who shot Cabel Bloxom, or I might not, and I might make him come back with me, or I might not. It doesn't matter yet. What matters is that I have the stars, the marsh, the smudge of the barrier islands again, that I can trace the Milky Way, that my feet remember the shape of this land. That for right now they're all mine.

CHAPTER XIII

2143

———

TEARS OF THE GODS

Time was, in the byandby days, people came and went across the bay, or around the hook, or through the marsh, just as they wished. And that might sound like a lovely thing, a world so big, but time run along and the oyster beds lay empty, and the sea tossed up great two-headed fish, and all the flitting seabirds hid their sandy nests. About that time we heard whispers from the mainland, about babbies being born dead or not at all, people going hungry or wandering around killing to get what they had to have, and the Bigmen not doing a thing to stop it.

Then the fever came. Some say it was a shivering fever, others say a sweating fever, but when the little ones are asleep, Wink tells it was a sick that rotted a man's parts from the outside in, and a woman's from the inside out. It came with the first chill of year's end, and our luck was no one much wandered over t'the Island when summer was done. Big Island people was dying like baitfish in a bucket, but we was holding steady, certain sure that all would be well, till the healer woman came with her dark wood chest and her follow-afters. She, what was the first Keeper ever we had, ever we needed, kenned what was to come, pitched her hut far from the village, told us what must be done if we would live. We were ready to hold them off, any that might come to our island with the fever on them, but the rain came first. And with it came the wind, and waves tree-high, and when blue sky came again there was no road back to Big Island. Just rubble speckled across the sucking mud and sunk deep in the reeking water to mark where it had been. People say boats came to find us at first, across the bay or tracking slow through the marsh's paths, which no one could follow lest they'd grown up there, but the tides threw them around and laid them bare on the rocks of Tom's Hook, or else the twisting of the creeks or the snakes'n'spiders'n'other nasties took care of them.

But that's not what this story is about. That's just a goes-to-show. Islandmen are laid out so that they can only see one way to fix a thing, mostly, and are just as hard to bring around as the tide itself. But I did work a bring-around, once, on Trower Bell no less, and this is how it happened.

Now you might think with us being an Island of fishers'n'farmers'n'trapping men, no one'd have a use for daughters, and maybe that's how things were, in the byandby days. A couple of sons is all well, but when they marry up, their hands go to working their own plots. A daughter will be cooing over you an' baking'n'brewing over you till you die, whether or no she's got a man t'home. So it's no secret that an Islandman, when his love grows round, hangs shells on the beach trees and sings for a girl child. A son is useful like an ass or a goat is useful, but you never seen a man delight in an ass, lest there was something odd about him. Too, you can plant and catch all you want, but if there's no one to preserve it, dry'n'pickle'n'pack it away neatlike, you may as well sun all the summer away. So it's no secret that Islandmen hang the trees for loves as well. Suppose I'm lucky, some men never get a love, and with all this pining after women what we do, sometimes a boy could get to thinking that no one in the world wants him. That's pretty much where I was when I found the copper gourd. But I'm getting ahead of myself.

When I got born, I was quick in the head but not in body. My right arm was stiff at the elbow so it wouldn't bend all the way, first two fingers stuck together and last two not there at all, with hollow places where some of the muscles should have been so it never got as strong as the other, and the shoulder slumped in. The right leg was off too, the foot clubbed and the hip popped. I could walk on it, but not comfortlike and not pretty, and couldn't do heavy work that took both hands. As I grew the bad side grew with me, not quite keeping up so I had a funny bouncing walk that I was shy of. It wasn't my fault, it was just how I was born, same as how Wink was born with no eyes, just two soft dark bumps where eyes ought to be. Lot of little ones born then had something off about them; it happens more than we would like. I was better off than a lot of them; Wink couldn't see a blame thing, and summa the others didn't live to their teething year. He mends the nets finer than a woman now, and keeps the stories, but there's only room for one Keeper on t'Island. I had the welcome to a piece of dirt and a stretch of corn like every other man that may, and the choice to work it how I could, or else hang on at some other man's hearth until I was turned out, and that was how I thought it would be.

⤙

When you're just a slip you don't notice them, think everyone's the same more or less. Then one day you look up and something's different.

We was all splashing in one of those beachy hollows what fills with seawater when the tide's up, not a stitch on and not thinking twixt about it. I'd seed Jillet a hundred times before, but when she skinned off her big loose shift, same as we all wore, and jumped in the water with us, the bottom fell out of my gut. I got right out of the water and nipped down the beach, fast with my sideways skip like I have to, before she could see the red in my face. The first beach tree I came to, one of the little twisted trees all torn by the salt wind, I dropped down and gathered up the holy shells and hung it all about.

My da hung the first tree I saw. Took me up on his shoulder one day and sung out that we was going off, and strode out with me up high through the whispering pines with the hard dirt sliding by so far down beneath his feet. He legged it through the wood and across the little marsh where the wild ponies graze to the sand, where all the little ones play and fishers launch their boats, and the Keeper has his hut of sea-licked wood between the soft hills of the dunes. He nipped along the water edge, till we come to a spindly tree stripped by wind and water till its wood shone polishedlike, and set me down. He picked up a great pile of white shells, all broken, and threaded them onto the bone-fine branches, all the while singing about daughters. Some say it's a prayer, others say it's magic. Wink says though Islandmen been hanging trees since time out of mind, it doesn't do you a lick of good to hang a tree like that and then sit back and not work at the reason you hung the thing. Think he has it right; we hung that tree 'n' sung the songs, and m'brother Wol came in the winter. So after hanging my tree and singing for want of Jillet, I sat down in the sand, and looked up at that naked little tree all dangling broken seashells, and gave it some thought.

Jillet's Trower Bell's daughter, his only daughter, and from what I'd seed she was his light'n'life'n'loveliness since his love passed on, and before. And if that didn't make it bad enough he was Bigman on the Island, with more chooks'n'goats'n'corn than anyone else. As I thought it, it wouldn't be long before all the young bucks would be looking to snitch her away from him, so he'd be watching doubly close, and not giving her up to just anyone. They'd be offering him gifts, but seeing as he was set comfortlike he'd be above what most of them could manage, untried boys as they was. And they'd be offering her gifts, but he'd brung her up smartlike and strong, and it'd take more than a lapful of roses 'n' the usual boys' empty promises to turn her head. As you might think, these was worrisome thoughts to a man with one side all shriveled and not much more than a herd of chooks to call his own. Hell, I had no knowing even if I could get a babby by her, given the chance.

I walked away from the sand that day heavy in the step, but I couldn't stop thinking about Jillet. Me'n'Wol had a plot of our own way back in the woods, what had been Da'n'Mam's afore us, and all the time I was working our corn, gathering in our clams, scrabbling after plovers' eggs or babbying my little herd of bantie chooks, I was thinking on Jillet.

Wol's a decent brother, as they go, and we worked fine together, but I knew he had his eyes on a lovely of his own. I remember when he was born, and the sad in Da's eye that he wasn't the daughter he hung the tree for, but Mam just crowed on that he had all'n his limbs. He follerd after me till he learned to run, and got in all manner of things I'd never bothered with, until Mam wondered out loud why she'd ever asked for a sound'n to make up for the Halfman she'd borne, meanin' me. Da had been drowned when Wol was in his walking year, going after fish on the back of the changeable sea. Mam hadn't lasted too much longer, just until Wol got to be some use around the place. Byandby, he became the leader 'n' I the follow-after, and the plot what usual goes to firstborn went to him. I had my little corner what he left alone, and my banties, and my way with finding clams and plovers' eggs, and we got on sweetlike'n'good with each other. Be that as it may, when he finally brought his love home to roost I'd be left hanging on at their hearth, and I never heard tell of a new-joined couple in their honeymonth what didn't deeply need their privicy. Otherwise I could take my chances with my own plot'n'herd, but a one-arm Halfman what can't run down his goats'n'chooks hasn't much chance alone on the Island. You can guess neither future filled me full of glowing.

Perhaps it was all that thinking that led me up to the old light-watch one day, when Wol was off courting his lovely and I had the time to wander. It sits on the highest point of the Island, a big red-white stripe finger rising out of the hardpack dirt and thick clustering trees, what used to warn away the ships back when we wanted them to land safe instead of smashing open on the rocks. Back when there were ships to land. It certainly was all that thinking that made me misstep off the edge of the gully up by the light-watch and go sliding down through the under-brush, and if I hadn't slidden down, I never would have found it.

When I fell, my gut stayed back up top, leastways it felt like it, but when I hit the bottom I landed in mounds of soft skeleton leaves, so wasn't bad hurt. Just lay there a while, watching the light-watch spinning up above me through the wavering trees under a clear blue sky. When it all held still again I flipped over and took stock, and found I wasn't hurt bad, just all banged up. The climbing back up with one strong hand took some time, but as I was going up the face of that gully my right knee fetched up against something that gave a hollow sound, and curiousome I stopped to see what it was.

Dirt had sifted down and mosses grown over, but a tick of scraping showed that the mother of the echo I had heard was a low square door, set into the earth of the gully at a slant. A thick heavy door it was, but no lock, and hauling it open near tore my good arm off. Breath of the grave seeped out of the opening, cold and dry all together. And I dropped inside, dustlight flickering in after me, but what I found puzzled me grievous.

A little cave had been cut in that gullybank, sandy and clean with neat tight-packed walls cut square, as big as mine'n'Wol's hut, with an iron table pushed up into the back. Setting on that table was a gourd, but it rung when I tapped it and shone coppery and spotted with greenish thumbprints. Its copper stem twisted up and over to hang above a little bucket on the floor, its bottom red with rust. The gourd had stubbly little legs, and beneath it was the sleeping bones of a snuffed-out fire. Some dust had sifted down from above, and a scattering of leaves'n'beetle bits littered the corners, but it was a tight'n'neat little place. I thought for a moment, if Wol turned me out when he brought his love back, I could sweep it out and make a tolerable snug home for myself, or at least a place to die privatelike. But I put that thought away sharpish.

Any idea in the world what that copper gourd was, I had none, but I knowed that it could maybe get me what I was after. That time, we were still finding pieces and bits of the byandby, things with biting edges, that weighed too heavy for their size or were smooth and hard and colored bright, shards of the sky that showed back your own face. Any little piece you could find was worth your while, because any little piece you could find, what was useful, could make you a very big man indeed. So I stood cogitating on that piece for a while, fetched it a clip with my finger to make it ring, and thought some more. The air in that space was dry and dusty, and my eyes began weeping, so I fetched out a little length of rope I kept with me, and fixed the gourd by its narrow neck around my waist, and most careful of its snaking, hollow stem I closed up the door and began the climb to the top again.

Wol was yet abroad when I scattered our kids'n'chooks and slipped back into our hut. Ours was a small hut, and that might have been enough of a reason in itself for Trower Bell to deny me his quicksilver daughter. But our hut was made of goat hides beaten soft and oiled thick, and though it was small the rain stayed out, and when the kids'n'chooks huddled in with us when the snows came down it was near too warm. I kenned the making of it too: Da had showed me how to work the hides to rabbit softness and stitch them together with the ends clamped in my teeth and trapped under my foot. It isn't a skill most men have mastery of, though they have use of both hands. I laid my bones down into our heap of skins and hefted the shining gourd above me. It was an odd and beautiful thing, as long as my arm and fat, but I didn't know the first thing to do with it.

Didn't take much studying before I lit on taking it to Wink. He may have been eyeless'n'loveless 'n' have the hands of a woman dancing quicktime through the nets, but he's the Keeper of all our memories, and it's his business to puzzle out what's been forgot. The Keeper before him was born with no legs nor arms, just feet'n'hands set stumplike into his body. That's the way of it, with Keepers: their bodies are broken so they use their heads, and get admired no end for it. Some say they charm the skies, pull the clouds to keep the worst of the storms away and bring us rain in drought, and that makes people more careful of them. Trouble is, there can only be one Keeper at a time, so all the other broken Halfmen fall by the wayside, and worry out their days at someone else's hearth, or else come to grief early on, on account of a father or brother what doesn't want the burthen of feeding them. Wink got lucky; the old Keeper was brother of his mam, and raised him up from his walking year to know our secrets.

I caught up my gourd in an old poke and went shuffling off to Wink's hut. He could have set up anywhere, in the center of the village or deep in the trees where the grapevines grow, but he'd chosed to raise his hut twixt a creek and the sea, in amongst the dunes where the winter wind blows fierce. That's no nevermind to him: the Islandmen raise the Keeper's hut from silvered wood they've caught off the back of the sea, and keep it covered with the softest kidskin and bind the cracks tight. The women lay the floor thick with rugs in all manner of colors, so he's set up sometime better than the Bigman for comfort, but mostlike all alone'n'loveless. I lit upon him set cross-legged afore his doorway, face up to the sun, someone's net spread across his lap and gliding through his hands quick as sand'n'water.

"Lo, Sim," he sung out when I'd got close enough for him to hear me walking.

"Lo, Wink," I answered and settled down next to him slow-like. I'd brought a bottle of sour applemilk, and I pulled it out then and gave it over. He sipped it slow, and I sipped it slow, and we felt it swimming inside us spicy-warm for a breath. Even Trower Bell treads careful around him, but when I was too small to know better I used to bring him applemilk and ask for stories of the byandby, and when I got some bigger I'd come not wanting aught at all, just company, and now I know better I can't do any different. The Islandmen hold a powerful fear of him, for what he knows and what he do, but I never learned that fear. When we may we sit like brothers, and he's never chased me off.

We sat'n'breathed, hearing the water slap the sand, but I could feel Wink waiting on me to talk. Eventual I started in on Jillet, how she looked'n'moved'n'breathed 'n' how my arms just ached to touch her all day long, and other parts ached with strange dreams of her all night long. Wink nodded through it all. We'd talked on such before, and as we knew that neither of us would ever have a love we'd sighed over it together.

And after I'd talked all there was about that girl, we set silent again. Then I fetched out my gourd from its wrap, twitched the net away, and set it in the hollow of Wink's crisscrossed legs. He ran his soft brown hands over it gentle-quick, and started grinning all over his face.

"You be knowing what you got here, Simian?" he asked me, and I shook my head afore I remembered that he couldn't see it.

"Not the first idea," I answered.

He turned it over slowlike in his hands, and said, "This little bit of copper, you take your applemilk or your wine or any bit of brew sieved fine, strike a fire underneath, and the very tears of the gods will drip out its stem. Burn like fire, they say, and bend a man's mind till he don't know hisself." He handed it back to me careful-like. "Takes a mite of work to make it run the way you like, but once you figure it, you'll be master of an art that most men would give their souls to know."

I studied on the gourd a bit, turning it about in my hands. "How'd it come to be lost, you reckon?"

"Dunno, rightly. No copperworkers, I suppose, and anyone with knowhow of the art died off eventual. Used to be a secretlike thing, some said it turned men's minds too far and they smashed them all to stop it. No knowing how thisn got hid away, but you're in luck having found it."

We set for a time then, not talking, just being companion-like, but I was thinking on how I could turn what I had into what I wanted.

I started at it the next morning, after Wol had driven the kids out to pasture. Laying up applemilk'n'wine is women's art, they keep it secret, but Mam showed me how when I was small, and I make enough for Wol'n'me, not the best but hot enough. I cast about and found a vine all heavy with fruit, and took and mashed it as for wine, and did the same with a measure of corn'n'oats, and whilst they worked I played every whichway with the copper gourd. Burned myself right smartly the first few times, and near cried with the frustration of it all, but every time I thought on quitting, up cropped a vision of that lovely girl again, naked on the beach and smiling at me, so I kept on. As time run along I figured the trick of it, slowsome, and as Wink had said, out dripped the tears of the gods. They clumb all up in my head and made me feel like a river of warm honey, it was that good. I took him the first fair measure I got out, made from applemilk, and he sipped it down satiny and smiled his square-toothed grin, and that's when I knowed that I had what I was looking for.

Time had run along smart while I was playing with that boiling gourd back in the trees where Wol wouldn't see, and the dams had dropped their kids again by the time I'd made a fair measure of the stuff. Jillet had grown some, not uplike but outlike, as women do, and as I'd been working on my boiling gourd I'd been working at her too, like a body works at a bashful kitten he wants a chance of petting. I'd started settling down near her, when she was weaving on baskets or rugs or pounding corn fine, and talked sweet and low to her. Her mam had passed on, so there warn't anyone to chase me off—Floss was there with her, whose mam and da both had passed on, leaving her to the keeping of the Bigman, but as soon as she saw me she scurried off, and for once I was glad of my shriveled side, if horror of it bought us some privicy. Floss hadn't spoke a word since her da died, so Jillet was lonesome. Wasn't a thing usually seen, man'n'woman set together during the day with work to be done, but most saw me as more woman than man, so no one gave it no nevermind if I worked my hides or wove my baskets while keeping company with her.

She laughed me away at first, saying she wasn't a dam to be cooed at like I wanted milk out of her, so I tried a different tack, and made her laugh until her belly ached. When they hatched,

I brought a basketful of my bantie-chicks with their mam for a visit, and as I'm the only man on the Island what bothers with banties—they being so small and all—she'd never had a lapful of happy hen afore, and that alone near turned her head. Soon she didn't stare at my arm'n'leg no more, and looked all bright-like when I came to sit by her, and I found that she was a sharp-some thing, and made me laugh harder than I made her. And then, I asked her, teasinglike, which of the young men she had her eye on, and she wouldn't answer. As I named them out one by one she laughed me away with a sideways grin, but when I named myself she doubled over with laughing, and though I knew she would, it tore me some to hear.

But I kept at it just the same, bringing my sitting work to keep her company with, and talking on this or that, till one day she reached out her hand while we was arguing on some point and rested it on my shriveled arm. Was like being hit with a lightning bolt, though she didn't let on that it was anything un-usuary. No one'd touched that side of me since Mam died, and that made me just the more set that I would have her. I kept on teasing her about what Islandman she fancied till she didn't laugh so long when I said it, and looked at me thoughtful-like instead. Till one day I asked her what would make her say yes to a man, but all she would give me was that when her father said yes, then so would she.

Course, I never let Trower Bell know the first of these goings-on, as it would shoot my planning all to flinders. But the afternoon of the first day that frost silvered the ground, after I'd figured the secret of my boiling gourd, I went out to find him. He was down by the mud flats on the fringe of the Island, where I expected, looking over his oysters careful-like. We've all got ourselves a bed of them, and keep them thinned'n'tended 'most like a garden, and when the tide's low they poke up from the slick black mud'n'rock like the ugliest flowers you ever saw. The shadows were growing long when I sung out to him.

"Lo, Bigman Bell."

Wink had told me how when the man was barely more than a baby, Trower Bell had stood up and said he would be the Bigman of the Island one day. Most would take that as child's natterings, but he had the stubborn to make it happen. Things were, once, being Bigman was cushiony work, and that's how we reckon the mainland went all to hell'n'flinders. Now it only means anything goes wrong, it's his lookout, for the whole Island. That's where Floss come from—fisherman called Mal passed on not long ago, so Bigman has the keeping of his only daughter, till he can set her up comfortlike in her own hut. If Mal'd had a hut full of babbies and an old, toothless grammy, Bigman would have done the same by 'em as if they were his own, as was his duty.

He turned slow to me. He's got a stiffening in his joints that plagues him something awful in the cold, but he won't let it nevermind him much. "Lo, Halfman Simian," he sung back, and came slow out of the oyster bed to me, black mud sucking at his legs. He's a short man, but broad in the chest like a pumpkin, and he came right up and took my good hand. "How's the world been treating you?"

"Fair and fresh, sir, naught to cry over." Then I got to the pith of my business with him. "I heared tell your aches been binding you something fierce with the frost, I been thinking I might've found something that could smooth away the pain of an evening."

"Who's had reason to say my aches?" he asked sharpish.

"Just the squirrels and the fishes, sir, no one impertinent," I said quicklike, and he had to know that we'd all seen how his walk had stuttered the past winter. "I'd be obliged though if you'd step on up with me and have a sit before wand'ring back."

He had to say yes to that, it wouldn't be polite to refuse. We wandered back to my hut, me leading the way and feeling his eye on me. I can move quick or I can move prettysome, but I canst do the same at once, and it felt like he was burning holes in my head as I clumb slowlike up the shore to our hut.

I hadn't the brawn to turf Wol out when I wanted privicy of an evening, but I'd told him that byandby he'd be getting a love, and she wouldn't be wanting me around during their honeymonth, or probable after, either. He'd kenned on that I had a plan brewing right off, and promised to be scarce whenever I asked. I'd brushed out our skins just as he was gone and laid them down smooth, and put my god's tears what I had stored up in hollow gourds where I could reach them easy, with a pair of little cups and some of last year's nuts and this year's berries and some oatcake, and when we got back it was all laid out as nice as if I'd had a love to take care of me. He settled himself gingerly across from me, folded his legs, and set his hands on his knees as polite. I had to crumple down less graceful-like, but he pretended not to notice. I poured him out a cupful of tears—they were Mam's cups, flat-shallow and the best we had—and he held it gentle in his palm while I filled mine, then we raised them to each other and sipped. His face went red. He'd taken too much at once, but he held the cup still and pretended that it wasn't bothering him any. I'd learned by then how hot the tears burned, and barely wet my upper lip, even though my belly was jumpin' in me and I wanted the whole gourd to give me courage; we'd never had a Bigman in our hut.

"It's like fire, sir, but that one cup will erase all of your aches, for a time," I said. He sipped it slowly then and settled more comfortlike.

"How did you find the secret of this?" His voice was satined by the tears, and I knew they would be warming his chest.

"I came at it in a sideways-fashion. Blindman Wink gave me the what of it, but I found the how on my own." He sipped again at the little cup, and I mimicked him to feel the warm slip down my own throat and up into my face, like a mouthful of tea come to life. I was gladsome and fortunate to have him in my hut. Had I gone begging, as a man does when wanting another man's daughter, he maybe could have pressed me for the secret. As a guest, though, he had to leave it at what I would tell.

"Oysters be manysome this year," he began, and we started in to talking in the slow weaving way men have, of this and that and nothing much. Though I'd listened often enough, I'd never joined in, and found it real comfortlike. It eased my belly inside me till I thought I might start in on what I was really after.

"Bigman," I said when he'd thrice emptied his cup, "winter's coming on quicksome. It weighs on a man, not having any company in the long nights, wouldn't you say, sir?"

"It has been right lonely since my Kit passed on, but I'm not thinking that's exactly what you're meaning," he said.

I shook my head in a no, and sipped again. He knew what I was after, but I didn't want to be so direct about it right off. He shook his head at me sadlike. "Weigh it may, but no man could ask it of a Halfman to hold and raise children, and no man could ask it of his love to go without." He'd kenned my purpose so

I changed tack sharpish, not quite certain how I was going to bring him about.

"Well," I said, "Keeper's a right high place to hold on the Island, wouldn't you say?"

"Right high," he said back and emptied the little cup.

"There's them that say no one can mend and make nets as fine as Wink," I added, and he nodded smartish. "And of course the Keeper gets his hut built fine for him of weathered wood, and has fish and fowl and all he would need set at his door, besides." He nodded at this too. "Well then, sir. I know Wink. He's a steady man, and set up comfortlike. It crushes him lifeless, being all alone through the cold."

"Never been a Keeper with a love before," he said slow, but I could see the thought working in his head like bread rising in the sun.

"True, but no reason it shouldn't be. Wink could hold and love her good as any, perhaps better, since he's so fair set up and doesn't have the eyes to be tempted away by other men's loves."

He nodded at this, then sat still a moment. "Mal died of gangrene this spring, you recall, and his motherless Floss has been resting in my hut since, quieter than a cotton boll. Man with hands that magic could tease out the words again, wouldn't you say?" he asked, and I could see a touch of mischief in his eye. The tears must have clumb up to his head, and got him in the temper I needed him to be.

"Fair plan enough," I answered back. "He'll be right happy."

"But now I wonder—" he turned back—"why you're frettin' on a love for the Keeper and not yourself? You've not brung me up here sole from your heart's kindness, Simian." I blushed at that. "What's preying on your mind?"

"You've said it, sir. What woman would have a Halfman?"

"Find the right woman, and all she'll fret on is whether she'll get a brood by you." He looked at me slantwise and grinning saying this.

"I'm right certain I can give that at least," I laughed it off. Truth was, I didn't know if I could, as many Halfmen couldn't, but I didn't want to even think it.

"Then the worry would be provisioning the brood you got, and keeping them comfortlike?" I nodded at that. "No Halfman I know of has ever done so."

"I know it," I said.

"Keeper would be one thing, but you . . ." He didn't say I was a nothing to the Keeper, but I couldn't deny it. He thought on more.

"But no Halfman has ever had this—" he raised his little cup, which I had filled yet again—"nor had the making of it. That could be the keepin' of you and yours."

"Keeper says it has its uses," I said. "Besides the warming and the softening of your aches."

"Simian," he said most sternlike, "you have the kenning of a marvelous gift, and the only man to have it. That's a treasure least as high as the Keeper's, and men will trade fish'n'fowl'n'what-have-you for a measure. What love you want can be yours."

He started out rattling off the girls of the Island, and for every one he named I had a reason or three why I wouldn't do for them. Some too tall, others too broad, some too small, others flitlike and deserving lively husbands. We were playful about it, and he rocked a bit in his speaking, but I was in dead earnest. Was scared about this part, truth to tell, but the thought in the back of my head of Jillet with another, of being a burthen at my brother's hearth, with a young love and all the sweetness between them turning me lonesome'n'bitter, drove me on. Came to the end of the girls, and he shook his head.

"Halfman, you are hard to please," he laughed.

"There's one you haven't sung out," I said. "Think this gift would be good enough to keep your Jillet?"

He started up at this, but unsteady. "My Jillet stays where she is."

I didn't answer right off, just poured out his cup again. I'd had time with the tears, learned how much softened my aches and how much tipped me over, so I was firm and steady yet.

"These here gods' tears are worth their weight and more in fish'n'fowl, didn't you say?" I asked softlike, and he nodded warm. "Time'll be, naught but the Keeper will have more laid at his door in trade, and never could I brew enough to keep every house with a full pot." I looked up at him, slowlike. "Wouldn't it be fitsome for the Bigman's pot to be everfull, without a fish nor a fowl changing hands?" He turned his cup in his hands, and thought on this. "T'would be a fitting gift for a new-bought son to give his father, a full gourd of tears, with the promise of as much as he could want without the bother of kenning the craft. And a goodly gift to have in the snow, when even a new-mint brood of grandbabbies won't keep out the cold."

It was most likely the mention of those grandbabbies what won him over, and we sat up all through the night, sipping at my pot of tears and naming all the grandbabbies I'd give him. But I knew he wouldn't like it when the tears had flowed out of him, so when his eyes closed and the cup dropped from his hand, I nipped out across the Island.

The moon was shinin fair'n'full, but the cold burned up through my good leg and made me stumble. Bigman's hut was full across the Island, and I was winded when I dropped to my knees aside it. His dogs knew me well by then, and scarce stirred when I stepped over them to get to his hut. All his great hulking boys was stretched out inside, like the dogs without, but I moved around to the back without going in. Jillet had her own little space, curtained off with kidskin for privicy, and I slit the stitching near the ground and put my head inside. She was all stretched out on her rug, warm'n'deep asleep, but soon as I touched her she sprang up smartlike. I whispered to her that her father had given his go-ahead, and we had to go quicklike if we aimed to keep it. I feared that she'd set back down at that and wouldn't budge, but instead she moved sharpish to the edge of her rug, asking me what had taken me so long, and fetched out a bundle that I reckoned held everything she'd be wanting to take. That caught me sideways unexpected: she had no way of knowing that I'd be coming for her. But there's no explaining lovelies, so it's not worthwhile trying to understand.

We legged it back across the Island, her trailing her silvery laugh in the moonlight all the way behind her, making for the light-watch 'n' the gully 'n' the hidey-hole where first I'd found that copper gourd. When my arms were all covered in burns 'n' I was thinking I'd never get a love I'd swept it out clean and cut a pair of windows in the bank for air, and when I started on thinking it might actually happen I laid away fish'n'fowl 'n' the thickest, newest sleeping skins could be had over the Island.

I got her in there close on to sunrise, when the sky was its darkest. She looked around and said how clever a place it was, smart'n'neat'n'secretlike, and how none of the other Islandmen would have set up a hidey-hole half as nice for his honeymonth. She took her bundle what I'd been carrying and began to unbundle it, and that's when my vinegar ran out. I dropped down and told her how I'd found the copper gourd and brewed up a liquor to turn a man's head, and used it to get her father's go-ahead, and how I expected he'd come for me when the sun rose. And I told her about all the nights I'd lain awake wanting to be settin'n'talkin' with her, and my fear of ending my days at another man's hearth without love nor child to call my own, and how I feared I'd never get her a child, till she stopped all my blathering with a kiss. It was the longest 'n' the sweetest 'n' the most comfortsome kiss I ever had, being the first one I'd ever tasted, and after that I shut my crying up tight.

She didn't stop at one, but kept on and showed me all the things no one'd ever bothered explaining, figuring I'd never have the needing of them. Wasn't nothing painsome about it, the two of us tucked away all snug and comfortlike there as the days ran along. Tradition went, we'd have a moon of privicy before we had to go out blushing to face the world, and I was glad of the time to let my new father simmer down. Wasn't nothing Trower Bell could do about it after that night; once a maid's been pierced there's no snitching her back, and he couldn't say I'd taken her against hers nor his nor anyman's will. Sometimes, curled up with her there, it got a bit mixed around in my head who'd been doing the piercing, as I'd felt like nothing more than an innocent maid that first night with only half an idea of what I was doing, and she as purposeful'n'knowing as they say a man is supposed to be. But about then she'd cuddle up and kiss my neck, and I figured I didn't care who did what to who, so long as I got to keep her.

Byandby, Trower Bell forgot his raging at being tricked out of his only daughter, and byandby we gave him a fat dumpling of a darling grandbabbie. He had naught but smiles for me and mine after that, and Jillet had never had naught but smiles for me from the start. I was just so full of sunshine from the knowing that I hadn't cursed Jillet to pass on without a brood that I wouldn've cared if it'd been a Halfman like me. Instead, I'd got her a perfect little daughter, nothing but smiles'n'sweetness. Everyone loved on her so much she barely touched ground between birth and her walking year.

I wasn't wrong about the tears of the gods I'd stewed up. Me and mine have all we need and more: a warm hut, thick skins, the best of the Island fish. It got me something I didn't expect to be getting, though: no one calls me "Halfman" no more, but talk up to me like I'm whole'n'sound as anyman.

Afternoons, I take myself sometimes over to Wink's hut in the dunes, and he'n'I sit quietsome, kenning how the grasses blow, sipping our silky-soft tears and whispering on the old times. His Floss works quietlike in'n'out 'n' all around us, but she never stops smiling, now. Our babbies crawl over our criss-crossed knees and tumble in the sand in front of us, and sometimes our hearts feel so full they're like to burst.